Promise Me Nothing

Dawn Vogel

DEDICATION

To Ariel, Marc, Nate, and Jeremy, for "Zee", "Chris",
Gerard, and "Et in Arcadia ego"

CONTENTS

CHAPTER ONE:
JUVIE PSYCH WARD BLUES

Something was coming. I could feel it.

I'd been in this weird juvie-slash-psych-ward for three weeks now, and things had been ... normal. Well, as normal as they can be when you're fae living in the mortal realm. Everything had seemed a little duller since I got here, a little less vivid and exciting.

But I also hadn't gotten into any fights, which was apparently very good, according to my counselor. I wasn't sure what I was supposed to do when I went in for a session. She didn't really ask me any questions about how I was doing or feeling. She made sure I was staying out of trouble, noted some things in my chart, and sent me back to the rec hall. When her pen scratched across the paper, it made my skin crawl, like nails on a chalkboard. It sounded about the same to my ears.

I felt all right, just strange, like I was waiting for the other shoe to drop. Since I had left my home in Idyll, this was the easiest my life had been. Instead of living in a park, sneaking into the locker room for a shower, and begging, borrowing, or stealing for meals, I got hot showers, warm food, and an actual bed. I could get used to this.

No, of course it couldn't be that simple.

It started in the meds line. The girls in line behind me were chatting and goofing around. I hadn't bothered to learn their names, because no one talked to me if they could help it. It was like they knew that something was wrong with me, and their deepest instincts told me to keep away.

One of the girls, who was either Catherine, Caitlyn, or Callie, had her back to me. When I picked up the flimsy paper cup filled to the brim with the cherry-red liquid meds they were feeding me, she stepped backward, right into my arm. Droplets splattered all over my hand, my shirt, and the counter.

"Oh, sorry," Catherine-Caitlyn-Callie said with a gasp. She whipped her head around, the ends of her blonde ponytail sliding across my face. Then she saw who she'd just apologized to and snickered, turning back to her friends.

I looked at the orderly at the dispensary window. He wasn't the usual guy. "Uh, my meds spilled?"

He shrugged. "Take what's left."

"Don't I need the full dose?"

Another shrug. "I'm just filling in. Take what's left, and I'll note it in your chart."

Goosebumps prickled at the back of my neck, but I gulped down the liquid left in the cup, not even a third of my usual dose, and set the empty cup on the counter. The orderly whisked it away into the garbage can and called out "Next."

He hadn't even looked at my chart, let alone noting anything in it. But I knew that when the orderly said "next," I'd best move on and deal with it some other way.

I licked the few droplets that were still on my hand as I walked away. I had no idea what meds they were giving me, but it tasted like the ripest cherries, not the weird artificial cherry flavor of most medicines. I thought about trying to get more out of where it had splattered across my shirt, but I knew sucking on your shirt was not something normal humans do. To be fair, it isn't even something normal fae do. But I've never really claimed to be either.

Regardless, I was hungry, and that was a distraction from my predicament. I glanced up at the clock. Still an hour before lunch. I had a few stale cookies stashed in my room, but they didn't sound appealing right now. I wanted a burger. Something greasy and horrible for you, not like the weird mostly vegetarian stuff they served here, with occasional meat for garnish.

Instead of heading to my room, I stopped at the bulletin board to peruse the menu. I did this a lot. Whatever bland food they had planned for us never seemed to stick in my mind. Or to my ribs. My stomach not so much grumbled as yowled. Sloppy joes for lunch. Which meant lentils and what they told us was "textured vegetable protein," which I was pretty sure was not any of those three things in the true sense of their meanings.

At least there was chicken noodle soup on the menu for dinner, and that meant real bits of chicken. I looked at the clock again. Only six more hours until chicken.

~

The feeling of being on edge didn't subside as the day went on. I was still starving, even after lunch. I'd eaten every single cookie in my room, despite how much they tasted like cardboard.

In the rec room, I slumped on the couch, idly brushing cookie crumbs off my red-splattered shirt and trying to find something to keep my mind off my hunger. I'd flipped through the same half a dozen magazines at least half a dozen times. I was pretty sure I could spout off the horoscope of anyone who asked me, though the predictions would be for some random month in the past. So now I was people watching.

Every time I looked in her direction, Catherine-Caitlyn-Callie was staring at me, whispering to her friends. So it came as a half-shock, half-complete-lack-of-surprise, when she dropped her tray on my table at dinner.

"You're Briar, right?"

I looked up and nodded. "Sorry, I don't know—"

"I heard you killed five people."

That was complicated, but not for the reasons most people would suspect.

On a frigid night, an entire "militia" compound had burned, and I had been there. The inhabitants were militarized, but I don't think their "militia" was on any official watch lists. As for me, I may or may not have actually slaughtered ... well, whatever they really were, with my own hands and teeth. I honestly didn't remember how many people I might or might not have killed.

That had been my last night of freedom, my last night with my friends. Me, Gerard, Zee, and Chris, even though Chris hadn't wanted to be there at all. We'd dragged him along anyway, because we knew he wouldn't want to miss the end result of stopping this group of people who were keeping way too close tabs on the supernatural kids in our school. Once things heated up, Chris was right there with us, though. And I had feasted like I hadn't feasted since I got to the backwater town of Artis. Nothing like the taste of human ...

Catherine-Caitlyn-Callie was still staring at me. "Well?"

Yes, I totally killed at least five people. Honestly, I lost count. And then I ate them. It's what I do. I'm fae. Not like the faeries you see in story books. I was created to be a killing machine. I'm more like the faeries of your nightmares.

But I didn't think any of that would go over too well. So I shrugged and gave a non-committal response. "I don't know. I might have."

She shoved her tray across the table, knocking it into mine and splashing hot soup and cold grape juice onto my shirt. She smirked. It hadn't been an accident. She was trying to goad me.

I looked down, feeling a sudden need to break the eye contact I had with her. The red spots all over my shirt from my meds were now joined by faint golden and dark purple. And something inside of me ... shifted.

I'd held my temper in for three weeks. Somehow, having Catherine-Caitlyn-Callie spill meds, soup, and juice on me all in one day was the breaking point. And I was so hungry, a hunger that even chicken noodle soup couldn't abate.

My vision blurred, and the next thing I knew, I was standing on the table, one hand twisted through Catherine-Caitlyn-Callie's hair, and my other hand a mess of nasty claws going for her exposed throat.

If the guards hadn't blown their weird shrieking whistle right then, I might have found out Catherine-Caitlyn-Callie's name at her memorial service.

"Williams! Stand down!"

It took me a moment to remember that they were talking to me when they said "Williams." I'd only used the name since leaving Idyll, because most humans, unlike the fae, had first and last names, and for some reason, "of the Brambles" didn't work as a last name. But between the whistle and the authoritative voice, something brought me back to my senses. I let go of Catherine-Caitlyn-Callie's hair and stood upright. My clawed hand brushed my leg, but then the claws retracted, and it was just my fingertips against the thin cotton of my pants. My stomach roared with defeat.

A loud sigh came from behind me, followed by, "Take them both to solitary till we get this sorted out."

Catherine-Caitlyn-Callie wailed. "I didn't do anything! She attacked me."

I didn't hear the guard's reply, as four burly guards surrounded me. I didn't resist. I just put my hands behind my back and let them cuff me. It was easier that way.

~

Solitary is supposed to be another word for alone, but in this place, it meant "more of the same." There wasn't much of a difference between this room and the room where I kept all my stuff. Well, this one was in the basement, and had a toilet and sink in place of a second bed. The door here was closed and locked, as opposed to standing open at all times. But the room still had a bed and walls, which made it the second nicest place I'd stayed since leaving Idyll, coming in just behind my normal room.

I didn't get much of a chance to make a lengthy comparative list of the pros and cons of gen pop versus solitary, though. I was still hungry, but as soon as I sat down on the bed, all I wanted to do was lay down. After that, I was out like a light.

When I woke up, I could tell I hadn't been asleep for long. The hunger still nagged at me, rather than settling down to a low rumble like it usually did when I didn't eat for a while.

At first, I didn't know why I'd woken up. I looked around through bleary eyes and spotted the guard in my doorway, calling my name. "Williams. Briar Williams?" She looked like the Platonic ideal of a guard—spotless uniform, thick arms and legs that were probably heavily muscled, lean but not skinny, with her highlighted blonde hair in a neat French braid.

I shook my head to clear it and realized she was waiting for a response. "Yes, that's me."

"Good. Follow me."

Apparently, I hadn't cleared my head enough, because all I could manage was a faint, "Huh?"

The guard glared at me. "Follow me. Now."

"Where are we going?" I didn't want to linger in my solitary room, so I got up, but I still trailed a few steps behind the guard.

"Transfer."

I tried to make sense of what she was telling me. I didn't understand all the ramifications of this place. Maybe this was just a temporary holding facility where they decided if I was legitimately crazy or legitimately a murderer. By their standards, I was both, at least to a limited world view that didn't allow for things like fae and other supernatural creatures who go bump in the night.

At the end of the hallway, another guard glanced up from his clipboard and looked me up and down. "Name?"

"Briar Williams."

"Date of birth?"

I didn't know my actual date of birth in terms of dates the human world understood. Time worked differently for the fae. But this facility had assigned me a birthday during the intake procedure. The normal meds dispensary guy made me recite it daily. "January 1, 2000." It seemed far too generic to be a good identifier, but then again, maybe I was the only person here who didn't know when she'd been born.

The male guard grunted in agreement, and the gate in front of me buzzed, then opened. The female guard who had retrieved me from my cell pulled my arms behind my back and snapped a pair of cuffs on me. Unlike the previous pair of cuffs, these were thick and heavy, and as soon as they made contact with my skin, my wrists began to tingle.

"Umm, I think I'm allergic to—" I tried to look over my shoulder to see the cuffs, even though I didn't need to see them to know they had to be made of iron. I really hoped this transfer wasn't going to take very long. Humans tend to get really concerned when your wrists start smoking.

"Can it," the female guard replied. I caught a glimpse of her nametag. Jackson.

"Officer Jackson, I'm really not kidding. This could be potentially life-threatening."

That gave her pause, but she shrugged. "Just following the instructions I was given. You don't have far to go."

I wasn't sure if that was meant to reassure me, but at least it shut me up, as I puzzled over who might have given a juvie guard instructions to restrain a seemingly random inmate with iron. There was only one reason to use something other than standard steel or aluminum cuffs, and that was if someone knew they were dealing with one of the fae.

If Jackson's statement hadn't shut me up, the blast of cold air that hit me when the outside door opened would have done the trick. When I picked Washington as my home away from Idyll, I chose it because it was supposed to have mild weather, which made living outdoors a little easier when I arrived. Maybe it was just the thin cotton of the scrubs-like pants and shirt all the kids here wore, but the wind went straight through them, even during the day.

Night. It was definitely night now. That still didn't mean that I had slept for long, though. Washington had also topped my list for the shortness of the days during the winter. Warmer than Alaska, but also not much daylight. Mild temperatures and lots of darkness sounded like heaven to the old me.

The wind died down, and I managed to take in the rest of what was going on. The facility was on a flat patch with mountains in the distance, though those weren't visible at night. You could see for miles, but right now, I only needed to see a few dozen yards.

Ahead of me was a solid black van, and standing beside it were a pair of tall, slender adults, dressed in heavy dark-colored coats. Both were gingers, skin even paler than mine, one man and one woman—not so similar that I thought they were related, but their hair matched perfectly. The woman's hair was pulled back, making her features look severe, while the man's hair was a bit less tamed and shaggy, and it whipped in the wind to obscure his features.

I drew back involuntarily. Their hair reminded me of the loyalist fae—the sort of fae I preferred to avoid when I was still in Idyll. If loyalists had come to retrieve me, that would explain the iron handcuffs. It also meant that I'd be safer if I went back inside and stayed in solitary, instead of being "transferred" to wherever they were taking me.

In drawing back, I moved away from whatever had been blocking the wind from me, and I shivered. There was no way the people near the van, nor the guards, hadn't noticed my reaction. But then I realized what—or, more properly, who—had been blocking the wind. It was an African-American guy a full head taller than me, his head shaved down to a barely visible layer of stubble, huddled into a Navy peacoat with the faintest scent of acrid smoke lingering within the fibers.

"Gerard? What the hell are you doing here?"

Gerard looked down at me and frowned. "I could ask the same of you. Been here three weeks. Since ... well, you know." His gaze shifted around as he finished up, and his voice grew quiet.

7

"There will be time for the two of you to catch up in the van," the woman standing beside it said. Her cadence was clipped, and there was a hint of an accent—thankfully not the sort of accent that the noble fae used.

I relaxed a little bit. Maybe there was another, logical explanation for the iron handcuffs, then.

Gerard, on the other hand, tensed up. "Where are you taking us? Who are you?"

The ginger woman sighed. "You will call me Miss Whalen. My compatriot is Mister Walkenhorst. You are being transferred to a facility that is better suited to further your rehabilitation."

I glanced at Gerard. His jaw clenched, and he murmured, "I don't like the sound of this, Briar."

I gave him a quick nod and turned back to Miss Whalen. "I don't suppose we can get a burger on the way? I missed dinner."

Miss Whalen exchanged a wordless wide-eyed look with Mister Walkenhorst. Her expression told me everything I needed to know. That, followed by Mister Walkenhorst immediately producing a stick of beef jerky from inside his coat and waving it at me, both put me at ease and terrified me. They *did* know what they were dealing with, and they knew exactly what I was capable of. I'd have been more worried if Miss Whalen hadn't looked afraid. It's nice to know you can still inspire a healthy level of fear.

I tried not to drool when I asked, "Can I get my cuffs switched out then, too?"

Miss Whalen glanced at Jackson, still behind me. "Yes, I think we can dispense with those for our journey." Her gaze slid to Gerard. "They have both been medicated, have they not?"

Gerard's jaw was pulsing now, but he nodded. "Every day since we got here, ma'am," he said, his voice stiff.

The tingling in my wrists abated, and I rubbed absently at them as I reached for the offered beef jerky.

"Briar, what are you doing?" Gerard asked, his dark brown eyes pleading with me. He didn't want me to take food from strangers, and normally, I was happy to help him out. But now was not the time for him to try to play on that tendency.

"I'm *hungry*. You know how I get."

His eyes widened for an instant, but then he shook his head. "Always thinking with your stomach. It's liable to get you killed."

8

"Might be," I said, as I accepted the beef jerky from Mister Walkenhorst. "But at least I won't be hangry while I'm dying." I winked at Gerard as I took a healthy bite out of the processed meat.

CHAPTER TWO:
EN ROUTE

Once I'd eaten my beef jerky and the van started moving, I was ready for more sleep. I had started to drift off when Gerard poked me in the side. "Hey, do you have any idea what's going on?" His voice was low.

I shook my head as I observed Mister Walkenhorst, who was driving, and Miss Whalen, who rode beside him. They hadn't been particular about where we sat, so Gerard and I had both gone as far back in the van as we could. They also didn't seem to be paying attention to us, but I kept my voice low as well. "They know what I am, at least. They put me in iron cuffs and had food on hand. I'd bet they know about you, too, since we're both here."

"Have you been taking the meds?"

"Mostly, yeah." I frowned. "I only got maybe a third of my usual dose today, though."

He frowned in response. "What are they giving you?"

"No clue. It's red, liquid, tastes like cherries? Not the weird like candy cherries. Like real cherries."

"Does it stop your powers?"

Powers was a generous term for what I could do, but it was the term Gerard understood. The short version was that I had the powers of plants, portents, and pursuit. A touch of my hand made any plant grow, like the world's greenest thumb. I could read signs and portents in the patterns of natural things. And as for pursuit, I was fast and sneaky, I had claws and a maw that put most carnivores to shame, and I could literally eat my way out of anything, if I had to.

His question sent a chill down my spine. "Yeah, but it stops the ... you know, hunger, too. How did you know?"

He shot another glance at Mister Walkenhorst and Miss Whalen. "I stopped taking mine a week ago. My powers started coming back as soon as I stopped. I'm still weak, but I've got something to try."

"Something like what? We don't know where they're taking us. What if they're helping us get out?"

He gave me a look, the one I was used to getting all the time in Artis—the one that was a visual representation of someone wondering how I could be so naïve. "Let's find out." He spoke louder. "Excuse me, Miss Whalen, could you tell us where you're taking us now?"

Miss Whalen turned in her seat to face us. "I could, but it won't change anything." She smiled what I expected was meant to be a sweet smile, but in the van lit only by passing headlights, it looked way more ghoulish.

I glanced at Gerard, whose jaw was twitching again. "Do me a favor," he muttered. "Keep her distracted for a minute."

"Why, what are you going to do?"

"Please, Briar? Just ... all I need is a minute."

I nodded, just barely, and then turned my attention back to Miss Whalen. "Well, we're just really curious, that's all. It's not every day that you have a couple of people come and remove you from a juvenile detention psych ward, or whatever that place was."

Miss Whalen chuckled. "I suppose that's as good a summary as any. As I said before, we're taking you to a place that is much better suited to help rehabilitate you."

"What makes you think we need rehabilitation?" I'd moved beyond just distracting her from whatever Gerard was doing. I was genuinely curious about this one.

Working her upper lip with her teeth for a moment, Miss Whalen hesitated. "How long have you been away from Idyll, Briar?"

She knew where I had come from. That made sense, seeing as she knew what I was. I pushed down the terror that had started to bubble up so I could respond. "That's not really an answer. That's ... why does that matter?"

"Please, just indulge me."

"Six or seven months, I guess."

"Very good. You spent roughly five or six months of that time living in Artis. You attended school for two of those months.

12

When you set foot in that school, you entered the administrative systems of the human world. According to the state of Washington, your name is Briar Williams, and you're fifteen years old. That makes you a minor. You are a minor with no family to speak of, making you a ward of the state. So when you fell afoul of those ... people—"

I interrupted her at that. "You and I both know they weren't people."

"Of course. But remember the *system*, Miss Williams. They were people according to the system, just as you are. Now then, you are under the age of majority and have been accused of multiple counts of murder. You could be tried as an adult, which would certainly end in a prison sentence for you. If you were to remain unmedicated, the humans would have a real problem on their hands, wouldn't they?"

I didn't know much about prison, except for what I'd seen in movies and on television. Generally, though, they didn't seem like the sort of place that was prepared for supernatural creatures like me. I understood enough to know that if you committed more crimes in prison, you had more problems. So I nodded.

Miss Whalen continued. "Mister Walkenhorst and I represent a different sort of institution. We provide a service to the state by taking some of their delinquent minors, particularly those with nowhere else to go, and turning them into law-abiding young people."

"Really?" That was all I could think to say after hearing her explanation. Why try to fix someone as irrevocably broken as me?

"Truly. We have a high success rate—"

"Then that means there are failures, too."

With a slight inclination of her head to the side, she said, "That is true, but there are other facilities with which we are affiliated that offer a more comprehensive rehabilitation, for those who are beyond our help."

I frowned. "Okay, that might make sense when dealing with a ward of the state, but what about Gerard? He's got a family back in Artis."

Miss Whalen's gaze left my face and lingered on Gerard's. I hoped he was done with whatever he was doing. When she didn't look back at me immediately, I turned to look at Gerard as well. He looked like he was sleeping, but his lips moved ever so slightly.

"If it's all the same to you," she said, "I feel it may be inappropriate to discuss Mister LeCroix's situation with you."

I didn't like the sound of that. More and more, I agreed with Gerard that something strange was going on here. Maybe multiple somethings.

Before I could say anything more, Gerard jerked awake beside me. "Buh-wha? Oh, hey, Briar."

I stared at him. "Hey, yourself. Did you just nod off?"

"Yeah, totally," he said, but he shook his head no. He smiled at Miss Whalen. "Sorry, you were saying?"

She arched one eyebrow at him. "Miss Williams was asking about how you and she wound up in similar circumstances, when your backgrounds are so very different."

"Oh," Gerard replied, his voice flat.

I glanced at him. Discomfort marred his face. "We can talk about it another time, Gerard," I said quickly. "Thank you, Miss Whalen, your explanation has been quite enlightening."

"Of course." She turned back toward the front of the van.

"What'd you do?" I muttered at Gerard, pounding my fist into his leg.

His voice was barely above a whisper when he responded. "Called Zee."

The two words made perfect sense, but at the same time, they were among the more baffling things I'd heard that day. Zee had been the leader of our little band of miscreants, in a way. Her family were hunters, not the sort that spent time looking for multi-point bucks, but the kind that stopped supernatural creatures who had gotten out of hand. In a different life, Zee might have been hunting someone like me, but instead, we'd become friends. If anyone knew how to save us, it was her. "What? Do you still have your phone?"

"Not like that," he murmured. "I *called* her. She's coming to get us out of here."

"Seriously?" I could barely keep my voice down. "When? Where?"

"Soon, that's all I know. She said she wasn't far when I reached her."

"Awesome!" I bounced in my seat. Zee had skills. She'd managed to disappear before the cops showed up the night we raided the compound. It seemed likely she hadn't wound up in a

14

similar institution to the one we'd just left. But even she had some limitations, and they probably included an inability to break us out of a place like juvie-psych-ward. Out here on the open road, though, was another matter entirely.

I looked out the window, half expecting to see Zee running alongside the van. We'd already reached the foothills of the mountains, and a few lazy snowflakes drifted around outside. One stuck to the window beside me, and my gaze was drawn to it.

That fragile little speck of frozen water drained my good mood of a moment earlier. I pressed my finger to the window. Even through the thick dark glass, the snowflake melted away to nothingness immediately.

"Nothing good lasts for me," I murmured, mostly to myself. Gerard might have had faith in Zee helping us, but in that moment, all I could think about was every time in my life that my hopes had been dashed to shards of nothingness, just like the melting snowflake.

"What was that?" Mister Walkenhorst asked sharply.

It was the first time I'd heard his voice. It pulled my fear screaming to the surface, overwhelming my dark mood. Mister Walkenhorst's accent sounded like a noble from Idyll.

I turned to look at him, eyes wide. His pale blue eyes seemed like they were suddenly highlighted in the rearview mirror. He locked his gaze with mine, and my stomach dropped.

His eyes were like a whirlpool, sucking me in, making me fall toward something I couldn't see. Whatever it was, it was massive and dark. And evil. Not casually evil, like people had believed me to be. Pure, rich evil.

The feeling didn't last long, as the van struck something solid. I shook my head, trying to make sense of what I'd seen in Mister Walkenhorst's eyes. Was the evil in him? Or was he just evil adjacent, to a point that it had saturated his soul? My powers hadn't come back yet like Gerard's had, as far as I knew, so it might not have been any sort of portent. Whether it was or not, I couldn't make any sense of it.

The van swerved, then continued on a steady course.

"What was that?" Miss Whalen echoed Mister Walkenhorst's words from a moment before, but her tone was far more frantic.

Gerard and I looked at each other, and both mouthed the same word. "Zee."

"We hit something," Mister Walkenhorst said. "Just a snow drift, I believe. The freeway up here can be treacherous at night." He glanced up at the rearview mirror and smiled stiffly. "Everyone buckled in back there?"

Gerard nodded as he glanced out the rear windows of the van. "Yeah, we're both buckled in. And you're right, it looks like an old snowplow push pile."

I turned my attention back to the front of the van, and saw a figure, dimly lit by our headlights, framed by the snow that raced toward the windshield like stars when the Millennium Falcon used its hyperdrive. "Here she is," I whispered.

In my imagination, I could see Zee standing there, weapons in both hands and strapped across her back, not even flinching, as the van stopped in front of her. Then she'd rip the doors off their hinges with her super-human strength, and Gerard and I would just walk out of here.

That's how it was supposed to go.

But that wasn't how it was going.

The van wasn't slowing down. There was no possible way that Mister Walkenhorst and Miss Whalen didn't see her, unless Zee had somehow learned how to make herself invisible to people who didn't know her.

Miss Whalen placed a delicate hand on Mister Walkenhorst's shoulder. "Kurt?" That single word, and the waver in her voice, made it apparent she could see Zee.

"The boy summoned someone in his sleep." His gaze flickered back to the rearview mirror and met mine again. "Or perhaps he wasn't sleeping after all."

Miss Whalen spun around, venom in her eyes. "You called to her in dreams, did you?"

"What? No," Gerard said, shaking his head.

"Please," Miss Whalen said as she rolled her eyes. "I am not so naïve. You may call it whatever you like, but you reached out to her while you dozed off." She arched an eyebrow. "You will learn to watch yourself around me, Mister LeCroix."

The engine roared as Mister Walkenhorst accelerated the van directly toward where Zee was standing.

"Move, Zee, move," I murmured. "Tell her, Gerard! Please!"

"I can't contact her that fast!"

We got a glimpse of Zee just before the van collided with her. Her face was stony, just like it had been the night at the compound. She was going to stand her ground, because every other time she'd done something like this, the van had stopped.

This time, it didn't.

I hadn't even realized I was clutching Gerard's arms until I felt the pressure of his hands on my arms too. For a moment, my mind fixed on the counterpoint of my pale hands on his dark, coat-clad arms, and his dark hands on my pale, bare arms. There was a symmetry there, and if my mind wasn't so cloudy with the drugs, I might have been able to read a sign or portent—something that could help us. But instead, I couldn't do anything more than shake my head to clear the image and focus on my surroundings.

"He just hit Zee." I whimpered. "There's no way ... how ... is she okay?"

"You just hit a girl!" Gerard shouted. "We gotta stop and see if she's alright, or if you just killed her."

Again, Mister Walkenhorst's pale blue eyes were all that were visible in the rearview mirror. "She'll be fine." His voice was cold, far more frigid than the weather outside. The van was slowly rolling to a stop, the only indication he gave that he might feel some remorse for what he'd just done. It wasn't enough for my liking.

I tried to lunge out of my seat, forgetting that Gerard had made me fasten my seatbelt when we got in the van. The beef jerky was barely keeping my hunger at bay, and now I was angry. Not a good combination for someone like me. My fingertips bristled with claws, and my vision started taking on a reddish hue at the edges. I fumbled with the button on my seatbelt with one hand and reached toward Mister Walkenhorst with the other.

My hand impacted something solid in the air, just ahead of the row of bench seats in front of Gerard and me. I blinked at it and swung again. Again, the same resistance.

Miss Whalen smirked. "If you're not willing to play nicely, then you won't be allowed to play at all. Sit."

I only snarled at her in response.

"Sit!" she barked out.

"Don't talk to my friend like that," Gerard growled.

"Then rein her in," Miss Whalen said. "I trust you recognize a barrier spell when you see one?"

"Yeah, I do."

"Then rein her in quickly, before I feel compelled to box you in a bit more snugly. Understood?"

Gerard touched my elbow gently. "Briar, you aren't going to be able to get to them." He dropped his voice to a whisper. "Not now, at least."

I seethed at my inability to reach either of the adults. Mister Walkenhorst was likely from Idyll, and Miss Whalen apparently could use magic. Somehow, just finding this out now made me extra mad. But Gerard was right. The only powers I'd gotten back so far were my claws and my hunger, and I wasn't sure the latter technically counted as a power.

I relaxed and sat back down beside Gerard. My claws retracted, and my vision cleared. And once again, I was tired and hungry. I slumped against Gerard, my head turned away from the adults in the front of the van.

As we started moving again, I hazarded a glance out the rear windows. In the red glow of the taillights, I couldn't see Zee, standing or crumpled on the highway.

"She's gone," I whispered.

Gerard shook his head. "She's tougher than both of us. Tougher than both of us and Chris."

"If she were so tough, she'd have gotten us out of here."

Gerard wrapped his arms around me. "She'll be fine. Promise."

My soul latched on to the word "promise." To the fae, it was the most sacred and binding thing anyone could do. Fae extract promises from humans to get what we want. A human who extracted a promise from a fae could do similarly, though most fae were too wily to allow such a thing to bind them.

I looked up at Gerard through my tear-filled eyes. He understood what he'd just said. I reminded him of the slip anyway. "You should know better than to promise when I'm involved."

~

I woke up again when the van stopped. My stomach still growled, but I felt a lot better than I had. I extricated myself from Gerard's arms gently, but he woke up in spite of my best efforts.

"We're not moving," he said.

"Yeah."

I glanced at the front of the van. Mister Walkenhorst and Miss Whalen were talking quietly.

Miss Whalen paused long enough to look at us. "Ah, you two lovebirds have awoken."

"We're not lovebirds," I said, my voice flat. I wasn't about to explain to her that I considered myself asexual, but Gerard knew that about me. He and I were good friends, nothing more, and we both were okay with that fact. "Where are we?"

"Just about to embark on the next portion of our journey," Miss Whalen replied.

Mister Walkenhorst opened his door and stepped out of the van. A moment later, fluorescent lights blinked to life, illuminating the interior of a large, industrial looking building. One end of the structure had a large, roll-up door that was currently closed. In front of it sat a plane that barely looked any bigger than the van we were in.

"We brought the belongings you had with you when you were checked into the institution. You'll find a pair of duffel bags containing those, some additional warm clothing, and a coat for you, Miss Williams. You'll want all that for the plane ride."

"Plane ride?" Gerard asked, his eyes wide. "You think I'm getting in that puddle jumper?"

"Yes, I do," Miss Whalen replied. "If you have a phobia, I can ensure the ride passes peacefully for you and does not remain in your memories."

"No, I'm good. No phobia. Just ... is one of you a pilot?"

"No, our pilot will be arriving momentarily," Miss Whalen said. "In the meantime, get moving! You'll find facilities behind the van, so you can change your clothes and freshen up a bit. I'm afraid there's no loo on the plane."

"Yeah, because there's nowhere to fit one," Gerard muttered. He nudged my leg with his. "Let's go see what they've got."

I nodded and got up, clambering into the back of the van. Though it was dark, it wasn't too difficult to find the duffle bags Miss Whalen had mentioned. I grabbed one and opened the rear door of the van, peeking into the bag as I climbed down.

The first thing I saw was my pre-paid flip phone, and my heart skipped a beat. What were the odds it had a charge left, after sitting in a locker somewhere for three weeks? Not good, I was pretty sure, but it was worth a shot.

As Gerard climbed out behind me, I murmured, "Your phone in there?"

He did a double take as he looked at me, then into his bag. "Yeah." His hand disappeared into his bag, then he shook his head. "Dead though."

"Maybe we'll find a charger. If you can get a signal, call Zee. And Chris." I hesitated. "And anyone else you think might help us."

Gerard chuckled softly. "Okay, if I can get my phone to power on, I'll see if I can get ahold of anyone."

I nodded and made a beeline for the door with the outline of a woman on it. I didn't really care if anyone saw me change my clothes, but if I was going to try to make some calls, I preferred the privacy.

The bathroom was single occupancy, and didn't even have an outlet, let alone my hoped-for charger. I stripped out of my uniform from the institution and started putting on the clothes from the duffle bag, trying to think of another way we could reach Zee and Chris. Maybe Gerard could call them from a dream again, but I suspected Miss Whalen wasn't going to let him sleep if she could help it.

The clothes in my bag weren't the ones I had worn at the compound. I suspected the juvie psych ward had burned those, since they were probably soaked with blood. What was in the bag all fit me loosely—baggy T-shirt, jeans, and a bulky black sweater, along with a coat with a fur lined hood. I had no sense of how long we'd driven. But apparently, wherever we were, or maybe where we were going, would be cold.

I rummaged through the rest of the bag. I hadn't had much on me other than my cell phone when the cops had found us at the compound, so I wasn't sure what I was expecting to find. When my fingers stumbled across a hunk of metal, I jerked backward, half expecting it to be iron.

It didn't burn or tingle. I prodded at the bag with my toe, as if it were a snake ready to strike. Without even thinking about it, I flipped open my phone and pressed the power button, hoping to use the light from the screen to get a better look inside the bag.

My phone chimed, and the screen lit up. It was turning on. My eyes widened. I must have turned it off at some point, or maybe the people at the institution had. Either way, I still had battery life! I bounced as I waited for the phone to boot up.

When the screen showed a selfie Zee and I had taken, I nearly whooped with joy. I watched the spot on the screen where the service bars would appear. And waited.

Nothing happened.

I held my phone out at arm's length and spun slowly, raising and lowering it slightly. Still no bars. Maybe the walls of the bathroom were too thick. I headed for the door, and then paused. Somehow, I didn't think that Mister Walkenhorst and Miss Whalen would take too kindly to me trying to call the girl they'd just run over, or the werewolf we had raided the compound with.

Instead, I closed the lid on the toilet and stood atop it, despite the sign exhorting me to not do exactly that. For a second, one faint bar flickered upward, but it disappeared just as quickly as it had appeared.

I decided to give it a shot anyway. I punched up Zee's number and waited.

It didn't even ring.

I still clung to hope. I called Chris.

Still nothing.

I shook my head as I climbed down from the toilet. But then I had another thought. Maybe I couldn't call them, but I could at least queue up some texts.

I sent the same message to both of them. "With G. No clue where. Call me!"

That would have to do for now. I tucked the phone into the T-shirt pocket.

As soon as I stepped out of the bathroom, Miss Whalen looked at me. "Where is your bag?"

"Oh, it's in there still," I said. "Am I supposed to bring it with? It's—" I started to say empty, and then remembered the metal. "I'll go get it."

Ducking back into the bathroom, I turned the bag upside down until the piece of metal fell out. It landed on the tile floor with a clatter, and I nudged it with the toe of the boots that had been in the bag. My eyes widened as I recognized it.

It was the ring that one of the people from the compound, the one who had come after Gerard in the first place, had been wearing. And I remembered the weird inscription around the band: *"pacem undique quaesivi sed nusquam repperi."*

I understood Latin. I'd learned it in Idyll. The phrase translated to "In all things I sought peace, and I have found it nowhere." I didn't understand what it meant, though. Apparently, I'd kept the ring after the compound burned. So it must have been important in some part of my brain.

Without a second thought, I scooped it up and tucked it into my shirt pocket beside my phone. I felt a faint shiver as it settled against me, with only a thin layer of t-shirt separating it from my skin. It wasn't unpleasant, not like the burning of iron, and the feeling faded almost immediately. I tossed the rest of my clothes from the institution into the bag and went back out into the hangar.

Gerard was waiting near the entrance to the ladies' room, his bag slung over his shoulder. "Any luck?"

"No signal. But I've got texts ready to send as soon as I we get one." I glanced past him to where Mister Walkenhorst and Miss Whalen were talking to an older man in coveralls. "Did you find anything weird in your bag?"

"Weird like what?" Gerard asked.

I stepped closer to him, making sure that I was hidden behind him entirely, as I fished the ring out of my pocket. "Like this."

"You kept one of their rings?" he asked in a whisper that almost felt like a shout.

"I ... maybe? I don't know. I don't remember. I really, really, don't. There's a whole lot of that night that's a blur." I shrugged. "But I guess so."

He shook his head. "I don't think ... Wait, you know what. Yeah, bring it with us. If it brings those racist rednecks down on our heads, they might accidentally help us get out of wherever we're going. Might end up being for the best. Who knows?"

CHAPTER THREE:
DEDWYDD

When we took off from the airfield in that tiny little plane, I thought wherever we were was remote, but when we landed again, the only lights for miles were the ones on the airstrip. The sky was clear, and I could see stars—far more stars than we could see even in Artis. I had no sense of direction aside from what little I could glean from the stars, so at least I knew we hadn't magically traveled across the world or something. What I did know is we were in the middle of nowhere.

Gerard echoed my thoughts. "Where are we?"

Gone was the weird tension in Miss Whalen's posture, which I hadn't even recognized as such until now that she was relaxed. She smiled, and it seemed genuine. "Almost home."

I tensed up at that word. "Where is home?" My gaze darted to Mister Walkenhorst. "Are you taking me back to Idyll?"

"Heavens no," he said, looking directly at me. Without the frame of the rearview mirror showing only his eyes, he didn't look half as terrifying. He, too, stood as though the weight of the world had dropped from his shoulders. "We're almost to Dedwydd."

"Deadwood?" Gerard asked. "In South Dakota?"

I shot him a confused look. "That's, like, a couple of states away from Washington, isn't it?"

"Yeah. Several. When I moved to Artis, we drove through there." He looked up at the stars, then turned his attention back to the adults. "There's no way we drove and then flew that far in one night. Not by normal means."

"Dedwydd," Miss Whalen said. Something in the way she said it made me realize it wasn't an English word. "It's a place of peace, or refuge."

A prickly feeling crept down my neck and across my arms. I realized I could feel the tingle of the ring again. What was it the writing said? *"pacem undique quaesivi sed nusquam repperi"*? *In all things I sought peace, and I have found it nowhere?* Suddenly, her words didn't seem quite as innocuous as they'd sounded before.

Miss Whalen continued. "It's also the name of the school you'll both be attending."

Gerard laughed. I hadn't heard that in a long time, and it gave me a warm feeling that almost counteracted the prickliness and the hunger still rumbling in my belly. But when he spoke, the words sapped that warmth from me. "School. You're taking us to supernatural reform school."

"That comparison has been made before—" Miss Whalen began.

Gerard interrupted her. "Do they have an anti-bullying policy?"

She nodded. "We do. Aside from that, there are a number of other policies and restrictions to ensure everyone's safe co-existence."

"Do they work?" he asked.

"They have in the years I've spent there," Miss Whalen replied.

Gerard smiled. Like his laugh, it was genuine. "Then I take back what I said earlier, Briar. This place won't be so bad."

I was less convinced. "The last school I—we—went to, I'm not really sure the things they were teaching us were useful. How is this any different? Am I still going to have to pass algebra?"

Miss Whalen chuckled. "All in good time, Miss Williams, but I do believe you will find this school preferable to your last one."

Mister Walkenhorst cleared his throat. "We should be going. Our pilot needs to return home, and we are standing on the runway."

"Yes, of course." Miss Whalen gestured to a point in the darkness that looked no different than any other point. "The van is this way."

As we made our way to the van, I tugged on Gerard's sleeve. "How can you think a supernatural reform school is a good thing?"

He slowed his pace to match mine, lagging behind the adults. "Look, I know you aren't that interested in school. I've got plans, and those plans need either a high school diploma or a GED. If we'd stayed in Artis, with all those racist rednecks living there, I'd probably have wound up dead or in jail before that happened. This

24

might be a new chance for me. If everyone there is like us, it could even be a *good* chance. Maybe it'll be good for you too, Briar."

I thought about that as we continued toward the van. Artis hadn't been great for me either. With no family, no income, and no real motivation to do the things I'd need to do to get either of those, I'd lived in the woods and scavenged for everything I had. I mostly went to the school to see if I could find other people like me, and because at least it was warm and dry when the weather got cooler and more rainy. Gerard, Zee, and Chris had been close to like me—at least other supernatural creatures—but they were a witch, a hunter, and a werewolf. Outsiders, but not fae.

Mister Walkenhorst had recognized the words I said in the van leaving the institution. "Nothing good lasts for me." There was a class of fae in Idyll, some of the non-nobles, that took those words as our motto. That suggested he was familiar with that group, which cemented my guess that he was fae, like me. It stood to reason that some of the other students would be fae as well. So maybe I'd finally find friends who understood what I went through every day. Maybe I'd find a family.

The biggest concern was what those friends or family would think when they found out why I wasn't in Idyll.

~

I dozed off again in the van. Apparently, getting angry and not eating much had me off my game. I imagined the drugs they'd given me at the institution probably didn't help either, but at least it sounded like it would only take maybe a week or so before I started feeling normal again.

When I woke up, Gerard and Miss Whalen were both gone. Mister Walkenhorst still sat in the driver's seat, reading a magazine, but he looked up and caught my gaze in the rearview mirror. "Hope you had a pleasant nap."

I shrugged and looked around. The faintest traces of sunlight had just crested the horizon, bathing everything in a pinkish glow. To the left was a wide field surrounded by trees, everything rimed in frost. To the right, a massive building. I leaned toward the windows on the building side of the van, trying to get a good look at it.

Compared to the buildings in Artis, this one looked old. The lower portions were made of cobblestones. The second floor was covered with dark wooden shingles, and the upper floors, at least what I could see of them, had slightly lighter wood that looked more like paneling than siding.

"This is Dedwydd?"

"Technically speaking, it's Dedwydd Academy. If you asked around about it in the area, amongst the humans, you'd be told it's a very posh private school for the scions of the finest families. Only that can't be true, because none of the locals ever get admitted." Mister Walkenhorst shrugged. "Guess they're not fine enough."

"Where are we, exactly?"

"Idaho. The nearest town is a few miles away, as the crow flies. It's far enough that the locals don't bother us, and we don't bother them." He turned in his seat. "Do you prefer to sit in here and talk or walk around outside? It's a mite bit chilly out, but I always feel a little strange sitting sideways in this seat and giving new kids the orientation talk."

"Orientation talk? Umm, how long is it, and when can I eat?"

He glanced down at his watch. "Breakfast is in about half an hour, and I can give you the basics before then. Sit or walk?"

"Walk," I said. I didn't care if he was comfortable in his seat or not, but I'd feel better out of the van. I'd feel even better in the woods, if he'd let me wander that way.

We both climbed out of the van, and I took a deep breath of the cold air. It was clean, tinged with the scent of wood smoke, and it felt good in my lungs. I smiled. At least that was better than Artis, with the choking factory smells always lingering in the air.

"Can we walk in the woods?" I asked.

"There are a few trails, but we won't want to go too far in. Students may spend time in the woods, but there's a fence out there, meant to keep you all in here, and it's not pleasant to touch."

I shuddered. "They're keeping us here with an iron fence?"

"It's more than just iron," he replied, "and it also serves to keep other things out, including nosy humans."

I walked toward the woods, my gaze darting around, looking for the fence he was talking about. The trees were a mix of deciduous varieties and evergreens. Few leaves clung to any of the former, which made it easy to see around them, but there were

26

enough evergreens to block the view farther in. At any rate, I couldn't spot the fence. That was something of a relief. It would have sucked if it was visible this close to the school. I anticipated I'd be spending a lot of time in the woods, if I could.

As we reached the first trees, I realized my hunger was less than I'd expected it to be. I wasn't accustomed to not being hungry, but here, it almost felt normal. I frowned at that realization.

Mister Walkenhorst spoke up before I had a chance to ask him anything. "Ground rules. Rule one: don't leave the school without permission. You'll need a month of good behavior before you can get that permission. Rule two: no powers. You won't be able to access them anyway, because of the warding here. Rule three: this place is safe because we keep the number of people who know about it to a minimum. We aren't going to take your cell phone, but you won't have much of a signal here. You may as well just turn it back off and tuck it away somewhere. Aside from those rules, we've got the usual sort of high school rules. No fighting, no bullying, no smoking, no drugs, no drinking, no boys in girls' rooms after ten, and vice versa." He paused to shrug. "You get the picture. Questions?"

I stared at him for a moment before I asked, "Can we start with the elephant in the ... yard? You're fae, right?"

Taking a deep breath, he nodded. "Yes, all the faculty here are recruited from supernatural groups. Some are previous attendees of Dedwydd Academy. I am not among those. But I was selected to accompany Miss Whalen to retrieve you and Mister LeCroix because the administration believed that perhaps the knowledge that there are others like you here might ease your transition into the school."

"Then clearly they don't know me," I muttered.

"On the contrary, they do." He straightened slightly. "You look at me and you see a fae of the noble class, and you are not incorrect in that assumption. Though it may not relieve you any to know this, I am the seventh son of a seventh son, or near enough that the implications of my birth order mean the same thing."

I bristled a bit when Mister Walkenhorst admitted to being of the noble class, but knowing that he was not in line for any inheritance was a relief of a sort. It meant at least he probably didn't want my head in the same way most of the nobles of Idyll did.

It didn't make us friends, though. And it presented more questions than it answered. "If you're a noble, why are you here?"

"By choice. My options in Idyll are constrained, much like the options of the non-nobles. While it is true that I have a certain level of freedom there, the lifestyle did not suit me. I wanted to do something, to make something of myself. So I left, came to the mortal realm, and found something that suited me here."

I eyed him skeptically. "And I should believe you why?"

"Do you have any other choice?"

He had a point. "I guess not."

"Very well, then. Any more questions?"

I scoffed. "Plenty."

"Unfortunately, if you wish to put your things in your room before breakfast begins, our conversation should come to an end."

Frustrated, I let out a long sigh. I had so many questions for him about the fae. As I thought about those questions, I realized what I was craving was gossip from Idyll. I wanted to know what had happened in my absence. The more I thought about it, though, I realized it didn't really matter. I had been exiled. Idyll was no longer my problem. And gossip from there wouldn't really help me out at a school for supernatural creatures. I gave Mister Walkenhorst a faint smile. "Sorry, you're right. Any tips outside of the rules?"

"Sure. Keep your head down, listen, and learn. If you run around trying to figure everything out right away, you'll just make yourself miserable, and you're liable to get yourself into trouble." He reached into his pocket and pulled out a key with a red plastic keychain. He squinted at it for a moment before he offered it to me. "Right. East wing, second floor. You're rooming with Lorelei Quinn till you're off probation."

I took the keychain. "Probation? You didn't say anything about probation."

"Keep your nose clean for a month." He shrugged. "That's the probation." Without another word, he walked back toward the van.

"Wait, what if I have more ... fae questions?"

He shrugged again. "You're a smart girl. You'll find someone to ask. I have places to be." He turned on his heel and walked away abruptly.

"Great," I said. "Guess I'll go meet my roommate."

~

The keyring Mister Walkenhorst had given me had once been painted with the number 217, but only the faintest remnant of the paint remained. Someone had rewritten the number in permanent marker on both sides. I made my way to the second floor, and then started checking room numbers.

I heard a click down the hallway, soft, but audible enough in the relative silence. One of the doors was slightly ajar, and the number on it was 217. If I'd just been walking down the hall, minding my own business, I might not have noticed. Now that I was standing outside of it, I wasn't sure how to approach this situation. Did I knock on the door to my own room? I knew that if I tried to put the key in the lock, the door would just swing open, and then I'd look ridiculous.

"Hello?" I called out as I nudged the door with my sneaker. It swung wide open, which meant my first introduction to the girl I assumed was my roommate was seeing her perched on the lap of a ginger-haired teenage boy in a wheelchair, their lips locked together. "Oh, sorry. Sorry, sorry, sorry."

She barely looked flustered as she pulled away from the boy. She smoothed her downright enviable wavy dark brown hair that nearly reached her waist. "Didn't realize the door hadn't latched. You must be Briar," she said, swinging off his lap. Straightening her short navy skirt, she smiled. "I'm Lorelei, and this is my boyfriend, Jasper."

Jasper nodded. At least he had the good grace to look as embarrassed as I felt, his face bright red, which highlighted his abundant freckles. He was awkward looking to begin with, and his embarrassment only heightened that. When he spoke, though, his voice was calm and smooth. "I should probably get going and let you two get to know each other."

Lorelei leaned down and gave Jasper a quick peck on the cheek before he wheeled his way past me and out the open door. She followed him and pressed the door closed until the latch clicked soundly. Leaning against the inside, she said, "So, can we keep that between the two of us? Technically we weren't doing anything wrong, but—" She trailed off and shrugged. "Some of the teachers are fussy about boys being in girls' rooms at all."

"Sure, no problem," I said as I surveyed the room. Two narrow beds, two desks, two wardrobes. One side of the room was very clearly Lorelei's—the desk surface piled with books and papers, the sheets rumpled, and the wardrobe doors hanging open. The opposite side of the room was starkly plain. I tossed my duffle on the bed.

"Welcome to Dedwydd," she said.

"Thanks." I looked at her outfit of a navy skirt and a slightly disheveled long-sleeved, white button-up shirt. She had the body to pull that look off, but I doubted everyone here wore their skirts that short. "Uniforms?"

"Yeah, they're basically the worst, but not everyone who comes here has, you know, family, or money, or—" She gasped and covered her mouth. "Oh, I'm so sorry."

I frowned. "Sorry for what?"

"Umm, all you've got is that one duffle, I'm guessing?" She gestured at my bag.

I held it up—at this point, all it held was my clothes from the institution, and it hung limply. "Uh, yeah. I suspect they burned the rest of my stuff."

Her eyes widened. "Your parents?"

"Uh, no. The parks department." I shrugged. "I didn't really have much to speak of. Uniforms are fine. Where do I get mine?"

"They'll drop them off later today. They'll bring you skirts and pants, so you can wear whichever you prefer, and if you want only one or the other, you can exchange the things you don't want."

"Don't I need to give them sizes or something?"

Lorelei shook her head, her shoulders relaxing a bit. "You've been brought in from somewhere else. The fact that I knew I was getting a roommate named Briar today should have told you as much. Someone, somewhere, already has your sizes. Don't worry. They fit everyone like crap."

I didn't think I should mention that hers fit just fine, lest she take it as some sort of unintended flirtation, so I changed the topic. "Uh, is the door always hard to latch?"

She shrugged. "Yeah, it's finicky sometimes. This is an old building, lots of weird creaks and other oddities."

"So, have you been here long?"

"About a year."

"Was it weird when you first got here too?"

She nodded. "A little. But Jasper and I both got sent here at the same time, so at least I knew someone."

"Oh, my friend Gerard is here too."

"Boyfriend?" she asked, a mischievous sparkle in her eye.

I shook my head quickly, not ready to start educating someone I'd just met about my asexuality. "No. We're just good friends."

"Okay, that's cool too. Having someone to talk to about the weird makes it a little easier at first. And then you get adjusted to the fact that you're going to school with witches and faeries and angels and who knows what else."

Her use of the word faeries instead of fae rankled a bit. Faeries always sounded so juvenile to me, and I hated it. But her mention of angels was more disturbing, since the people at the compound had claimed to be good Christians, with powers that reminded me of some of the stories I'd heard about angels. I had no way of knowing the truth, but the concept of angels on Earth was concerning. "So which one are you?" I asked.

Lorelei's eyes narrowed. She dropped her chin fast, but not so fast that I couldn't see her flaring nostrils before her hair fell forward like a veil.

I didn't know if I should apologize or run.

"Okay, I'm going to explain this to you once," Lorelei said, her words clipped. She looked me dead in the eyes with eyes so dark brown they almost looked black. "We don't ask that question here. It's rude. Think of it like asking someone who's not white where they're from."

"Okay, got it. Sorry."

Lorelei's expression cleared almost as quickly as it had darkened. "Sorry, I'm just touchy." She forced out a small laugh. "We're just tripping all over each other today, huh? I'm sure we'll get used to each other soon enough."

I nodded. "Yeah, I've never actually had a roommate, so I'll have to take your word for it."

"I didn't either until I got here. Worst month of my life." Then she stammered, "Oh, I don't ... I mean, I'm sure you'll be much nicer than my first roommate."

"I'll try," I said. But my mind whirled. Mister Walkenhorst had said "no powers," but I still didn't know if my sometimes-voracious hunger was a power or just a side effect of who I am. I didn't think Lorelei would take too kindly to waking up to me nibbling on her arm. "Do you mind if I ask you some other questions?"

Lorelei chewed at her lip. "Sure, I guess not."

"Is this place like a real school, or what?"

"Sometimes? I guess it depends on the specific, um, needs of the individual student. Like I'm in pretty much the same sorts of classes I was in at my old school. Jasper takes a lot of the same classes, but he has physical therapy instead of P.E. Not that it does him much good." She took a deep breath. "I'll just tell you now. He was in an accident, and it severed his spine. It was sort of my fault. That's all you really need to know about that, okay?"

I nodded, not entirely sure what to say. If Jasper was fae, or probably even a witch, a severed spine would eventually heal. I tried to remember what else Lorelei had mentioned before she got mad at me trying to find out what she was. Angels? They'd heal well too, I suspected. Something she hadn't mentioned? That seemed more plausible.

But there *were* other fae here. I felt the cold weight of the ring in my pocket and wondered whether I could make friends or if I was going to need to watch my back here.

"Almost breakfast," Lorelei said, interrupting my thoughts. "I'll walk down with you, if you want. But I'll warn you, it's usually disgusting greasy junk."

"Last thing I had to eat was a beef jerky stick sometime around dinner time. I don't really care what they're serving. I'm eating it. Tell me more about the classes while we walk."

~

The cafeteria here was much classier than the one in Artis, but it felt the same. Lorelei had ditched me as soon as she spotted Jasper, and they were too busy being madly in love with each other or something to invite me to sit with them.

Everyone else in the cafeteria was either blatantly staring at me or trying to pretend they weren't checking out the new girl. I saw more than a couple hands covering mouths as they whispered into someone else's ear. Then there were the ones shooting venomous looks in my direction, as though their glares might cause me to wither up and be banished from their sight. I was used to those glares from fae nobles, not so much from my peers. I could only assume that my reputation had preceded my arrival. So maybe Lorelei already knew what I was, and what I had done.

Looking around, I couldn't tell for sure what any of the other students were, except for teenagers. Clearly, from what Lorelei had said about fae and witches and angels, there must be some of those represented here. But to me, it just looked like a much wider assortment of people—ethnicities and genders and disabilities and who knew what else—than we'd had in Artis. I was glad to see Gerard wouldn't be the only African American kid here, and I thought he'd be pretty happy about that as well.

Speaking of Gerard, I didn't see him anywhere. I wondered if his orientation had lasted longer than mine. I certainly could have used a longer talk with Mister Walkenhorst, or anyone who was willing to put up with all my stupid questions.

My stomach roared and reminded me I was standing in the middle of the cafeteria, holding my tray of aptly described "greasy junk." I spotted an empty table, sat down with my back to the other students, and dug in.

I was so focused on eating that I jumped when another tray clattered down onto the table across from me, the bottle of orange juice teetering off the edge and rolling until my tray stopped it.

I looked up at a sheepish looking boy with sun-kissed tan skin, messy sandy blonde hair, and the same startlingly blue eyes as Mister Walkenhorst. He grinned at me and said, "Hey, sorry about that. Um, could you roll my juice back over here?"

I forced a smile and rolled the juice toward him, then turned my attention back to my breakfast.

He didn't take the hint. "So, you new here?"

I looked back up. "Yeah." Then I took a deep breath. I might not want to talk to people, but if I wanted friends here other than Gerard, I should start things off on the right foot. I set down my knife and extended my hand across the table. "Briar Williams."

"Keegan Morris." He smiled broadly, showing off brilliant white teeth, but didn't take my hand. "So, what'cha in for?"

That took me aback enough that I couldn't respond immediately. According to Lorelei, it wasn't acceptable to ask people what they were, but Keegan had no compunctions about asking what I'd done. To me, the latter seemed more offensive. Maybe it wasn't. Or maybe it was, and I should get angry at him. Either way, I felt like I might be doing a pretty good impression of a fish, which was not exactly an answer. And I was still holding my hand out across the table.

He laughed aloud. It didn't seem like he was laughing at me, but it still made my skin crawl. I pulled my hand back and tried to ignore his laughter by stabbing another bite of food.

"Sorry, it's a joke, mostly." He nodded toward the rest of the cafeteria. "A lot of us here did stuff on the outside that would have gotten us locked up in the real world. Dedwydd's not exactly the real world."

I hesitated before I responded. I knew why Gerard and I were here. We had, according to the cops, murdered a lot of people. From what Lorelei said, Jasper had been in some sort of accident that had been her fault. Drunk driving? "Is everyone here a criminal?" I blurted out finally.

"No, not everyone. Some of them are 'witnesses.'" Keegan put his hands up to make air quotes. A ring sparkled on one of the fingers of his left hand, but both his hands vanished just as quickly as they had appeared, before I got a good look at the ring. "Sometimes, when someone encounters the supernatural, they can't forget about it, and it breaks them. So they bring them here to show them that not all supernaturals are the same as the ones who hurt them."

"I take it you're not a witness?"

He shook his head. "Nope, but it was just a misunderstanding that landed me here. Me and Dave, one of my buddies from the football team, decided to go into San Diego, and his dad got pissed. Called the cops, told them I had kidnapped Dave, because there was no way his son would willingly go with me." He rolled his eyes. "His dad thought I turned Dave gay. Whatever. He was gay before I showed up. So, what about you?"

"I wasn't gay before you showed up. I mean ... I'm not. Then or now." I sighed. "Sorry. That's not even what you were asking."

"Nope. And hey, you know, good to know." He smiled again, all gleaming teeth. "No, I told you how I landed here. How about you?"

"Murder," I muttered, barely audible. I gave him a sheepish grin. "Multiple."

"Hard core," he said.

"Really? I thought this school was all about rehabilitation."

"Oh, yeah, totally." He shook his head, turning his statement from one that seemed to confirm my understanding to a negative. "But, you know, there's sort of relative degrees of impressiveness here. There are the people who are here on drug charges. Meh. And then there are the murderers on the other end of the spectrum. You get a lot more respect that way. You've violated a higher sort of law than those who are here on what most people would say are technicalities."

"That's not exactly encouraging, telling me I'll get respect because I murdered people." I glanced around at the other students near us, hoping no one was listening in on our conversation. "It makes me think that the other students would be gunning for more respect by doing worse things, right?"

Keegan shook his head again. "No, if you cause too much trouble here, they boot you out and send you to some other school. Something closer to a prison, I guess. There are lots of rumors about where it is and how it works. It sounds pretty awful, so that keeps most people in line."

Somehow, him telling me this didn't make me feel any better about it. If anything, I was starting to feel sick to my stomach, though I couldn't be sure if it was from the greasy food or an actual feeling of remorse. Either way, I was done with this conversation. "I've gotta go." I clambered out of my chair and then froze. "Uh, do we have to bus our own tables here?"

He inclined his head toward the opposite side of the cafeteria, where a small pass-through window was partly obscured by a cloud of steam.

"Okay, catch you later then," I mumbled as I hurried away.

CHAPTER FOUR:
HOW DID I GET HERE?

———

By the time I got back to my room, my stomach had calmed, and I found myself wishing I had grabbed something to nibble on. The bits of my breakfast I had eaten before Keegan showed up weren't going to get me through until lunch.

Lorelei had still been in the cafeteria when I dropped my tray off, so I figured I'd have my room to myself. I could use a few minutes alone, just to get my head on straight before launching into the next round of weirdo supernatural reform school.

Of course, I couldn't be that lucky.

There was a guy leaning against our door. He looked like he could have been Lorelei's brother—same dark hair, same tawny bronze skin, and same dark eyes. He wore his uniform white shirt unbuttoned and his tie undone, over a black t-shirt and slacks, topped with a motorcycle jacket. The t-shirt somehow managed to show off the fact that he had chiseled abs. Where Lorelei seemed like your average teenage girl, this guy seemed to be going for the bad boy rebel vibe. It was setting my teeth on edge. Badly.

"Hey, that's my door."

He looked at me and arched a perfectly sculpted eyebrow, the rest of his face impassive. "Then you must be Briar Williams." He held out a piece of paper, far enough from his body that it was an obvious offering, but near enough that I'd have to step closer to retrieve it. "Your schedule."

"Schedule?" I snatched the paper from him, getting only as close as I had to, but didn't look at it.

"For classes."

I frowned. "What, are you like some sort of office aide?"

"Yeah, actually." He extended a hand to me. "Nic Flores."

I reached out to take his hand, but as my skin neared his, I felt a weird electric tingle from the ring, still in my shirt pocket. I withdrew my hand quickly.

"Ooh, burned," he said, shaking his head. He looked into my eyes quizzically. "Demon?"

So some people would just ask. That was an interesting development. I supposed a yes or no question was a little less intrusive than "what are you?" I shrugged. "Uh, no. I mean, I guess it depends on your worldview, but I don't consider myself to be a demon. I just ... sorry, I don't mean to be rude, I'm just kinda overwhelmed by this whole ... everything."

He nodded. "Right, I get that. And I'm preventing you from getting into your one safe place. My bad. I beg your pardon." He bowed as he stepped away from my door.

The way he said the last bit struck me as old fashioned. He wasn't saying it in the way some people in Artis did when they didn't understand you or hadn't heard what you'd said to them. He said it genuinely, and I felt like I should respond somehow. "Um, okay, I give you my pardon?"

"Thank you." He smiled at me. If ever a smile really was as bright as the sun, Nic had it. It wasn't all flashy teeth and laughter like Keegan's, it was a real smile, from the heart. I felt it, and his gaze, until I slipped into my room and closed the door behind me.

I let out a long, shuddering breath, and flopped onto my bed. The mattress was far more comfortable than the one in my room at the juvie psych ward. Was this what I had been missing living in my cave? I mentally punched myself for not figuring out a way to live like this without having murdered people. A girl could get used to this.

A girl might not be able to get used to this ring giving her creepy feelings all over the place, though. It had come from alleged Christians, so maybe it was blessed, which gave me an uncomfortable feeling when near something they considered evil? The rednecks at the compound hadn't liked me and Gerard in particular, so maybe it detected fae or witches, which was why it was a little tingly to me. Was Nic some kind of fae or witch, and the ring was warning me away from him?

I sighed. There were far too many possibilities, and asking was out of the question, according to Lorelei. If the ring was trying to warn me about Nic, it was going to have to be a little clearer, because so far, I saw no reason to fear him. In fact, even on our brief interaction, he seemed nice and easy going.

He'd asked me if I was a demon, though, which was an oddly specific question. Did that make him an angel? If that were the case, what was he going to think if he found out about me murdering people?

I had so many questions, and no good way to get any of them answered. I wondered if I really had to go to classes right away. I wanted a day or two to acclimate to this new place and maybe look for some answers, so I wasn't struggling to figure it all out while I got settled.

Then it occurred to me I didn't know what day it was. I'd lost track of time while I was drugged, and I had only a rough sense of how much time had passed since Miss Whalen and Mister Walkenhorst picked me and Gerard up. I'd been in the juvie-psych ward for about three weeks, give or take, but I didn't think it would have taken more than a few hours to get to Idaho. I supposed I'd figure it out soon enough and unfolded the schedule Nic had given me.

English. History. The dreaded Algebra. Psychology of Terror.

I frowned. That seemed oddly specific for a high school class. It sounded interesting, though I had no idea why I would be in a class like that.

P.E. Ugh. Anger Management? Okay, that one might make a little more sense.

I bolted off my bed and poked my head out into the hallway, hoping to spot Nic.

"Problem?" A voice asked right beside my head.

I turned and found myself face to face with Nic, and alarmingly near him. He was now leaning against the wall just to the left of my door, rather than leaning on the door itself. He smelled, surprisingly, of freshly baked gingerbread, spicy and sweet at the same time.

I shook my head to clear it, to get his scent out of my nostrils, so I would stop thinking about him as food. "This schedule. Why do I have classes on the Psychology of Terror and Anger Management?" I scanned the rest of the schedule. "And Group and Individual Therapy sessions?"

"Everyone's schedule is tailored to the things they most need in order to learn how to function in the outside world. It's the rehabilitation aspect of the school."

"How do they know what I need?" I asked.

He shrugged. "Years of experience, I imagine. This place has been here for decades—centuries, maybe."

A cold shiver trickled down my spine. "So if this was ready for me first thing this morning, does this mean they've been keeping tabs on me for a while?"

Another shrug. "I've been here a year and a half, and there are things I still don't entirely understand about Dedwydd."

This wasn't a mystery I was going to solve immediately, it seemed. "What if they've got something wrong about me? Who do I talk to about changes to my schedule?"

"Your therapist. You'll see the same person for group and individual therapy. Failing that, you could take it up with the Headmistress if you want, but I don't advise it."

I felt my temper rising, but it didn't feel the same as it normally did. It felt like it was smothered under a heavy blanket, rather than boiling up to the surface. My fingers felt normal, too, with no claws poking out of them. I ground my teeth, and those felt like they were of a human size and shape as well, rather than a mouth full of razor-sharp fae fangs.

"Look, I get it," he continued. "It takes some time to adjust to things. Just give it a chance and talk to your therapist at your individual appointment when you get there if you still feel like you're in the wrong classes."

I didn't like his answer, but he said it so calmly and reasonably that I couldn't help but see the rationality of it. I took a deep breath and nodded at him.

"See, that's already better. And hey, if you need anything, just look me up. I'm more than happy to help, day or night." He winked, and there was that slight bad boy vibe again. "Want me to walk you to your first class?"

I looked down at my schedule. As much as I wanted to tell him no, especially after his not-so-subtle wink, I had no idea where Main 75 was located. "Sure, why not," I muttered.

~

My English and History classes flew by as I tried to catch on to where the rest of the class was. It wasn't like we were picking up where I'd left off in my classes in Artis, and even if we had, I wasn't sure I'd remember what we'd done three weeks ago. I also didn't see anyone I recognized until I reached the Algebra classroom. Gerard stood beside the teacher's desk, and I joined him there.

"Hey, how's it going?" I asked.

"So far, so good," he said, wrapping an arm around me to give me a side hug.

I leaned into Gerard. I wasn't much for hugging, but right then it seemed like exactly what I needed to ground myself before dealing with the dreaded Algebra.

That caught the teacher's attention. "Please keep public displays of affection to a minimum, Mister LeCroix. Miss—" She reached out a hand for my schedule. Slender was the only word my mind could find to describe her, other than angular. Her dark hair was stick straight, and her facial features looked like they'd been carved from a smooth, coppery stone. Even her clothing was severe, high necked and long sleeved, but without the usual frills you'd expect on a teacher's blouse of that style.

She sniffed as she looked at my schedule. "Miss Williams. Very good. I am Miss Hale. Please find your seats, and we shall commence." Her diction was impeccable and perfectly fit my initial impression of her as sharp in a prickly sense. I knew the sort all too well from my time in Idyll, and I was more than happy to move away from her desk.

The classroom was small enough that none of the student desks were far from one another, with only about a dozen in total. But the only two seats with no one occupying them were on opposite sides of the room. I grimaced. I really wanted to catch up with Gerard.

"Door or window?" Gerard murmured to me.

"Gimme the door," I replied. "I'll get caught staring out the window too much otherwise."

He nodded. "We'll catch up later. I've got some news." Then he headed to the far side of the classroom, leaving me to fret about his news and getting through my least favorite class with a teacher who didn't seem like the type to let me coast through on partial credit.

~

If lunch hadn't been immediately after Algebra, I think my head would have burst. I waited in the hallway until Gerard came out, and I practically attacked his arm like a hungry leech when he joined me. "What's the news?"

"Chill, Briar," he said with a chuckle. "Gods, you're high strung."

"Whatever. I want to know."

"We're in Idaho."

I blinked a couple of times. "I already knew that. Mister Walkenhorst told me."

"Oh. Well then you just spent the past forty-five minutes being hyped up about something that didn't even matter."

"I guess." I shrugged. "But also—hi! We have a class together, and now we can go to lunch together!"

Another low chuckle rumbled in his throat, and he nodded. "Yeah, let's go eat mystery meat and dubious vegetables and talk about boys we like."

"You like boys?" I asked.

"Not in particular. It's just an expression."

"Ah, too bad. I met a guy you might like, otherwise. Well, maybe." I considered that. If Gerard did actually like guys, could I genuinely recommend Keegan or Nic to him? Doubtful. Both of them weirded me out, though in very different ways. They both seemed like trouble, though.

Gerard had to poke me to pull me out of my reverie.

"Huh?" I asked.

"Did you meet your roommate yet?"

"Yes. Her name's Lorelei. She's got a boyfriend, Jasper, who I met too. Slightly awkwardly."

Gerard arched his eyebrow at me. "Oh, do tell?"

"They were making out in our room when I got there." I lowered my voice slightly, even though we were entering the bustling cafeteria. "Also, don't ask people what they are. It's rude."

"Good to know," Gerard said. He jerked his chin toward a boy with hair so blond it may as well have been white, and skin even paler. He was willowy and lithe, and looked about as opposite from Gerard as he could be. "Blondie over there is my roommate. His name's Sean. He seems alright so far. Really quiet, which suits me fine."

I spotted Lorelei and Jasper across the cafeteria and pointed them out to Gerard. "That's Lorelei. Jasper's in the wheelchair."

"Oh yeah? He's in my occult studies class."

I stared at Gerard. "You have an occult studies class?"

He shrugged. "Yeah, what's your schedule look like?"

"Food first," I insisted. "Then we can compare."

Once we had our trays of aptly described mystery meat and dubious vegetables, I placed my schedule side by side with Gerard's. They were upside down to me, but I could read them just as easily that way.

"So we've got Algebra together," Gerard said. "And you're in group 6. I'm in group 1."

"Everything's conspiring to keep us apart," I wailed.

"If I didn't know you, I'd say that's a tad overdramatic, Briar." Gerard shrugged. "We can get lunch together after Algebra, and I don't think they have rules about hanging out outside of classes."

"Okay, but I'm just not really good at making friends, you know?"

"Maybe things will be different for you here." He shoveled a bite of food into his mouth and looked around. After he chewed it, he continued. "I mean, I don't see too many people with fake tans and bleached blonde hair and fancy nails and the latest fashions, though that last part could have to do with the uniforms. The people here seem a lot more down to earth, and a lot more like us."

"Like us isn't necessarily a good thing from my perspective," I said, taking a bite of my lunch and surveying the room. Gerard was right about the students here looking very different from the ones in Artis. But the possibility of running afoul of fae who might have heard of me wasn't far from my mind.

With a shake of his head, Gerard chuckled. "They've got the classes I need for college prep, they're feeding us food of a mostly edible nature, and we're not in dead-end Artis. I think we've hit the jackpot."

"If you say so," I muttered around a bite of food. But I couldn't shake the feeling that the other shoe was about to drop.

CHAPTER FIVE:
WHAT KIND OF SCHOOL IS THIS?

After a morning of standard high school classes, I was actually looking forward to seeing what Psychology of Terror was all about. I'd determined that it was Monday in my morning classes, and I'd finally puzzled out that P.E. met on Mondays and Fridays. It was replaced by Group Therapy on Tuesdays, with study hall on Wednesdays and Thursdays. So while that still left Anger Management to wonder about, it looked like an easy afternoon, especially since Nic had let me know that I wouldn't be expected in P.E. until my uniforms had been delivered.

I was starting to get used to the layout of the building, with its wings of classrooms on the first floor and dorm rooms above, so I was a little surprised when the room for this class was on the second floor. As I wandered down the wide hallway, Nic came out of one of the rooms and locked it behind him.

"Hey, Nic, could I get your help again?"

He smiled, with that grin that lit up the room. "Psychology of Terror, right?"

"Uh, yeah. Am I in the right place?"

"Just about." He nodded a little farther down the hall, where a door on the opposite side hung open. "We're in there."

"We?"

"Yeah, I'm in that class too. Study buddies, huh?"

I shrugged but headed into the room he'd indicated as he crossed the hallway to join me.

The room was about the same size as the room I shared with Lorelei, but rather than the setup we had, this room had a couple of sofas and several chairs, mismatched and threadbare, but cozy looking. A woman with an impossible mass of curly red hair and so many freckles they almost made her look tanned sat perched on the arm of one of the sofas, chatting with Lorelei, while four other students sat around the room. A girl who looked like the spitting image of Wednesday Addams sat beside a nerdy looking pale-skinned boy with round-framed glasses, while two of the chairs were occupied by a slim girl hunched over a notebook, a curtain of jet black hair obscuring her features, and an athletically built African American girl who glared at me the moment I walked through the door.

"You must be Briar," the woman said. She patted Lorelei's shoulder gently and rose. "I'm Finola Donaghue, and I insist that students in my classroom call me Finola." She looked me over briefly, then nodded. "Sit here with Lorelei for today, and we can rearrange later if need be."

Nic plopped into the remaining chair, while Finola reperched on the edge of the sofa that I was now sitting on. I gave Lorelei a little smile, but she was focused intently on the nerdy boy, who was most definitely not her boyfriend. If I hadn't already met Jasper, I would have suspected Lorelei was dating this guy.

"Introductions all around, please," Finola said, pointing to the other students in turn. Isabella was the goth girl, Mason was the nerdy guy, Dhani was the athletic girl, and Mei was the dark-haired scribbler, who I identified as Chinese once she looked up from her notes.

"Alright, so, quick recap for Briar on our discussion from yesterday? Mei?"

Mei carefully avoided eye contact with me when she looked up, her attention focused on Finola. "Fairy tales as a metaphor for humanity's deep-seated fears."

I cocked my head to the side. This was likely to get interesting quickly, especially coming from a non-human perspective. And while I couldn't easily identify what anyone else in the room was, in terms of their non-humanity, the only other person I thought could be fae was our teacher.

Then a darker thought hit me. What if Mei was avoiding making eye contact with me because she was one of the "touched by the supernatural" students. She could have been taken by the fae, and afraid of looking me in the eyes because of it.

Suddenly, I was sweating and nauseous. I had taken part in stealing mortal children and taking them to Idyll, a fact I had not enjoyed, and one I felt much worse about as I got to know humans in Artis. Now, I might be brought face to face with someone who had been victimized by the fae. In this setting, that felt worse than awful. It felt unredeemable.

I had to get away. "Um, can I be excused?" I asked, not waiting for an answer, but rushing out into the hall as fast as my legs would carry me.

~

I'd made it to the center of the wide second floor hallway and curled up in a ball before I heard the classroom door click behind me, followed by quiet footsteps.

I looked up, half expecting to see Lorelei or Finola. Nic was the third person on my list of people in that room who might check up on me, though I didn't know why he would.

He had concern etched across his features as he looked down at me. "Are you okay? The ... I mean, if we need to not start your first day with fairy tales, Finola says that's fine. We can try a different topic."

I took a deep, shuddering breath. "I don't know. Everything was going fine, and then all of the sudden, I felt sick and worried."

He crouched beside me, about a foot away, and lowered his voice. "I'm trying hard not to pry, but does it have something to do with your past?"

I nodded, though my head shook from nervousness as I did.

"I totally get that. We've all shown up here with baggage, and sometimes that comes out in weird ways."

"It's not my baggage I was worried about," I muttered.

Nic sat opposite me, his legs folded beneath him. "No? Then whose?"

"That's what I don't know. Nobody talks about what they are, I get that. But not really knowing what anyone is, what extent of creatures are here, or what sort of 'touched' some of these people are is terrifying. I'm worried that I'm going to piss someone off and not realize what I've done."

"Yeah, that's kind of inevitable," he admitted, rubbing at the back of his neck. "I mean, this is high school, and it's not easy to get along with a bunch of other teenagers you don't know well. Can I offer you a bit of reassurance?"

I shrugged but nodded. "Sure."

"Despite the fact that this school is weird, and there are a bunch of different kinds of people here, the teachers and Headmistress know what they're doing. They're careful about who they put into classes together. It's why a class like Psychology of Terror is so small. Our section is only 'creatures,' as you put it. None of the 'touched.'"

I wanted to believe him. He was so genuine, his eyes warm and brown and filled with concern. Concern for me. He didn't even know me, but he was worried about me. On top of that, his explanation made sense. They hadn't just thrown me into this classroom on a whim to see what would happen. This was part of a plan. Knowing that, maybe I could get through this.

I still had some lingering doubts, but now I felt like I could articulate them. "But there are people here who are 'touched' by the—" I had almost said fae, but I stopped myself in time. "There are people here who have been 'touched' by the type of creature I am. How do I make sure not to trip over that and trigger them?"

Nic shrugged. "As soon as I figure that out, I'll probably be promoted to class president. In the meantime, you'll feel like you're walking on eggshells for a few days, and then things will sort of fall into a routine. At least that's how it worked for me."

I nodded and took a deep breath. "Yeah, okay. I guess—" I trailed off and looked around the hallway. This was a completely new place, and it would take time to adjust, just like it had in the first few days and weeks after I was thrown out of Idyll. At least here, I had some idea about how humans interacted with one another. And I was living at a much more comfortable level than I had in Artis.

Nic was looking at me expectantly, and I realized I hadn't finished my earlier thought. With another deep breath, I forced a smile. "I guess it will take a little time."

He nodded, rose, and offered me a hand up.

I took it, unsurprised at the zap from the ring in my pocket this time.

Nic, however, narrowed his eyes. "What is it about you, Briar Williams?"

I smiled, finally feeling better enough to crack a half-joke. "That'd be telling, now wouldn't it?"

~

The discussion we came back to in Psychology of Terror had shifted to whether the blame should be placed on Goldilocks or the bears, which seemed a lot more light-hearted and easier for me to deal with. I couldn't be sure if they'd picked a new topic of discussion for my benefit or not, but either way, I appreciated it. As class ended, Finola stopped me as I headed for the door. "Are you alright now, Briar?"

"Yes, ma'am," I said. "Thank you."

She shook her head, grimacing. "Please don't call me ma'am. Seriously. I'm not that much older than ... well, at least not much older than you all seem to be. Just let me know if we tread on any problematic ground, okay?"

"It's not problematic ground for me, exactly." I looked at her thoughtfully. "I assume they give our teachers our full files?"

She nodded. "As full as they are when the school receives them. At a minimum, that's where you came from, originally and most recently, and what you've done."

I glanced into the hallway. A few clusters of students waited nearby, either waiting for this classroom or another similar one on this floor. None of them were near enough to overhear me if I kept my voice quiet, but I also felt the need to couch my words as cautiously as I could. "I had a pang of conscience, related to the ... topic for today."

"Understood." She bit at her lip. "Look, I'm not a therapist, so I can't really advise you on that. When you do meet with your therapist for your individual appointment, though, make sure that's on the list to discuss, okay?"

I nodded. "Thanks for the tip. I should get to my next class."

"Of course. See you tomorrow, Briar."

I hurried away, consulting my schedule to see where my study hall met. But my mood was buoyed slightly by Nic and Finola's concern for me. Maybe this wouldn't be so bad after all.

~

My good mood got me through the study hall they'd assigned me to in lieu of P.E. for the day. There were only half a dozen of us there, and pretty much everyone arrived and got straight to studying. I recognized pretty much everyone as someone I'd had classes with in the morning, though I hadn't caught any of their names. The only person I "knew" was Jasper, and with the way he made quick eye contact and then looked away, we weren't going to be chatty.

Since I had a couple of assignments from my morning classes, I had plenty to keep me busy, though I couldn't help but fret about Anger Management. I'd be the first to admit I needed help with my temper, but I doubted anything here could help me. Anger was an inherent part of the sort of fae I was. It fueled me. But it also had gotten me in trouble, more times than I cared to count.

From the limited amount of time I'd spent in the mortal realm, plus the years of studying it from afar, I'd seen that anger management was shorthand for a variety of techniques from meditation to art therapy. If I was honest with myself, I'd never actually tried anything to control my temper. In Idyll, I reveled in it, at least to a point. And that point had been when my temper threatened my careful planning. Then, I'd choked it down for as long as I could, only to have it rear up ten times worse when I couldn't hold it in any longer.

I found myself thinking about what Nic would tell me if he knew I was having worries about my last class of the day. He'd probably tell me to give it a chance and talk to my therapist if I didn't feel like it was the class I needed. Nic was all about giving things chances. I couldn't find any fault in that plan, at the moment. At any rate, it probably wouldn't hurt me to try whatever techniques they used here at Dedwydd to teach a bunch of supernatural troublemakers to stop getting into trouble.

I had to bite my tongue to keep myself from laughing out loud. How had I gone from "who is this random guy lurking near my door?" to "what would Nic Flores do?" in the space of a handful of hours? I had no idea. He'd been super nice, though, and helpful. I didn't think it was an act, which put him high on my list of people I could trust. Before, that list had been Zee, Gerard, and Chris. Now that it was only me and Gerard here at Dedwydd, it made sense to bolster the list with some new blood. I wasn't ready to include Lorelei or Jasper on that list, but Nic had gone out of his way to help me, so he rated inclusion.

Maybe I was making a new friend.

~

Anger Management was the last thing on my schedule for the day, and I found myself back up on the second floor in one of the tiny classrooms. That was a good sign. Hopefully, this wasn't some sort of additional therapy where I'd have to talk about my feelings.

The room was arranged similarly to the room for Psychology of Terror, with couches and overstuffed chairs. Mei was in this class too, already in the room, hands folded in her lap, and so still that if I hadn't known I'd walked into a different classroom, I'd have suspected she just stayed here between Psychology of Terror and Anger Management. She didn't look up when I walked in. None of the other seats were occupied, so I had my choice. I stood in the doorway, considering, until someone tapped my shoulder from behind.

I found myself looking at the stomach of a guy who was filling the entirety of the doorway, ducking so he didn't knock his head on the top of the doorjamb. He sported a nearly black buzzcut, sharply contrasting with his pale skin. He had to be at least seven feet tall and about three feet wide.

"Hey, sorry," I said, stepping out of his way and letting him move his bulk into the classroom.

He sat gingerly on the opposite end of the sofa from Mei, delicately enough that he barely moved the cushion he sat on, and he, too, focused on his hands in his lap.

I took my cue to sit, picking the couch seat opposite him. I wanted to introduce myself, but I wondered if he and Mei were already meditating or something. I wasn't sure if spending forty-five minutes thinking about my past would be better or worse than talking about feelings.

Two more students entered the room quietly, one a short dark-haired girl with a roundish face, whose gaze flickered across me before she took one of the armchairs. She wore a sweater over her uniform blouse that matched her skirt, and knee-high socks in the same color, all of which combined to look a lot cozier than just the blouse and skirt combination that Lorelei had been wearing this morning. I hoped I'd find a sweater waiting for me when I returned to my room after classes. Cozy seemed perfect right about now.

The second student was an average looking African American guy who sat in the other armchair. His tie was a little looser than most people wore theirs, and he had a blazer on over his uniform shirt. I considered whether there might be blazers for the girls as well. Was I actually getting excited about clothing? Then I remembered that some of the uniforms might actually be brand new pieces, not things I'd found discarded or dug out of a donation bin, and I accepted the fact that yes, I was excited about the prospect of *new* clothing.

With the latest two arrivals taking the chairs, and class about to begin, my thoughts shifted away from the uniforms. Would I be so lucky to get the sofa all to myself?

Before I could break the silence to ask if anyone else would be arriving, another familiar face entered the room.

"Briar," Mister Walkenhorst said, giving me a nod.

Oh, of course. A teacher. That was what we were missing. I nodded back. "Mister Walkenhorst."

He pursed his lips as his gaze swept over the other students. "Has anyone seen Jaylin?"

"I'm here," a voice said behind him.

Mister Walkenhorst turned, keeping the bulk of his body still in the doorway, but revealing a student with dark shoulder-length wavy hair and slender face. They wore slacks and a sweater, neither of which gave away their gender.

What was more interesting was the way they looked at me. Their expression morphed from confused to terrified to furious in the space of about as many seconds.

"Mister Walkenhorst—" they began, their voice now considerably louder and less relaxed, breaking on the final syllable.

Mister Walkenhorst raised his hand, palm toward the student, a gentle gesture for them to stop. "Jaylin. Take a seat."

Jaylin's eyes widened. "Next to her?"

I had no idea what was happening, but I scooted as close to the arm of the sofa as I could, trying to clear space for Jaylin. I was still wearing my clothes from the outside, and though they'd seemed clean when I put them on, I wondered if I stunk. Maybe I'd gotten some of my lunch on my shirt?

The short girl rose from her armchair and said, "Briar, right? Swap me seats."

I gave her a quick smile and moved to the armchair, which was still nearest to the end of the sofa near where Jaylin would be sitting.

Mister Walkenhorst interposed himself into the space between the armchair and Jaylin's end of the sofa. "Okay, better?" he asked, eyeing both me and Jaylin.

I shrugged. "I'm fine, but—"

He cut me off. "Good." He watched my face for a moment longer, then nodded. "After class," he mouthed.

Jaylin took their seat, pointedly looking away from me as Mister Walkenhorst closed the door. "Alright," he said, returning to his post between us and picking up a CD case. "I think we'll do some quiet meditation today, to the dulcet tones of 'Springtime Medley'."

I didn't know if I was in trouble or going to finally get some sort of explanation. Either way, even as the sounds of soft breezes and birdsong filled my ears, Anger Management was not off to a good start.

~

I waited in the classroom for the others to leave, feigning as though I'd fallen asleep during the meditation. It wasn't too far of a stretch. I almost had, a few times, but some level of alarm always kept me from slipping too far under.

Mister Walkenhorst left the classroom door open but perched on the arm of the sofa nearest me. "That could have gone worse. I'm not sure who made the decision to put you and Jaylin in the same section of Anger Management, but I'm going to run it by the Headmistress immediately."

Something gnawed at the inside of my stomach when Mister Walkenhorst mentioned the Headmistress, but I said, "I don't understand."

"I take it you've never met them before, then?"

I shook my head. "I can count the number of student *names* I know here on ... well, I guess I'm up to fingers and toes now. Gerard is the only person I know well enough to say I *know*."

"What about before that?" he asked.

I frowned. "Like, in Artis? Definitely not."

He continued to press me. "Before that?"

"You mean in Idyll?" I shrugged. I'd caught on to Mister Walkenhorst's use of "them" with regard to Jaylin, so I followed his lead with gender-neutral pronouns. "They don't ring any bells?

Except maybe some vague alarm bells in my head that I don't understand, that are getting louder now that I'm thinking about it?"

"Jaylin deals with a lot of anger, due to their past. I think it's safe to assume that they recognized you for what you are, which made things a lot worse today."

The truth of it finally clicked. "They're a changeling child?" My stomach roiled, just like it had when I'd run out of Psychology of Terror earlier. I almost bolted again. "But Nic said I didn't need to worry about that!"

"In Psychology of Terror, no, you wouldn't." He shook his head. "The rules have been a little looser for my class, because it's not been an issue before. I'll see what I can do. You might have a new schedule tomorrow. Just hang tight."

I nodded, but the pit of my stomach still churned. I didn't recognize Jaylin, I was sure of that.

But they sure recognized me.

CHAPTER SIX:
SPOOKY ROOM

One of the girls from Anger Management, the short one with the round face, was waiting in the hallway when I finally left, and I braced myself for more hate thrown my way.

"You're Briar?" she asked, dark brown eyes searching my face.

I winced but nodded.

Her words came out quickly. "I'm Echo, she/her. Welcome to Dedwydd. Not enough people say that on a new student's first day, so I've decided to become a one-woman welcoming committee. Also, what are your pronouns?"

Between the speed of her speech and the tension that had been building up in me all day, I nearly fell forward with a burst of laughter. "Thank you," I managed to say. "I'm sorry I'm laughing. It means a lot to me, but today has been a really hard day. Oh, and she/her."

"Cool. It's always rough to start at a new school. I remember how awful my first week was. Hence why I like to welcome new people." She paused. "You're rooming with Lorelei, right?"

My laughter finally subsided. "Yeah."

Echo nodded. "I'm sure she's not too happy about that. She hasn't had a single room for very long."

"Yeah, I could see her wanting a single room." I almost started to tell Echo about walking in on Lorelei and Jasper making out, but I remembered Lorelei had asked me not to. I'd already mentioned it to Gerard, and now I felt a pang of conscience. Lorelei hadn't specifically told me not to tell other students, and she hadn't asked me to promise not to tell, but I also knew that if gossip got around, she'd know exactly who blabbed. The whole thing was more drama than I wanted to deal with, especially on my first day.

I realized that I was probably staring off into space and might have missed anything that Echo asked me, so I tried to pick the conversation back up where I'd left it hanging. "I've never had a roommate before, actually. Any advice?"

"Ooh, never?" Echo asked. "No, don't answer that, I don't want to pry. As for Lorelei, I don't think she's a bad person, once you get to know her, but she's got a lot of barriers up. She's kind of prickly if you run into one of them."

I nodded at that. "Wow, that's really insightful."

Echo shook her head and looked away. "Whatever."

"No, I mean it. I'm really not very good at people? Like, I've only been one for six months?"

Narrowing her eyes, Echo returned her sharp gaze to me. "Wait, what?"

Ah, crap. I'd probably given too much away. "I ... it's complicated."

She chuckled, and her gaze softened. "Yeah, okay, I get that. So, anyway, assuming you don't have anything you need to do right now, would you like to meet some more friendly people?"

I shrugged. "I guess I've got some homework, but it's nothing I can't finish later."

"Great, follow me!"

Echo led me up to the third floor. I hadn't been up there so far, but reaching it, I found it to be basically a copy of the second floor. She approached one of the doors and knocked.

"Whozit?" came a girl's voice from within.

"Echo."

The lock clicked, and a taller girl with her light brown hair teased artistically into a wide, soft fauxhawk lunged out of the door and kissed Echo full on the lips. Then she giggled and looked at me. "Wow, I'm glad you were in the lead, Echo, or this would have been a much more awkward introduction." She stuck out a hand. "Hi, I'm Aimee. Welcome to Spooky Room."

"This is Briar," Echo said. "She/her."

"Right, the pronouns, sorry," Aimee said. "I'm also she/her."

I shook Aimee's hand and let her pull me into the room. It didn't look terribly spooky to me, but I guess some people might have been weirded out by the trappings of occult activity strewn about as decorations. Both beds had black comforters, with dark colored pillows propped against the walls to make them more like couches than beds, and there was a black lace scarf draped across the curtains, but otherwise, it didn't look much different from my room, just more lived in and cozy. I kind of liked it.

Aimee pointed at the room's other inhabitant, another shorter girl with about an inch of dark roots showing beneath bleached blonde wavy chin-length hair, who had been writing in a notebook until my arrival with Echo. "That's Mads. Well, Maddie. We all call her Mads."

"Because it's faster," Maddie said softly.

"Yeah, we know," Aimee said, scoffing. "This is Briar, I guess?"

I nodded. "Nice to meet you."

Aimee pulled Echo onto the second bed in the room, where they began making out. I stood awkwardly in the doorway until Maddie looked at me a bit shyly and patted the bed beside her. "I promise I don't bite."

I hesitated, both at her use of the word "promise," and what she'd said. "What if I do?" I asked.

Maddie's blue eyes widened, but she shrugged. "Please don't bite me?"

I offered her a smile. "I guess that's a fair request, since you invited me into your room and all."

Maddie looked at me more closely when I sat beside her. "Okay, you're not a vampire, because they don't allow those here. No self-control. Same with werewolves." She narrowed her eyes. "Oh, are you just being flip?"

"Flip?"

"Ummm, right, regionalism. Sarcastic?"

"Oh. Ummm, I guess sort of yes and sort of no? I do bite, but I won't bite you, since you asked me nicely not to." I cocked my head to the side. "Where are you from?"

"Massachusetts," she replied with a groan. "You?"

"Washington, most recently. Not the interesting part, though. Out near the Pacific where no one lives."

From across the room, Aimee asked, "Okay, we gotta know, and I hate twenty questions. If we tell you what we are, you willing to spill?"

I glanced across the room, where Echo was adjusting her shirt and Aimee was playing with Echo's short hair. Had Echo befriended me just to get information out of me? Or was I being paranoid? As I thought about it, I didn't feel threatened by any of these girls. Maybe this was just how you made friends here at Dedwydd.

Maddie spoke up before I could. "Okay, I'm just going to tell you, because if we don't, someone will. We're witches. We started out independent of one another, but we're a coven, now. A bunch of the other students think we're up to no good, but we're just as restricted as everyone else on campus. All we can do is study."

I nodded, excited. "My friend Gerard is a ... well, I don't think he calls himself a ... crap, I probably shouldn't have said that."

"Gerard LeCroix?" Aimee asked, approximating Gerard's Southern drawl. "Yeah, we met him. He's in Occult Studies, which pretty much pegs you as a witch of some derivation."

"Right, he mentioned that class." I took a deep breath, ready to spill the beans. "Yeah, so I'm a fae."

"Ooooh," Aimee said. "Now that's a fun one. What kind?"

Echo placed her hand on Aimee's shoulder. "Go easy on her, hun. It's her first day." She turned her attention to me. "So one of the things that a lot of students here do is a bit of *quid pro quo*. You know what that means?"

I scrambled for the Latin translation. "Something for something?"

"You speak Latin?" Maddie asked.

I nodded. "A little, yeah."

She hugged my arm that was nearest to her. "New best friend!"

"Hey!" Aimee and Echo both shouted at the same time.

I extricated my arm from Maddie's grasp. "Also, not much of a hugger. And my Latin's really kind of rusty." I didn't want to go into the rest of the details right away, about how the noble fae in Idyll used Latin, and I'd only used it to help with my own plans. That was too much information for new friends sharing, I suspected.

"Anyway, yeah," Echo said. "Information for information. It's basically the currency of the realm, so to speak. So we've established the basics. We're witches, you're fae."

"Seeing as about half of us at Dedwydd are witches or fae, yeah," Aimee said, rolling her eyes.

I was a little surprised by the percentage, since as far as I knew, I hadn't met any other fae. "Really?"

"Rough estimate," Echo replied. "To be fair, it's more like witches and fae are the largest groups of a single type of supernaturals. Overall, maybe everything else combined outnumbers us, but we represent probably the two largest blocks."

"So who else is fae?"

Aimee shook her head. "Nope, our turn. What kind of fae are you?"

I hesitated with my answer, unsure whether Aimee knew what she was actually asking me. "In what sense?"

"Like if you had to identify with any one character from a fairy tale, who would it be?"

I laughed at that one. "Most of the fairy tales you know are nothing like reality."

"Oh, we know," Maddie chimed in. "But it's a real question. So?"

I bit at my lower lip as I considered the question. They probably anticipated an answer like the elves that made shoes or Rumpelstiltskin or something like that. But my answer wasn't a fae at all. "The Big Bad Wolf?"

All three of their gazes landed on me. Aimee looked amused, and Echo looked startled. I hazarded a glance at Maddie, and she just looked confused.

"I'm not like a wolf fae or anything, it's just my answer." I paused. "You didn't ask why, but I think that's another question, and it's my turn now. Are you up to no good like everyone thinks?"

"No," Aimee said, rolling her eyes as her shoulders slumped. "Like Maddie said, all we can do is study. No spells on campus. And if we get caught doing spells off campus, we get detention."

I latched onto that. "Detention? Is that what happens if you get in trouble?"

"It all depends," Echo said. "But that's more information for later."

"Yeah, I have a much more important question," Aimee said. "Have you done the history homework yet?"

"Huh?" But it clicked as I looked at Aimee a bit longer. She'd been in my History class in the morning. Maddie had been in my English class. "Oh, no, I haven't." I paused. "That's seriously your deep and burning question?"

"Yeah, okay, that's a pretty dull one," Aimee admitted. "So you get a dull one next."

I pondered that for a moment. Most of the questions I wanted to ask were the big ones, the ones that apparently were going to require some big reveals from me. I wasn't sure I was entirely ready for that yet. Echo, Aimee, and Maddie seemed nice enough, but it was hard figuring out how to get close to people. I'd been lucky with Zee, Gerard, and Chris, in that we'd all been thrown into a bad situation and had to work together to get out of it. I wasn't sure these three girls would still like me if I explained why I identified with the Big Bad Wolf, either.

So I asked my most burning question that had nothing to do with supernatural creatures. "Is there anywhere on this campus where I can get a cell phone signal?"

~

Maddie and Aimee might have nicknamed their room "Spooky Room," but the space they'd sent me to after dinner where I *might* be able to get a signal on my cell was far spookier. They directed me to a narrow staircase, chained off with a "Do Not Enter" warning, up to the fourth floor. The fourth floor was more like an attic space, with sloped ceilings that were almost too low for me to walk under comfortably. Then there was a hallway that required turning sideways to navigate, a rickety looking spiral staircase, and then a dust and cobweb filled space. Thinking about the shape of the exterior of the building, I had a rough recollection of a sort of garret in the center of the roof. That had to be where I was.

I shone my phone's screen around. It was an octagonal room, smaller than my dorm room, with shuttered windows covering every wall. The shutters were on the inside, which seemed a little odd to me, but as I peeked through one, I discovered there were shutters on the inside and the outside. Even with the double layer of slatted wood, this room was still cold, and the high-pitched whine of the wind filtered through a crack somewhere. The whole place smelled of disuse.

But the witches were right. I had one bar of service on my phone if I held it up as high as I could. The text messages I had typed to Zee last night hadn't sent yet. I moved around the space, watching the single bar disappear on one side of the room, and flicker back into existence on the other. So there was service, but it was fickle. And my messages still hadn't sent.

The spiral staircase creaked below, and I pulled my phone to my chest, shielding its glow with my body. Maybe it was just the noises that old buildings make, and I was being paranoid. Or maybe I was about to get in trouble.

Maddie had warned me that technically the fourth floor and beyond were off limits to students. But she had also said the odds of getting caught were pretty slim. Based on our interactions so far, I didn't think the witches would have told me about this place to set me up.

But the staircase continued to creak. Ignoring the unsent text messages, I tiptoed toward the stairs.

I caught a faint glimpse of something wispy floating near the bottom of the staircase, and the hairs on the back of my neck bristled. Was that ... a ghost? Was this place haunted?

I thought back over the conversations I'd had with Lorelei in the morning and the coven after classes, and I didn't recall anyone mentioning ghosts among the students here. Or maybe they had, and I hadn't given it a second thought. Ghosts and fae didn't often interact with one another.

As I watched the bottom of the staircase, the floor creaked again, and I watched as a thick wad of cobweb wafted across the entry to the stairs. It was high enough up that I must have ducked right under it. It was decidedly not a ghost.

More movement caught my eye. I didn't recognize the disheveled blond hair until Keegan looked up and smiled a lopsided grin, waggling his eyebrows a bit. He continued up the staircase and whispered once he was nearer. "Fancy meeting you here."

His presence here certainly suggested that the witches had not set me up. But I thought I'd ask anyway. "So this place does work for cell signal?"

He shrugged. "It's hit or miss. Texting is easier than calling, that's for sure." He pulled his phone from his pocket and slowly rotated, then shook his head. "Doesn't look good tonight."

Sure enough, my own phone had dropped back to no signal, the text messages still unsent. I sighed. "So much for that plan."

"Plan?"

I shook my head. "It's not that important."

"The best place to get messages out is in town. School's technically a dead zone."

"And getting into town can't happen until I've had a month of good behavior?"

"Yeah, them's the rules, as they say." He smiled. "If you just want to draft up messages to go out, there are plenty of people who've been here for more than a month with town privileges. You don't even have to unlock your phone or anything."

I smiled. "Are you offering to take my phone to town for me? What would you want in return?"

"Ah, learning already," Keegan said, smiling more broadly now. He nodded. "It's my brother's birthday today, and I want to text him. Can you head back down to the third floor and make a ruckus if you see any staff coming?"

I nodded, not offering him my hand this time, since he hadn't shaken my hand at breakfast. "Deal."

"Thanks, Briar," he said, grinning.

I brushed up against his shoulder as I passed him at the top of the stairs. A shock ran through my body, the ring still tucked in my pocket almost burning for a second. I almost yelped aloud, but then I realized he hadn't responded. Maybe he, unlike Nic, hadn't felt the weirdness that seemed to happen with some of the people I made physical contact with.

I scooted back down the stairs, through the skinny hallway, thinking about which students I'd touched during the course of the day and which ones I hadn't. Gerard hadn't caused the ring to give me a jolt, and neither had any of the witches. Nic was the only person other than Keegan I'd touched, I was pretty sure. So what did the two of them have in common?

The teachers were even more mysterious than the students when it came to what they actually were, and as far as I could recall, none of them had offered me a hand to shake. But I knew Mister Walkenhorst and Miss Whalen were fae and a witch. I might have to talk to Mister Walkenhorst about the ring, either to see if he could identify it, or to see how it reacted to him.

Still lost in thought, I reached the wide third floor hallway.

And nearly collided with my Algebra teacher, Miss Hale. Thankfully, both of us recoiled in surprise rather than making contact. I wasn't about to just go around touching random people to figure out this ring.

She narrowed her gaze at the staircase behind me. "Were you on the fourth floor, Miss Williams?"

I'd told Keegan I would raise a ruckus. It hadn't been a formal promise, but a deal was pretty close. So I weighed my options and raised my voice a little louder than it needed to be. "Uhh, yeah, sorry, I was just seeing what was up this staircase."

Her gaze flickered to the cheap metal chain that hung across the bottom of the staircase. "Disregarding the clear indication that said staircase is unsafe?"

"Technically, that sign says nothing about the staircase being unsafe," I said, shrugging.

Miss Hale arched an eyebrow at me. "And you took 'do not enter' to be only a suggestion?"

"Curiosity did kill the cat."

With a tight-lipped grimace, she said, "While I am aware that this is your first full day at Dedwydd Academy, it is my responsibility to ensure that the rules are followed. It is also my duty to report this to the Headmistress."

So much for good behavior. Maybe the Headmistress wouldn't be as fussy as Miss Hale. At least having Miss Hale take me to the Headmistress's office would mean Keegan could get his text to his brother. All in all, it seemed like a fair trade, especially since my month countdown to semi-freedom had barely started. I tried to look contrite. "Of course. Should I come with you?"

"Indeed."

CHAPTER SEVEN:
NOT EXACTLY AS PLANNED

The Headmistress's office was in a wing of the building I hadn't seen yet, off the first floor at a strange angle. It looked kind of like it might have been added on as an afterthought, but the décor blended with the rest of the school—the same dull brown walls, interestingly patterned but mostly threadbare rugs, and fake plants. The doors lining this hallway had fancier doors, with a frosted glass panel in the top half of each, and gold paint designating which office belonged to which teacher.

The lights were out in most of the offices, and I didn't recognize the names on the doors of the few that still had lights on. The light in the office behind the door at the end of the hall was also on, and the door was the same as all the others, but somehow more imposing with the inclusion of the word "Headmistress" below the name "Kiyoko Yamashita."

Miss Hale stopped when we were a few steps away from the Headmistress's door, and I paused beside her. "Wait here," she said, and then proceeded to knock.

When Miss Hale entered the Headmistress's office, I considered running. I'd made sure Keegan had the chance to text his brother, so I'd fulfilled my end of that deal. I didn't see much reason to stick around here, other than to find out how much of a punishment I could expect for my first infraction. I suspected this was a routine sort of thing, and I didn't actually need to be present for doling out of punishment—someone would let me know what it was.

But I remembered the way Nic had recommended taking up schedule changes with my therapist, and not the Headmistress. He didn't seem afraid of her, per se, but leery about her. My curiosity won out, wondering what sort of woman could make the unflappable Nic Flores, well, flap.

Miss Hale emerged from the Headmistress's office but left the door open behind her. I couldn't see much beyond the doorway, other than more of the same general boring décor choices that seemed to prevail in the public areas of the school. "She'd like to see you now."

Ominous. Of course. I didn't feel fear, though, at least not about getting caught breaking what seemed like a small rule. I shrugged and walked in.

On first appearance, the Headmistress didn't look like someone to worry about. She was an older Japanese woman, her face gently lined with age, and her hair mostly white with a few sparse strands of black still mixed in. My gaze caught her bright pink lipstick and armload of gold bangles, her totally average looking middle-aged woman blouse and scarf. Somehow, though, my focus kept glancing off her actual face—her eyes, in particular. I squeezed my own eyes shut for a moment and then looked at her again.

My gaze connected with hers. Fire danced in the background of what otherwise looked like normal dark brown eyes. That might have been the cause of my lizard brain slipping off her face before. Now, I couldn't look away. The flames felt real. They warmed my face, and I could almost hear them crackling before they scorched everything in their path.

"Briar Williams," she said, and that was, thankfully, enough to break the spell. The sense of burning vanished, both the heat and the illusion of flames. The Headmistress gestured to an overstuffed armchair. "Have a seat."

I did as she instructed and managed to keep my gaze near her but not on her, letting whatever effect was keeping me from looking into her eyes again do its job.

"I must tell you that we were warned about your potential for bad behavior." She flipped through a few sheets of paper, what I suspected was my file. I was curious about what it said, and my stomach twisted a bit from the nervousness I always felt when something was written down about me, but I was still rattled enough that it didn't hit me as hard as it normally did.

She seemed like she was waiting for a response from me, so I said, "Well, I'm just getting a feel for this place, seeing as I've been here less than twenty-four hours."

"I see." Her voice took on an icy edge. "I assume you've been informed that off-campus privileges are reserved for students who manage to maintain good behavior for a period of one calendar month."

I nodded.

She picked up a pen and made a notation in my file. The pen scratched across the surface, raising the tiny hairs on the back of my neck. Then she closed the file. "Your calendar month begins tomorrow."

I sat for a moment, trying to figure out what had just happened. Was that it? Was I taken to the Headmistress so she could make a note in an antiquated paper file, and it was done? No chiding or threatening (if you didn't count her fire eyes)?

I wasn't used to this, in Idyll or in Artis. When I'd gotten in trouble at the high school, it always involved lecturing. In Idyll, it had been worse.

I couldn't keep my tongue still. "So that's it?"

She nodded, then gave a half-shrug, a surprisingly out-of-place gesture for someone of her apparent age. "I advise you to read the student manual carefully to avoid further problems."

I let out a deep breath and rose. "Alright, thanks, then."

"You're welcome."

The words were common enough among humans as a response to "thank you." But somehow, when Headmistress Yamashita said them, they made me feel anything but welcome here.

~

Miss Hale was waiting for me when I came out of the Headmistress's office. She looked slightly more relaxed than previously, and she even attempted a friendly smile. "I feel like we may have gotten off on the wrong foot."

I was pretty sure yelling at a teacher was going to land me straight back in the Headmistress's office, and I had no idea what the consequences might be if I wound up there twice in rapid succession. Technically, the Headmistress had said my month probation started tomorrow, so maybe I could break as many rules as I liked tonight. I doubted that was really the case, so I tried to play it cool. "What do you mean?"

She gestured for me to follow her down the hall, away from the Headmistress's office. "I mean that believe it or not, teachers have rough days too. I wasn't on top of my game in Algebra this morning. I'm also not a big fan of after-dinner hall duty. As a result, you've been on the receiving end of that, twice."

I wasn't sure what she was doing by giving me this explanation. Was she actually trying to be nice to me? It seemed like a trap. I shrugged. "Oh, okay."

"Those of us who choose to teach at Dedwydd usually do so for one very important reason. We understand what it's like to be an outcast from society, and we want to do our best to help you succeed, so you can return to the world, if that's what you want to do, after high school."

Did I want to return to the world? Given the alternatives of going back to Idyll or death, I supposed being here sounded better. But I couldn't resist a quick dig at Miss Hale, even if I was trying to play nice in response. "And Algebra is going to help me learn to cope with the real world when I'm secretly a monster?"

She chuckled. "No, but Algebra will allow you to move on to other math classes, which will allow you to earn a diploma granted by the State of Idaho. A diploma allows you to apply to colleges or get a job. You know, normal people stuff."

I shook my head. "But we're not normal people."

"Maybe not. But with appropriate training and self-discipline, you can be more than, as you say, 'a monster'." She paused, cocking her head to the side. "Take me, for example. I'm just a boring Algebra teacher and a stickler for the rules, right?"

I sensed a trap. "You wouldn't be teaching here if that's all you were."

"Correct. If you met me on the street, you would never suspect that I'm a supernatural creature."

Shrugging, I said, "It just means that you're something normal-ish."

"I assure you, I'm not." Miss Hale's dark eyes sparkled faintly, but at least they didn't suddenly show me flames like the Headmistress's had. "The lesson, the overarching lesson at Dedwydd Academy, is about learning to hide what you are from humans. Learning to blend in."

I frowned. "And if I don't want to blend in?"

"Then you may be in the wrong school."

I latched onto that. "Is there another school? One for the real problem children?"

If I hadn't been looking straight at her when I asked the question, I might not have noticed the slight droop to her shoulders. She glanced toward the Headmistress's office before she answered. "There are other schools similar in nature to this one, but generally speaking, they're not what students from Dedwydd need."

That sounded a little ominous, and also like the voice of experience. Had she gotten someone kicked out of Dedwydd? Did something horrible happen to them? I was curious, but I doubted she'd tell me more. I'd have to see what the gossip on that topic was. "If a student did get kicked out of here, where would they go?"

"That depends on a number of factors. It's a bit more than I'd like to get into at the moment. I *know* you have Algebra homework to complete, and I am still on hall-monitor duty. Suffice it to say that when you were selected to come here, someone saw potential in you. If not, you'd have been sent to a different school, or left to rot in the system. There are far worse alternatives."

I didn't think anyone I'd met here could speak to any potential I might have, and I doubted my teachers at the high school in Artis would have spoken highly of me, either. "Who should I be thanking, then?"

She smiled, seemingly genuinely. "That's a mystery you'll need to figure out on your own."

We'd continued walking along the main corridor as we talked, and now we stood at the bottom of the stairs to the second floor. She didn't look like she was going to head upstairs, so I put my foot on the lowest step, ready to head up to my room and my now long-delayed homework.

"One more thing before you go, Briar. Have you been through the extracurricular packet?"

I paused my ascent. "The what now?"

"I suppose you got here just before breakfast, so you haven't had much time to check out anything other than food and classes. There's a packet in your room about the extracurricular activities. Take a look and see if anything grabs your attention. It beats wandering around looking for trouble after classes."

I laughed aloud at that. Miss Hale was clever, turning this all back to what she'd busted me for in the first place. She moved up a slight notch in my estimation. "Alright, I'll take a look."

"See that you do, Briar. Have a good evening."

~

I made a big production of fumbling with my room key as I approached the door to my room, hoping I could avoid walking in on Lorelei and Jasper in the throes of teenage passion.

I heard Lorelei's voice. "Seriously, you're just going to make it worse."

I froze, listening for Jasper's response, waiting to see if maybe I should just go up to Spooky Room to see if they would let me do my homework there tonight.

I didn't hear a response, but Lorelei huffed out an exasperated, "Fine, whatever."

If I didn't know for a fact that our room had no cell phone signal at all, I'd think I was hearing half of a phone call. I waited another minute to see if I heard anything more, and then rattled my keyring against the doorknob a few times as I fitted my key into the lock.

Lorelei was at her desk, a textbook in front of her illuminated by her desk lamp, and she shook her head. "Hello, Miss Popularity."

"Huh?" I looked around, checking that no one else was in the room. "Who were you talking to?"

"Uh, you," she said, rolling her eyes.

"No, I mean, before I came in."

She shrugged. "Just talking to myself. Haven't had a roommate for a bit, so I've gotten in the habit of talking myself through problems."

I thought about what I'd overheard. It seemed a little weird, but I was willing to accept her explanation. "Right, so ... why am I Miss Popularity?"

"Your friend Gerard stopped by because he missed you at dinner. Then Nic Flores came by looking for you. And you just missed Keegan Morris. They all left you notes." She smirked as she gestured at my desk.

Gerard stopping by made sense—I hadn't seen him at dinner, and though we hadn't made definite plans to talk later, meals seemed to be the best time for us to hang out. Nic made slightly less sense, but he might have been checking in on me if word about Anger Management and Jaylin had gotten back to him. As for Keegan, he'd probably overheard my brief conversation with Miss Hale at the bottom of the fourth-floor stairs, so he knew I'd gotten in trouble. "Yeah, I don't think it'll happen that often."

"I dunno, new girl and single? You're fresh meat."

I grimaced at that, but Lorelei didn't seem to notice. I still wasn't ready to explain that I wasn't interested.

"Also, for the record, Jasper doesn't have a roommate. We'll make sure to keep our naked times limited to his room. So you don't have to make a racket every time you come in."

"Right, okay. Did any of those guys say what they wanted?"

Lorelei shrugged. "No, they seemed interested in talking to you, not me."

I approached my desk and picked up the stack of notes. Gerard's and Nic's both contained variations on "hope you're okay, see you tomorrow."

Keegan's, on the other hand, was an apology written in such a florid, flowy hand, that I wondered if he had studied calligraphy under a fae noble.

I frowned and looked at the writing more closely. Docra, the fae calligraphy master, had given up on teaching me after two days, calling my handwriting "brutish." But during my time in Idyll, I'd seen enough formal handwritten documents to identify the style. On closer examination, Keegan's writing had similarities, but there were too many things someone like Docra would have trained out of him. He was just a fancy writer. Who apparently felt really awful about me getting caught by Miss Hale.

I chuckled softly as I refolded his note.

Lorelei turned to look at me. "So? Any gossip you want to dish?"

I shrugged at first. I didn't care about gossiping about these boys. Two of them were my friends, and I had an arrangement with Keegan that would let me get messages to my other friends, the ones who weren't here. I leaned against my desk, wondering if maybe Lorelei would know any gossip about other things, instead. "What do you make of the Headmistress?"

Lorelei rolled her eyes and shrugged. "I dunno, a lot of people act like she's this horrible monster, but she's always been fine when I've dealt with her."

I nodded. "Yeah, she seemed serious, but not like—" I trailed off, recalling the flicker of flames I'd seen in her eyes. "I dunno, she seems okay. Miss Hale's the other one I can't figure out. She was—"

Lorelei narrowed her eyes. "So you *did* get in trouble."

I blinked a few times, not sure how she could already know that. "Rumors travel fast around here, huh?"

"Pretty close to supersonic speeds. Also, that would explain why Keegan seemed *really* concerned that you weren't back when he stopped by. What'd they get you for?"

"I was on the fourth floor. Where cell phones work?"

Lorelei sighed loudly and rolled her eyes. "Oh my gods, do not listen to the Spooky Girls. You have to stand on your tiptoes in the exactly right spot to get half a bar."

I shrugged. "Half a bar is better than no bars."

Shaking her head, Lorelei said, "Just wait a month and you can text to your heart's content on the weekends. Honestly, by then, you're not going to have much to say to people who knew you before."

I tilted my head to the side. "Really?"

She shrugged. "It might be different for you. I didn't really have anyone still outside other than my mom—well, my parents, but I haven't really talked to my dad since he left my mom. Jasper was here, and Jade—" She shook her head suddenly. "Yeah, you know, ancient history. If you've got friends outside, they'll have moved on by the time you get to leave campus and go into town."

I pursed my lips, ready to disagree with her, but decided it wasn't worth it. If anyone could find this place, it would be Zee. By the time a month was up, I might not even be here anymore. If I was, I knew Zee would still be looking for me.

"Do you know anything about other schools like this one? The ones for kids who get kicked out or whatever? Or, like vampires?"

Lorelei scrunched up her nose like she'd just smelled something foul. "What? Why? Are you trying to get kicked out or something? Or find a vampire?"

"I'm just curious. I mean, I've heard enough to know that some students get kicked out. So then what happens?"

"I don't know, and I hope to never find out. Say what you will about Dedwydd and their ridiculous rules, but it's not half bad as far as schools go."

"I just don't know that I can adjust to this place so easily."

"You'd be surprised. Sure, it's boring classes, boring homework, the usual. If you're lucky, you'll make some friends and go on like it's your old school, just with new people."

She had no idea how my four months of school in Artis had been, but I didn't really want to explain that to her. I did have a sudden thought, though, considering my limited non-Idyll experience thus far. "Wait, did I miss Christmas?"

Lorelei's brow furrowed. "Um, it's January, so yes."

"Wow, juvie didn't even have Christmas. Birthdays either, I guess. I knew I hated that place."

"Are you a Christmas birthday?"

I shook my head. "January first, according to the State of Washington." I tilted my head to the side. "Wait, do you have Christmas and birthdays here?"

She shrugged. "It's sort of odd, but yeah. They make sure everyone who wants to can get into town to talk to their family for Christmas, and their birthday too. My mom sends me presents— sundresses I can wear on the weekends, when it gets warmer. My dad sends gift cards for chain stores that they don't have in town, so I can't use them, but that's pretty much typical Dad fail. There's also a big Christmas dinner, and they celebrate Hanukkah and Kwanza and Winter Solstice too. Chinese New Year is coming up in a month or so, so that's the next holiday other than Valentine's Day."

"That all sounds kind of nice," I said with a smile. "I've never gotten to celebrate Christmas or my birthday. Those were things I was looking forward to."

Lorelei squinted at me. "I can't figure you out. You keep dropping me all these hints, but I still don't know where you came from. You're not like Jehovah's Witness or something?"

"I don't even know what that means." I considered my options, recalling the *quid pro quo* the witches—the Spooky Girls, according to Lorelei, which did go along with their proclamation of Maddie and Aimee's room as the Spooky Room—had offered. "I'll tell you if you tell me."

Lorelei stiffened, all the color draining from her face.

Backpedaling, I said, "Hey, you're the one who told me it was rude to ask outright."

"I know." She took a deep breath. "It's just hard to talk about."

I shrugged. "Then I'll go first. I'm a fae."

Lorelei didn't react much to my announcement, but she chewed at her lip for a moment. "My best friend was possessed by a demon. Jasper—Jasper's twin sister. Jade. Jasper and I got in her way and ... accident. And Jade's ... well, she wasn't so lucky."

I swallowed hard, imagining how I would have felt if Zee, Gerard, or Chris had been killed during our raid on the compound. "I'm sorry."

She nodded hastily. "Ancient history. So I'm one of the people they call witnesses here. I know too much." She shrugged. "Anyway, I'm sure you've got homework, because I've got a mountain of it."

"Yeah, I do." I turned back to my desk to see what I needed to do.

A thought caught my attention before I could find my assignment lists. Nic had assured me that the other students in Psychology of Terror were all supernaturals in our own right, not the victims of supernaturals. If he was right, then Lorelei shouldn't have been in our class.

Or she was lying to me.

I almost spun around to call her on it, but I kept steady. I'd known plenty of liars in Idyll. I'd just keep an eye on her and wait till she tripped up in her lies. Then I'd have the advantage.

I shook my head. Only one day here, and I was already back to thinking like I had in Idyll. I'd buried that part of me while I was in Artis, trying to be more human than fae. Some people had tried to tell me that high school was like a shark tank—one drop of blood, one hint of weakness, and they'd be all over you. I'd seen that plenty in Artis, but I managed to skate through most of it without any blowback. Here felt different. Here, we were all real monsters, not just teenagers. It was more like Idyll than Artis, a terrifying thought.

Lorelei and I worked on our homework in silence, but I kept turning over everything she'd told me in my mind, like I was polishing armor or weapons.

I still didn't know what to make of it by the time she yawned, loudly and dramatically. "You can turn on the light on your desk if you're still working, but I'm going to go get ready for bed and turn out the overhead light."

I faked a sympathetic yawn. "Yeah, sleep is a good idea. Bathrooms and showers down the hall, right?"

She nodded as she began collecting her things.

"Where do I get a toothbrush?" I asked, sheepishly realizing that I had no toiletries at all, nor pajamas.

"Second drawer down on your desk should be stocked up. If you need anything that's not there, you can get it at the office in the morning."

I slid the drawer open and marveled at the neat rows of toiletries arrayed there. "Well, what do you know. Much better than my old school."

Lorelei chuckled. "Oh, your uniforms are hung up in your closet, and they put socks and underwear in the dresser drawers. There are T-shirts and sweats for PJs and gym clothes."

"Oh, good." As I slid the desk drawer shut, it moved the comforter that was spread across my bed, shifting it so my pillow was visible. A crisp white pillowcase enveloped what looked like the fluffiest pillow I'd ever experienced.

And right in the center of my pillow, that pristine whiteness was marred by the presence of a polished dark green stone with what looked like red veins running through it.

Heliotrope.

CHAPTER EIGHT:
HELIOTROPE IN MY BED

I'm not sure what noise I made when I saw the heliotrope. Based on Lorelei's terrified shriek, I'm guessing it was a guttural growl, something no human vocal cords should have produced.

"What ... is that a rock or chewing gum?" Lorelei asked.

"Heliotrope." I hadn't touched it, so I did still possess the capacity for human speech. Just not the temperament for conversation.

It sat in the middle of my pillow, a taunting sign that someone had figured out exactly what I was and planned to use that against me. It was a clever technique, because cold iron would have tipped me off the moment I walked into the room. At the lesser concentration that iron occurred in heliotrope, it didn't set off warning bells, but it was just as dangerous. The iron that gave the heliotrope its veins would seep into my bloodstream if I so much as touched it. If I noticed the sluggishness that followed before the paralysis hit, I'd just be weakened until I could get rid of it. Once the paralysis hit, I'd need someone else to get it away from me. If that didn't happen, I'd die.

"So—" Lorelei began.

"I need you to move it. I can't."

Lorelei stood beside me, arms crossed over her chest. "What's the big deal? It's just a shiny rock. The hippie store in my hometown carried those."

My panic was starting to abate, letting me think a little more clearly. Had Lorelei planted it, even before I told her what I was? "Please, Lorelei, just take it out of here, throw it away as far from our room as you can."

"Why?"

I hedged my bets and gave her the condensed version. "Contact with it is harmful to the fae." I wasn't about to tell the roommate who probably didn't want me here that she could get rid of me permanently with a common rock from a metaphysical shop.

"Huh." She leaned over my bed and picked up the heliotrope, looking closely at it just inches from my face.

I backed away, knocking into my desk chair.

For a moment, Lorelei's eyes gleamed with mischief, but then she wrapped her hand around the whole stone, obscuring it from my view. "Alright, I'll be right back."

I regained control of my breathing once Lorelei left the room, collapsing into my chair. If she had placed it there, she'd likely come back with the stone still on her, or she'd stash it somewhere to retrieve later. I wasn't going to be able to sleep if I kept on that line of thought.

Moving past the possibility that Lorelei had put the heliotrope in my bed, there were three other potential candidates: Jasper, who seemed to come and go from our room as he liked; or Nic or Keegan, both of whom had stopped in to check on me. I discounted Gerard immediately—he wouldn't do anything to hurt me. I didn't think Nic was a likely candidate either, not with how kind he'd been to me so far. Still, I didn't know him well. Jasper and Keegan were in the same boat. And any of those three could have easily hidden the stone on my pillow.

Without confronting one of them, though, I had no way of finding out who had put it there, or why. A direct confrontation didn't seem advisable, either—anyone I asked about heliotrope would have a weapon to use against me that they might not have previously had. I'd have to ask my questions more subtly, and I'd have to watch my step around Lorelei, now that she possessed knowledge of something I was terrified of.

"So, where'd it come from?" Lorelei asked as she returned to our room. She held up both her hands, showing they were empty. "Don't worry, I washed them too."

I let out a deep breath. "I don't know. Do the ... are there staff who have access to our rooms while we're in class?"

She shook her head. "Nope. I let them in to put your uniforms away, but they can't come in if one of us isn't here, except in an emergency. They brought the sheets up yesterday, and I made your bed before you got here. You're welcome."

"Do you think ... could they have left something on my bed?"

Lorelei shook her head again. "No. Miss Whalen brought your stuff in. She's so fussy, I think she was half afraid to even be in here. Anyway, I was reading while she was here, and she didn't go beyond your closet."

I breathed a little easier with Lorelei's information. Miss Whalen knew what I was. If she had wanted to do anything horrible to me, she'd had plenty of opportunities the previous night. If she didn't want me here, it would have been very easy to stop in the middle of nowhere and toss me out of the van. Or not even bother to stop first.

Lorelei's answer also made me realize something else—I still hadn't read the student handbook, so I had no idea how a lot of things might work here. I figured it couldn't hurt to ask her. "So this isn't like a hotel, where there's maid service and stuff?"

With a chuckle, Lorelei said, "One could only dream. No, we have to make our own beds, take out our own garbage, do our own laundry, and sweep up at least once a week." She paused. "I'll keep doing the sweeping up if you'll take the garbage bag to the chute when it needs it."

I nodded and said, "That sounds fair."

"Great." She hesitated a moment, her eyes narrowing. "So whoever put that rock in your bed must have known what you are, right? Who else have you told so far?"

I didn't need to give it any thought at all. "Maddie, Echo, and Aimee. Gerard knows too, of course."

She chuckled, then sneered. "Oh, the Spooky Girls. Yeah, that sounds like their kind of experiment."

Did it sound like their kind of experiment? I didn't know them well enough yet to say. But Lorelei's sneer made me wonder if she'd somehow been at the butt end of one of their experiments before. Regardless, her suggestion didn't make sense. "They didn't come by here tonight, did they?"

Lorelei shrugged. "No, just all those boys. Gerard, Nic, and Keegan."

I leapt to defend Gerard. "Gerard's a good friend. He wouldn't try to hurt me."

"Okay, I'll buy that. You've certainly got more reason to trust him than you would most people here. As for the others, Nic and Keegan have both been here a while. Keegan's never gotten in trouble, as far as I know. Nic—" She paused to shrug. "—he's always trying to look like he's bad, but I don't think he's done anything wrong his whole life. Either that, or maybe he's just really good at covering it up."

That sounded like what I'd seen of Nic, and maybe what I'd seen of Keegan. Keegan was harder to pin down, since my interactions with him had been limited to breakfast and a coincidental meeting on the fourth floor. We had made a deal regarding getting my messages out to Zee, so I had reason to talk to him later. And I'd see Nic in class tomorrow. I'd have to approach both of them cautiously.

I was still on edge, but I waited for Lorelei to head to the bathroom before I stripped down my bed, checked for any more hidden stones, and remade it. I heard her come back in, but I lay facing the wall and breathing quietly, hoping she'd figure I had fallen asleep without brushing my teeth.

My mind was still racing through the possibilities of who had put a piece of heliotrope in my bed. My thoughts drifted back to what I had overheard Lorelei saying before I came in. What if she hadn't really been talking to herself? She'd lied to me at least once, so why shouldn't I suspect she'd lied more than once?

And while I had been told we weren't supposed to be able to use our powers here, but what if someone could? There were a lot of supernatural creatures I knew nothing about. Were there people who lived their life invisible? Would they wind up in a place like Dedwydd?

I realized that my breathing had become fast and agitated, which was not a good way to convince Lorelei that I was asleep. I forced myself to calm down. I tried to remember the music Mister Walkenhorst had played during Anger Management, in the hopes it might help.

It wasn't until I heard Lorelei breathing slow and quiet that I managed to calm down enough to sleep myself.

~

I didn't see Nic or Keegan at breakfast or lunch, which wasn't entirely surprising, seeing as there were probably a hundred students all getting food at roughly the same time. Breakfast thus far seemed to be spread out a bit more, since it had a wider window of availability. Lunch was much more concentrated, everyone making their way through the cafeteria during the same hour-long lunch break.

Maddie flagged me down as I was scanning the cafeteria at lunch and gestured to an empty seat beside her. Seeing as no one else was offering me a seat, I headed to sit with the so-called Spooky Girls.

"Hey, how's it going?" Maddie seemed super excited that I'd taken her up on her offer, wiggling in her seat like a puppy.

"Eh, weird." I poked at the food on my plate. I wasn't sure what was in this "curry," but I could smell some sort of meat buried beneath the sauce. At least here, it was easy to get meat with every meal, even if they insisted on garnishing it with a few scraps of vegetables they called a salad.

"Weird?" Aimee waggled her eyebrows. "Do tell us more."

"*Quid pro quo*," I replied. "Who here hates the fae?"

All three of the girls took deep breaths. Maddie's eyes got huge, Echo shook her head, and Aimee smirked. "Changeling children, of course," Aimee replied. "Now tell us what's weird."

Changelings made sense, but that didn't fit any of my suspects at the moment (since I hadn't entirely let Lorelei or Jasper off the hook). Anyway, I'd have to answer more questions to pull more information from the Spooky Girls. "Do you know what heliotrope is?" I asked.

Echo nodded. "The plant or the stone?"

"The stone."

"It's purported to have mystical properties, mostly related to blood and bleeding, hence why it's also called a bloodstone." Echo frowned. "I'm not sure what this has to do with—"

I interrupted her. "It's called bloodstone because it has hematite inclusions that look like blood. And hematite is an iron oxide. And iron—"

"—is bad for fae," Maddie interrupted me to conclude, her eyes still wide.

Aimee looked back and forth between Echo and Maddie, then narrowed her gaze at me. "And this has what to do with anything?"

I leaned over my lunch and whispered. "I found a lump of heliotrope on my pillow last night. Including my roommate, there are only a handful of people who were in my room or could have been in my room. Hence my question about who hates fae here."

Aimee tapped her index finger against her lips. "What would happen to you if you touched heliotrope?"

I took a deep breath. Between Echo's confusion over my interest in heliotrope, Aimee's question, and the fact that none of them could have gotten access to my room without Lorelei knowing it, I felt better about giving them the whole truth. "If I just touch it, it'll make me queasy and sluggish. Prolonged contact can weaken a fae to the point of death."

Maddie pulled a notebook out of her bag, not to scribble in it but to flip through until she found a scrawled list. "Zoe, Logan, and Jaylin."

I hadn't heard the other two names, but Jaylin—Mister Walkenhorst had confirmed that one for me the previous day. My shoulders slumped. "Okay, so maybe I have another suspect, but I'm basing this on what Lorelei told me about who was in our room last night. She didn't mention Jaylin coming by."

"Maybe Jaylin didn't personally. Who are your suspects?" Maddie asked.

I shrugged. "The people who had access to my room, at least according to Lorelei, were her, Jasper, Gerard, Nic, and Keegan. I've already discounted Gerard."

Echo frowned. "Sure, that makes sense. And I suspect Jasper is in your room about as much as I'm in the Spooky Room. Why were the other two there?"

"Nic seems to have adopted me like a new puppy, maybe? He left me a note just saying he was checking in on me. Keegan—" I trailed off. I didn't want to blame the witches for sending me to the fourth floor and inadvertently getting me in trouble, but if I thought about it, they were kind of responsible. "I ran into Keegan on the fourth floor. He wanted to text his brother, so I covered for him, in exchange for a favor, but Miss Hale spotted me, which got me a visit to the Headmistress's office. So Keegan left me a lengthy apology note."

Maddie bit her lip. "Sorry. Most of the teachers don't really check on the fourth floor, but sometimes they have to walk past it."

I shrugged at her apology, not really sure if it required a response more than that, and continued. "At any rate, it doesn't make much sense that it would have been Nic or Keegan, but I'm not sure why Lorelei or Jasper would have tried that without knowing what I am. I only told Lorelei last night." I left out the part about Lorelei lying to me about what she was. That wasn't necessarily relevant. Unless it was.

Maddie scribbled in her notebook, then showed it to me. She'd written Nic and Keegan's names in her notebook. The "N" in Nic had little horns on either side of it, while Keegan's "K" was flanked with question marks.

I frowned at the page, and Aimee snatched the notebook out of Maddie's hands. "*Quid pro quo*, Mads. Information is money here. It's gotta be a fair trade."

Maddie glared at Aimee until Aimee tossed her notebook back. Then she turned to me. "Keegan could be a changeling child. I just don't know yet."

"Do you just carry around that notebook for anyone to potentially grab?" I asked.

Maddie's already pale face grew whiter. "Well, yes, but—" She held up her pen and twisted it to retract the tip, then gestured at her notebook. The page was as white as her face.

I gasped. "How'd you—"

"Some of us have little trinkets that still work in spite of the prohibitions against powers," Echo said, gaze darting around. "Keep it under wraps, Mads."

Maddie tucked the pen back into her bag, glancing around furtively.

Meanwhile, I had a thought. I'd moved the ring from the compound to my uniform shirt pocket when I had gotten dressed that morning. So far, it hadn't given me any weird tingles, but I also hadn't touched anyone recently. "How do you know if an item is a trinket that works here?"

Aimee shrugged. "You don't, necessarily, unless you try to use it for something, and it works. So it's a lot of trial and error. Why, you got something?"

"I don't know if I do or not. It's ... complicated."

"Maybe you can tell us later," Echo said, rising from her seat and giving Aimee a quick peck on the cheek. "Briar, I'll see you in Anger Management, unless your schedule gets switched. Either way, come by our room after classes?"

I nodded. Information was money, like Aimee said. Though I was still a little bit leery, I felt like I'd stumbled upon a goldmine with the Spooky Girls.

~

Nic snagged my arm on the way into Psychology of Terror that afternoon. "Hey, you okay?"

I flinched, now accustomed to the little shock the ring gave me, but still not big on physical contact that I hadn't initiated, and he released my arm. "Yeah, I'm alright. Why?"

"I heard you got in trouble last night, and there was the thing with Jaylin, too."

I shrugged. "It's all fine."

His brow furrowed. "Are you sure?"

I frowned. If what Maddie had told me at lunch was correct, Nic was some sort of devil or demon. But Lorelei had said he was someone who wanted to look bad, but really wasn't. I trusted Maddie's information more than Lorelei's assessment, though. "What does it matter to you?"

Nic's shoulders slumped. "Sorry, I'm just trying to be nice. You know, welcome to Dedwydd and all that."

I took a deep breath. "Yeah, sorry, I'm just kind of rattled." I chuckled softly. "Nothing like coming back to your room after your first day in a new school to find out that multiple people have stopped by to check on you."

"Multiple?" Nic's eyebrows rose.

I waggled my eyebrows at him, seizing the opportunity to joke around with him. "That's right. You're not the only gentleman caller knocking at my door, Mr. Flores."

He bit at his lip and gave me an eyebrow waggle in return. "Are you flirting with me, Miss Williams?"

I shook my head firmly. "Whoa, no, sorry. Just messing with the fragile male ego."

"Funny how those things are so often conflated," he said, but the smile he gave me assured me that he understood it as the playful joke I'd intended it as. Maybe he was super perceptive because he was a demon. Or maybe he was a nice guy trapped in a bad situation himself. I could relate.

I didn't realize it until halfway through class, but he'd fallen off my list of possible suspects for the heliotrope, leaving my roommate, her boyfriend, one or more of the changeling children (somehow), Keegan, or some invisible friend of Lorelei's that she hadn't seen fit to tell me about (possibly for fear that I'd think she was making it up). Of those, Keegan seemed the most plausible, but I really couldn't see him being sneaky enough to drop a note on my desk and tuck a small rock beneath my comforter without Lorelei noticing. The only possibility was that she'd been so sick of boys knocking on our door to leave notes for me that she'd just ignored him while he wrote, giving him the privacy he needed to hide the heliotrope.

With suspects still whirling through my thoughts, I stepped out into the hallway after class to be greeted by Keegan, leaning against the wall near our classroom. His eyes lit up when he spotted me. "Briar! Hey!"

Nic glanced at me. I couldn't tell whether it was him thinking there was something between me and Keegan, or a worried look. "Later," he whispered.

I nodded and looked back to Keegan. "Hi, Keegan."

"Did you get my note?" He looked at me like a big lost golden retriever, a mix of excitement and worry in his expression.

"Yeah, thank you. Umm, apology accepted." I shrugged. "It wasn't really your fault. I leaned hard on the 'new girl' card, and it didn't work."

He let out a sigh of relief. "Okay, good. I didn't want you to be mad at me."

I thought about the heliotrope. "Why? Should I be?"

"No reason," he replied, apparently hearing my questions as a single one. "So—"

I held up a hand to quiet him as the hairs on the back of my neck stood up. I looked over my shoulder, but there were just a handful of students walking from one classroom to another. They looked dimly familiar, but not enough that I could have picked them out of a sea of faces. I could have had a class with them or just seen them in the cafeteria. Either way, they didn't seem to be paying me or Keegan any undue attention.

"You alright? You seem kinda jumpy."

I shrugged. "Yeah, a little. Still settling in, you know?"

He nodded. "Yeah, I get that." He paused, then his eyes lit up. "I got an idea. In exchange for that whole nonsense last night, what if I were to give you a tour of the school after dinner, show you the no-go places, and give us a chance to chat?"

He'd leaned closer to me as he spoke. Where Nic and I waggling our eyebrows at each other had been a ridiculous display of the way some people flirted, Keegan seemed to have learned his technique from bad movies. I'm sure if there had been lockers nearby, he would have leaned against them with one arm, forming a sort of barrier far above my head. I'd seen it in plenty of movies, where the boy had to have some sort of physical dominance over the smaller girl, who would clutch her books to her chest and look up at him adoringly.

Yeah, that wasn't my style, even if I did have to look up to look at his face. "Thanks, but no. I've got plans."

"Oh." His expression fell, once again giving him the look of a puppy, this time one who was being admonished for doing something bad. I knew there weren't werewolves here, but I wondered if he was some sort of shapeshifter with a predilection for canine forms.

"Hey, anyway, I've got to get to my group therapy," I said, giving him a light punch on the shoulder, ignoring the shock from the ring in my pocket. I'd learned that from movies too, as a way of saying "we're pals!". "I'll catch you some other time."

That was probably more hope than I ought to have given him, but whatever. At least it got him to stop looking like he'd been caught chewing on my shoe, and instead looking like I'd thrown him a bone.

"Yeah, that sounds great! See you later, Briar!"

CHAPTER NINE:
GROUP THERAPY

Group Therapy was in the wing where the teachers' offices were. It felt weird to be there again, with the Headmistress's office looming at the end of the hallway. I mean, she wasn't mean, just creepy. But there was something slightly menacing about her office with the door closed. Was someone else getting in trouble right now? Or was she the sort of person who always kept her door closed, even throughout the day?

The sound of wheels clunking onto the hardwood floor in this hallway pulled my attention away from the door. "Oh, hey, Jasper!"

He nodded stiffly. "Briar." Turning his wheelchair, he rolled into the office labeled "Dr. S. Pudi." The same office I was expected in.

Huh, so Jasper was in my group for group therapy. I still didn't know what exactly this group therapy would do, but here I was. At the very least, maybe it was a chance to see if Jasper would talk more about why he and Lorelei were at Dedwydd, rather than the lie Lorelei had fed me. I followed him into the office.

I recognized the other three students from my morning classes, though I didn't know them quite well enough to put names to faces. There was the Indian guy who wore a lot of bracelets on his right arm, the African American girl who wore a lot of bracelets on her left arm, and the Indian girl who had a gorgeous little jeweled bindi on her forehead. I felt awful about reducing each of them to an ethnicity and an item of jewelry, but between our school uniforms and not much interaction thus far, that's all I had to go on.

All three of them looked to acknowledge Jasper and then turned their gazes toward me. I couldn't quite read their mix of expressions, with all of them trying to quickly tamp down whatever reaction they had to the new girl.

The room was large for an office, with bookshelves flanking a door in the back wall and a desk just in front of that. The floor was covered with a lush burgundy and gold rug surrounded by a mix of cushions and low-slung chairs, with a space cleared on one side for Jasper and a slightly taller chair where our therapist was seated.

I hadn't seen him before. He was Indian too, with the first touches of gray at his temples and in his sparse beard, and some of the most intense brown eyes I'd ever seen. He smiled when he spotted me. "Briar Williams?"

"Yeah, that's me."

"I'm Dr. Pudi. Welcome to Group 6." He gestured to the other students, introducing them in turn. "Jasper, Trinity, Chana, and Logan."

So Trinity was the African American girl, Chana was the Indian girl, and Logan was the Indian guy. Hopefully I could keep them all straight. As I repeated their names in my head, I remembered Logan being on Maddie's list of changeling children. Did this mean Group Therapy was a place where the supernatural and the touched by the supernatural kids were going to interact? I wasn't sure that was a good idea for something that was supposed to be healing.

There was a cushion beside Logan and a chair on the other side of the room available, so I took the chair, placing myself opposite Jasper. He was doing his best to ignore me, but I wanted to keep an eye on him, and to sit far enough away from Logan that I wouldn't make him uncomfortable.

Dr. Pudi rose from his chair to shut the door and spoke again after he sat back down. "So, Briar, can you tell us a little bit about yourself, and what brings you to Dedwydd?"

I shot a worried glance in his direction. "Like what do you want to know?"

"Whatever you're willing to share with us. The things we discuss in here are kept in confidence among the group."

I wondered how strictly that was enforced, given how rumors seemed to perpetuate themselves in most high schools. But I wouldn't know if I didn't try. "Okay, I'm Briar Williams, I came here from a little town in Washington called Artis, and, umm, I guess I might have murdered some people." Sure, why not just get it all out in the open?

"Might have?" Dr. Pudi asked, his eyebrows raised.

I shrugged. "I don't remember a lot of what happened. I know that I was at a place where some people died. I don't know which, if any, of the deaths I was responsible for."

Dr. Pudi nodded, steepling his fingers in front of his chin. "Okay, that's a good start. Would anyone like to add anything about similar experiences?"

Dr. Pudi's gaze flickered toward Jasper, but Jasper's attention was focused on his hands in his lap. Now that was an interesting addition to what Lorelei had told me. She'd never said Jade was dead, but she'd implied it. Had she and Jasper somehow been responsible for Jade's death? Maybe they were both innocent bystanders who saw too much *and* murderers. The plot thickened.

"I just want to say that I know what it's like to have some gaps in your memory," Chana said. Her voice was soft, but her eyes glowed when I looked at her. She nodded and gave me a smile. "It makes it hard for you to know what's real and what's not, even after the fact."

I nodded. She was right. It probably hadn't helped matters that after the compound, I had wound up in juvie and was drugged to keep me from accessing my powers. That was bound to be confusing. For all I knew, I might not have killed anyone. Oh, sure, I injured plenty of them, but maybe their injuries by my claws and fangs weren't fatal.

I didn't respond aloud to Chana, but my nodding seemed to have sufficed. "Anyone else been to Washington?" Dr. Pudi asked.

"Seattle is awesome," Logan said, his face and hands animated. He gestured in a way that seemed vague to me, but likely made sense to him as he continued. "I lived in Bellevue for a little while, which is close enough that I could do things in the city without living right in the middle of it."

"Did you go up in the Space Needle?" Trinity asked, her eyes wide. Her accent made me reconsider my earlier assessment of her being African American. She sounded more like she'd been born in Africa, and that English wasn't her first language.

Chana asked Logan something in a different language, and Dr. Pudi cleared his throat pointedly. Chana gave him a quick nod and switched back to English. "Did you see any orcas?"

With Logan, Trinity, and Chana all chatting about Seattle and its environs, I managed to fade out of the spotlight and focus my attention back on Jasper. He also wasn't taking part in the conversation, but he glanced up from his lap and looked at me, then immediately back down to his lap. He was looking very shifty right about now, moving him up a few rungs on my list of heliotrope suspects.

Could he have figured out what I was and hidden the heliotrope without Lorelei noticing? It seemed plausible, since he had access to our whole room, not just Lorelei's side. His wheelchair didn't have the smallest turning radius. He'd likely have to wheel over to my side of the room in order to exit, and Lorelei might have missed him putting something on my bed if she was distracted at the time.

And what if the whole Jade story was just a cover? Jasper could very easily be a changeling. Fae was less likely, given his apparent inability to heal from whatever injury had landed him in a wheelchair. But what if Dedwydd also impacted our healing factor?

I did recall, though, that Jasper was in Gerard's Occult Studies class, which suggested that he was a witch of some sort. That also didn't mesh with what Lorelei had told me. I was beginning to think that if I was going to figure anything about them out, I'd have pick up on the inconsistencies to find the lies, and with those, wander to the truth.

Lost in my own thoughts, I didn't bother tracking the conversation, and Dr. Pudi didn't attempt to draw me or Jasper into it. So I was a little surprised when he cleared his throat. "Thank you all for a lively conversation. I'll see you all for individual counseling before we meet again."

Great. Individual counseling. I'd almost forgotten about that, but there it was, asterisked on my schedule. Friday, after Anger Management, just one more thing in the way of the weekend and a break from all of these classes. Great.

I shuffled out of the office, ready to head upstairs for the last class of the day. I had a few minutes between classes, and Jasper hadn't wheeled himself very far down the hall. I wanted to play my hunch, so I jogged to catch up with him.

"Hey, so I guess maybe we didn't formally meet yesterday," I said, thrusting my hand toward Jasper. "I'm Briar Williams, and I'm rooming with Lorelei."

Jasper looked up at me, eyes narrowed. He didn't take my hand. "Yeah, I know. And?"

I shrugged. "And nothing. I just figured we might, you know, interact some in the future, so I wanted to try to start out on the right foot?"

Jasper scoffed. "Yeah, the right foot. Great plan." He wheeled away from me.

I realized what I'd said and clenched my eyes shut. "Oh, I didn't mean ... look, I'm sorry."

Jasper spun his chair around to face me, almost a stationary 180. Maybe it did have a tighter turn radius than I'd thought. His face had reddened, and his expression was fierce. "Look, I don't need your pity, and Lorelei doesn't need your friendship. She and I are in this together, and neither of us needs your help with anything. So leave her out of whatever you've got going on here. Got it? Just keep your head down so you can get moved to a single sooner rather than later."

I took a step backward, surprised by his sudden vehemence. The way he was dictating what Lorelei "needed" made my skin crawl. And what did he mean about "in this together" and not needing my help? There was definitely something odd going on with those two, and this only piqued my curiosity.

I managed to keep my temper under control and not yell back at him. Mister Walkenhorst would be so proud. Thinking of that, I remembered I had a class to get to. I gave Jasper a stiff nod. "Gotcha. Loud and clear." I sidestepped Jasper's wheelchair and headed for the staircase nearest to the Anger Management classroom.

Jasper was still on my list of suspects, but it seemed like talking to him wasn't the best way to find the information I was looking for. Maybe I'd talk to Lorelei later about my suspicions, though I figured I'd have to couch it in the gentlest terms possible. I didn't think she'd take it too well if I complained about her boyfriend without her being witness to his behavior. Or maybe I was just going to have to drop the entire thing. So long as no more deadly rocks found their way into my bed, maybe that was the best option.

I found myself wondering whether the ring would have given me a shock if Jasper had shaken my hand, and what it would have meant if it did. It occurred to me that I'd punched Keegan in the shoulder, and the ring hadn't reacted to that. But all that told me was that Keegan and Nic weren't the same sort of creature. If Nic was a demon, that might mean I had a demon detecting ring. And that didn't quite mesh with what I knew of the people at the compound, where the ring had come from in the first place. I'd have to ask the Spooky Girls if they had any ideas after classes ended for the day.

Jaylin wasn't in the Anger Management classroom when I arrived. Mister Walkenhorst gave me a silent nod when he entered the classroom, so I assumed that meant I was still in the class. The other four students all seemed to relax when that happened, most notably Echo, who I sat beside on one of the couches.

"No offense to Jaylin," Echo murmured, just loud enough for me to hear, "but they have some serious anger issues. It'll be easier without them here."

I still wasn't entirely sure why they'd put a changeling child in a class for students with anger issues that definitely had supernaturals in it—I mean, Echo was living proof, even if I didn't know what the rest of the others were. I comforted myself in knowing that *I* wasn't the one who had screwed up in this case.

I didn't place any blame on Jaylin, either. At least not for this. The jury was still out on the heliotrope thing, even if I couldn't pin down how they could have been in my room without Lorelei knowing. Maybe they'd worked with Jasper—Jaylin knowing what I was, and Jasper having easy access to my bed. With Jasper yelling about me getting a single room, that suggested he was motivated to get Lorelei back to having her own room, so he might have been more than happy to help Jaylin out with getting rid of me.

Mister Walkenhorst started the meditation music, and I tried to quiet my thoughts and all of that good stuff. But my mind kept wandering back to the heliotrope, who might have put it in my bed, and what would have happened if I hadn't found it. I spent most of the class envisioning a variety of horrible personal scenarios, most of which ended with me lying on the floor of my dorm room and gasping my last breaths. Clearly, I wasn't going to be able to just drop it.

Echo nudged me at the end of class. "You still coming upstairs?"

I nodded. "Definitely, though I wanted to stop by my room first." I gave her a grin. "Thanks for taking me in, by the way. It's nice to have some friends here."

"Other than Gerard, you mean?" she asked

"It's nice to have *girl* friends. In the most strictly Platonic sense of the word."

Echo returned my grin. "Yeah, I get that."

We walked out of the classroom and toward my room. A cluster of four or five students milled around at the landing between the second- and third-floor stairs, right in the path of where Echo would be going to get to Maddie and Aimee's room.

Logan looked up from within that group and caught my gaze. He pressed his lips together and shook his head, then mouthed "sorry."

At that, I gave the rest of the group a closer look. Some of them were people I'd only seen in classes or the cafeteria, and couldn't identify, but one of them stood out. Jaylin.

They strode out of the group, crossing their arms over their chest, and glared at me.

Under her breath, Echo muttered, "Ah, crap."

I felt the same, but I tried to put on a brave face. "I'll see you in a little bit."

"Don't ... you don't have to fight them," Echo said, her voice still quiet.

"Wasn't planning on it."

"Yeah, well, they want to fight you. You might not get a choice."

"Don't worry. I'll be good."

"Good luck with that," Echo said, then scurried away from my side.

It had felt strange for Echo to have my back for a moment, and now it felt strange without her there. But I didn't want to run from this confrontation. I just had to play it right. "Hi! Jaylin, right?"

Jaylin rolled their eyes. "Wow, you're a quick one."

"Right. Can I do something for you?"

They sighed. "Well, dying in a fire seems unlikely, but you can leave me and mine alone."

Dying in a fire was specific. Had they said "dying in your bed," I'd have been a lot more concerned. "Dying from heliotrope" would have been a dead giveaway. But their second request wasn't half as bad. I nodded. "Sure, that seems doable. Can it be mutual?"

Narrowing their gaze at me, Jaylin asked, "I'm sorry, did you just presume you get a say in this?"

With a deep breath, I pushed the issue. "No, I just presumed that maybe if I'm going to leave you alone, you should try to do the same. It doesn't work out too well if I'm trying to leave you alone, and you're getting in my face." I crossed my arms over my chest, too, glad to not feel the prickles of my claws where I gripped my upper arms. "Who am I leaving alone, then, aside from you?"

Jaylin glared at me. "Logan. Zoe. And Walter."

I nodded as they listed the names. Logan and Zoe had both been on the list in Maddie's notebook. I'd have to ask Maddie what she thought Walter might be, though my money was on changeling. "I don't know Zoe or Walter."

Jaylin jerked their head backward at a slender African American girl with skin so dark it was nearly black, waist-length braids, her tie worn loose and her shirt untucked. "Zoe." Jerking their head to the other side, indicating an African American guy who was fairly slight in stature and wearing his uniform as close to regulations as possible, they said, "Walter. Got it?"

I nodded. "Gerard LeCroix and the Spooky Girls are my list."

Jaylin frowned. "You want us to leave the Spooky Girls alone? Why would we even—" They trailed off. "Yeah, okay, deal."

"Do you know who Gerard is?"

"The other new guy, yeah. Not a problem."

I glanced at the others, unsure of what would happen next. Despite the fact that I'd been rebuffed twice now when presenting my hand to other students in introduction, it seemed like an arrangement like this needed to be formalized. I was also a little curious as to what the ring would do if Jaylin and I shook hands. I extended my hand toward her, trying to keep it from shaking. "So, do we shake on this?"

"Hell no," Jaylin scoffed. "I wouldn't touch you if I was dying."

I pulled my hand back, but I couldn't resist a dig at them, and a possible clue in my investigation. "Not even with a fistful of heliotrope?"

Jaylin frowned, their eyebrows furrowing. "What?"

Crap. They didn't know what heliotrope was or what it did, and I'd just tipped my hand. "Don't worry about it," I said, forcing a smile. But I already knew it was too late. Zoe's gaze had narrowed, which meant she either knew what I meant, or she was about to go figure it out.

Either way, I'd probably just given the person here who seemed to hate me most the ammunition they needed to cause me serious harm if I got in their way. I was going to have to give Jaylin and what I presumed were the other changeling children an extremely wide berth.

And yet, I still didn't know who to blame for trying to kill me in my sleep.

CHAPTER TEN:
LEARNING THE LAY OF THE LAND

I headed up to Spooky Room immediately, moving fast enough that I wondered if I'd catch up to Echo on my way there. Instead, she was waiting in the doorway for me, concern etched across her features.

She relaxed when she saw me. "All good?"

I shrugged. "Complicated, but I didn't get in a fight. So sure, it's all good." I gave her two thumbs up and a half smile.

She gestured into the room with a tilt of her head, and I followed her in. Maddie and Aimee were both sprawled out on their beds working on homework, but with our arrival, Maddie scrambled to clean up her books and notebooks to make room for me on her bed.

Aimee put her book aside and shook her head. "Man, Briar, you're just trouble." She grinned broadly, so I knew it was a joke. "Welcome to the club."

"Does this trouble club involve an inability to take a single step in this place without tripping over something major?" I asked, returning her grin.

"Something like that." She paused to catch Maddie's gaze. "So we're agreed?"

"Totally!" Maddie exclaimed. She bounced slightly on the end of her bed, jostling me as I sat down beside her.

"Yes," Echo replied.

I looked at the three of them in turn, watching their shared glances and nods. "Agreed on what?"

Aimee turned toward me. "Congratulations, you've been nominated, seconded, and approved as an honorary Spooky Girl.

I'm not gonna lie, I voted for hazing you before we went forward with the approval, but I got overruled."

"Thanks, I think?" I had no idea what was going on, nor why. Honorary Spooky Girl sounded pretty cool, though.

"We're adopting you," Maddie said. "Or letting you join our clique. Or something like that."

"Oh, okay. Then yes, thank you. I'm honored. Right?"

Echo nodded. "I mean, you can be honored if you want to be. Mostly, you seem like our type of weirdo. And you did a good job defusing Jaylin."

I frowned. "I did? I'm pretty sure they still want to fight me."

"I overheard you put us on the list of your friends for Jaylin and their friends to not mess with," Echo admitted. "You didn't have to do that, but you did. So we thought we'd let you know that you're one of us now. You know, if you want to be."

I chuckled. "Ah, yes, now it makes more sense. And yes, I think you guys are my kind of weirdos too. I would be proud to call myself a Spooky Girl."

"Cool, now you get the tattoo," Aimee said, opening a drawer beside her bed.

"Wait, what?" My heart started racing. I had no idea how human (or witch) tattoos worked, but I knew about fae tattoos, and the sheer amount of pain they were said to inflict was terrifying.

"Kidding," Aimee said. "Sorry, Briar. You basically have to assume that ninety percent of what I say is me messing with either you or Maddie. It's just what I do."

Maddie shrugged beside me. "You get used to it."

"Right," Echo said, clearing her throat. "So Jaylin's got it out for you."

I nodded. "I don't know if they've got it out specifically for me or for fae in general. And there are a lot of gradations of fae that I don't think they quite get."

"Gradations? Can you elaborate?" Maddie's pen and notebook had appeared out of nowhere, or possibly they'd just been beside her on the bed all along.

I eyed the notebook. "Do you have to write it down?"

She waved the pen around. "Magical pen."

"Still?"

Her shoulders slumped, but she set the notebook and pen on her desk, only pouting a little.

"Thanks. It's not that I'm worried about you guys learning this, I just ... I really don't like it when people write stuff about me. Call it a phobia, almost."

Aimee tilted her head to the side. "Now that's one I've never heard before. What would we even call that? It's like scopophobia, but with writing instead of photos. Hmm, what's Greek for writing?"

"Grafí," Echo said. "But that would be for a fear of writing." She looked at me and shrugged. "I'm not sure that's quite right."

"You know Greek?" I asked.

Echo nodded. "A little. My dad's side of the family is Greek. I've poked at a little bit of Ancient Greek just for fun."

"Because my girlfriend's a nerd," Aimee said, chuckling. "But that works out fine, because so am I."

"Well, if you want to call it graphophobia, I guess that's as good a name as any." I took a deep breath. "And it's related to my explanation of the gradations of fae. There are two broad classes of fae: the nobility, and everyone else. And in that structure, the everyone else tend to be the ones who are only written about when there's something bad to record." I grimaced slightly. "It's kind of why I'm not there any more."

"And likely why you don't want to get in trouble here, too," Echo said. "Can we ask what you did?"

I hesitated. I knew my actions in Idyll had been against the rules there, but they were the right thing to do in the situation. The nobility had overstepped their bounds, and commoners were getting hurt. My rebellion had been for the greater good. I was fairly sure the Spooky Girls would understand this, but the details were something I hadn't even really told my friends in Artis—they only knew I'd been kicked out.

After a long moment, I finally shrugged. "I started a revolution against the nobility and got captured in the process. They had plenty of evidence for me as the ringleader of it, because I was. So they kicked me out."

"That's all?" Aimee asked, frowning. "You just wanted to smash the patriarchy ... I mean, fae-archy?"

"I mean, it's treason, technically," I said, shrugging. "I guess that might be a slightly bigger deal in Idyll than here?"

"No, treason's still a thing," Maddie said. "It's just less of a thing amongst people who would also like to smash the patriarchy. Or fae-archy. Was it a patriarchy?"

"Aristocracy, if you want to be technical about it," I said. "Without getting too far into the details, there's a council of governors, picked from amongst their peers. There are men, women, and fae of other genders on the council, but it's an aristocratical dictatorship."

Aimee shrugged. "Yeah, okay, smash the dictatorship, too. They have a definite tendency toward sucking."

"Anyway, what Jaylin probably doesn't understand is that my stance in the rebellion was for better treatment of all non-nobles, which includes changeling children. I wanted the nobles to stop abusing anyone 'beneath' them."

"So how do changeling children happen?" Maddie asked. "Is it like in the fairy tales where fairies take children and replace them with changelings?"

"No, there's not always a replacement left behind, these days. The nobles just take people—" I began, then paused. "Okay, that's not ... I mean, it's done at the behest of the nobility. It's done *by* everyone else. Like we're their errand people."

Maddie's eyes went wide, and she gasped. "You've kidnapped babies?"

My stomach sank. I'd just found these new friends, and they'd hit upon the thing I most hated to admit. They weren't going to want to be my friends anymore once they realized what I'd done before getting kicked out of Idyll. I tried to downplay it. "Uh, babies are usually more trouble than they're worth. But yeah. On orders."

Echo nodded, but her lips were a tight line, like she was judging me quietly but trying to not let that slip out. "Okay, you know what, that was then, this is now. You're different now, right?"

Did she actually get it? I nodded enthusiastically. "So different."

"So then what you need to do is get that information to Jaylin. Maybe they already know and don't care. But if they don't know, it might calm things down, right?" Echo asked.

I shrugged. "It could, I guess."

"Then if I were in your shoes, I'd try to talk to Logan, Zoe, or Walter, if you can pry them away from Jaylin," Echo suggested.

"See if you can get one of them to listen to reason and take it back to Jaylin."

I nodded. It was a solid idea. I didn't know Zoe or Walter at all, save for our brief introduction just previous, but maybe I could get Logan to talk to me. It should at least be easier than trying to explain myself to Jaylin.

"Since you guys asked me a couple of questions, can I ask you some in return?" I asked.

Aimee sighed. "You're one of us now, so we're technically not doing *quid pro quo* any more. Ask away."

I fished the ring out of my pocket. "So I've got this item, and I think it does something supernatural. I don't know what it's doing though, exactly."

"May I see it?" Maddie asked, holding out her hand.

I held the ring between the thumb and forefinger of my right hand and took Maddie's hand with my left hand. Nothing happened when I was in contact with her, like nothing had happened when she hugged me previously, so I let the ring drop into her upturned palm.

"What was that about?" Echo asked.

"Testing," I admitted. "What the ring has done so far is to tingle in Nic's presence, and then it actually shocked both of us when we shook hands. Oh, and it shocked me when I brushed up against Keegan, but he didn't react to it. Nic did."

"Shocked like surprised, or shocked like zapped?" Maddie asked as she held the ring up to the light and scrutinized it.

"Zapped."

She squinted at the interior of the ring. "What does it say in the band?"

"It's Latin," I replied, reciting it without looking. "'*pacem undique quaesivi sed nusquam repperi.*' It means 'In all things I sought peace, and I have found it nowhere.' But I don't know where the phrase comes from or anything like that."

"Where did the ring come from?" Echo asked, walking over to look at it more closely.

"The compound, in Artis. The one where my friends and I probably murdered people. All of the people there had rings like that, and they acted like they were religious symbols." I hesitated, chuckling. "I don't actually know how I wound up with one, but apparently I had it on my person when I went into the institution I was at before I came here, because it was with my stuff when I got out."

Maddie pursed her lips and shook her head. "I can't get anything out of it without a spell." She handed it back to me. "It's probably magical. If it reacted to Nic, maybe it detects demons?"

"If he's actually a demon," Aimee said. "That's our best theory. Also, you said it was a tingle in his presence, but a shock with physical contact, right?"

I nodded.

"And it does nothing in the presence of witches?"

"Presence or contact," I confirmed. "I've had it in my pocket basically since I got here."

"Have you put it on?" Echo asked.

"What, like my finger?" I asked, taken aback. "Isn't that how bad things happen to people?"

The Spooky Girls looked at one another, then shook their heads in unison.

I pieced together my confusion quickly. "You guys have different versions of fairy tales here. Okay. There are a lot of what you'd call fairy tales that are told in Idyll as cautionary tales. Wearing a ring that doesn't belong to you tends to bind you into the service of whoever's ring it was."

"Oh, yeah, that's different alright," Aimee said.

"It's okay, though," Echo said. "If you're already getting some information out of it without wearing it, maybe it doesn't need to be worn. If you want to try it out though, whenever, just let us know." She glanced around and lowered her voice, even though it was just the four of us in the Spooky Room. "Do not tell anyone, not even Gerard, but I have a warding circle crafted into a rug in my room. It's the safest place to try anything potentially dangerous with items."

I blinked a few times in response, but then nodded. "Okay, lips are sealed. And I'll let you know if I want to try it later. But right now, I want to eat."

~

As I was taking my tray to the drop-off after eating my dinner, I spotted Logan in the cafeteria near the self-serve cereal and made a beeline in his direction. I wasn't a fan of the sugary junk, but I could at least pretend to be browsing while I chatted with him.

"Hey," I said, trying my best to act casual.

His gaze flickered over me, and his face paled slightly. "You shouldn't be here."

I sighed. "I'm not here to mess with you. We go to the same school. We're going to run into each other. It's not like I can just stop going to every class I have with one of you."

Logan's gaze shifted around nervously, and he breathed out through his nose loudly. "Okay, fine. But I'm not socializing with you."

I took a deep breath. "Could you just tell Jaylin—"

"Tell Jaylin what?" Jaylin's voice was crisp as they stepped into view from the other side of the cereal island.

I took a deep breath, looking them in the eyes. "There are some things you should know about the politics in Idyll."

They scoffed. "Really? I know plenty. And you're stepping where you shouldn't be. Or have you already forgotten our arrangement?" Their gaze stretched out to a point behind me, and I didn't need to turn around to know they were looking at where I'd been sitting with the Spooky Girls.

I put my hands up. "I just want to clear the air."

Jaylin shook their head. "There's nothing to clear. I was in Idyll for what felt like a hundred years. I probably know more about it than you do, and nothing you say is going to change my mind on that count. Now leave. Us. Alone."

"Have it your way." I turned away, ready to go back to the Spooky Girls, but they had already vacated, likely when they saw Jaylin get in my face. They were great friends, but they were very violence averse. And I guess I was too.

I headed back toward the upper floors, debating if I wanted to go back to Spooky Room or to my own room. I had homework to work on, but I was pretty sure the witches wouldn't mind if I worked on it upstairs. After all, now that I knew them, I'd realized I had a class with each of them.

At the very least, my books were in my room, so I'd need to stop by there to collect them before going anywhere else. Or maybe if Lorelei wasn't there, I'd just enjoy the quiet of having the room to myself for a bit.

There was one door in the hallway before my room, and the door had been closed every time I'd passed it so far. At the moment, though, it stood wide open, so I took a peek to see who my neighbors were.

I recognized Trinity from my group therapy session immediately, but I didn't recognize the girl she was making out with. Of course, all I could see of that girl was a mass of brown curls, deeply tanned skin, and willowy limbs. Her facial features were sort of lost in the act of smooching Trinity.

Why they were making out with the door wide open was beyond me, but human sexuality wasn't something I really understood. Being born in Idyll, I understood the way fae sexuality worked, and there were a number of commonalities. Public displays of affection were not among them, plus Miss Hale had warned Gerard off from even hugging me, so seeing Trinity and this other girl making out was awkward for me.

I kept walking, thinking maybe they hadn't noticed me, but I heard Trinity call out after me. "Hey, Briar?"

I froze just outside my door. "Uh, yeah?"

"Could you come here a minute, please?"

I shuffled back to the open doorway and lingered just outside.

Trinity smiled at me. "This is my girlfriend, Val. She wanted to meet you."

Val smiled, and her whole face lit up. Her features were fine, almost elfin, but it was hard to see that with her smile as broad as it was. "It really is you!"

I peered at her, having no idea who she was (other than Trinity's girlfriend). I felt like maybe she was in one of my morning classes, but the people in those classes were mostly a blur to me, as I paid more attention to the subject matter rather than the other students. "Sorry, have we met, and I've forgotten?"

She shook her head. "No, we haven't met. I've just ... I've heard of you."

I blinked. "Sorry, what?"

"From Idyll." She lifted the bottom edge of her T-shirt and tugged at the top of her leggings to reveal her right hipbone, branded with the sigil of House Van Drande, one of the noble houses of Idyll. The nobles didn't mark themselves. They marked their property. And the Van Drandes were among the vilest and most abusive of the nobles.

From the way the brand had healed, I could tell she was fae, not a changeling child. On a fae, the branding looked elegant. On a changeling, it usually scarred horribly, no matter how careful the brander or the branded was about preserving the mark.

I blanched, feeling suddenly nauseous thinking about the process of branding and the Van Drandes, and looked away. "Sorry. I'm so sorry."

"You have nothing to apologize for," Val said, hurrying to cover her hipbone again. Then she rushed over to the doorway. "I wanted to meet you so I could say thank you. You're a huge part of the reason why I got out of Idyll. Your rebellion paved the way for a lot of fae and changelings to leave."

I turned back toward her, eyes wide. I'd made an impact? "Really?" I managed to ask.

Val tilted her head to the side, eyebrows furrowing. "I thought you knew. Rumors say that's why you got thrown out."

I shook my head. Val knew a lot about me that I didn't even know, and it was sort of throwing me off. But she was fae. She was, maybe, the first fae I'd met here, other than Mister Walkenhorst, who most certainly had not fanboyed over my presence here. "So wait, you know a lot about what's going on in Idyll, even now?"

Val shook her head. "Not so much now. A year or so ago, yeah."

"A year or so? I've only been out six months."

"Time's a little different on this side," Val said, "and I was among the early departures. We heard rumors that you were still in the wind for a while, then nothing. I guess maybe that's when you got exiled."

I bit at my lip, unsure about pursuing my next question. "And do you know Jaylin?"

Trinity took a deep breath, loudly enough that both Val and I looked at her. "I really don't like them."

"Yeah, me either," Val agreed, but a frown crossed her face. "Wait, they're pulling their usual 'you treated me like garbage' nonsense?"

"Uh yeah, I guess so. They pretty much flew into a rage the first time they saw me, and now we have this maybe temporary truce?"

Val continued to frown. "Did you try to talk to them?"

"Yeah. They don't seem to be interested."

"That's weird. They're not a fan of the fae, but they generally have a lot of questions for new fae. Something doesn't seem right."

"Can I ask you how many of us are here?"

Val hesitated for a second, but it wasn't a hesitation of not wanting to tell me so much as she seemed to be counting. "With you here, there's fourteen, across all of the grades. Six in our year now."

My mouth gaped open. "Seriously? Who?"

Now Val frowned, and I could tell she wasn't compiling a list. "Sorry, I've probably told you too much already. But listen, if you want to know more about Jaylin, talk to Keegan. They both showed up here about the same time, and he seems to be the only fae she's spoken to beyond an initial conversation."

So Keegan was fae, not some sort of canine-based shapeshifter. That was a huge piece of information, one that even the Spooky Girls didn't have. It also made my interactions with Keegan so far seem a little weirder. Did he know who I was, like Val did? Was he trying to get to know me because we were both fae?

The ring had shocked me when I'd touched him, both accidentally and when I punched him in the hallway. I wondered how weird Val would think it was if I suddenly tried to touch her. I hesitated a moment, and then asked, "This is going to sound really weird, but can I shake your hand?"

"I'd be honored," Val said, her eyes filling with tears. "I mean, I want to hug you, really."

I shook my head. "I'm not a hugger." I extended my hand to her, and she took it.

In my pocket, the ring sent out a tiny zap, smaller than the ones I'd felt when touching Nic or Keegan.

Val tilted her head to one side. "Static?"

I decided to play it off, since I still wasn't entirely sure what the ring was reacting too. "Yeah, it's a whole lot worse here than it was in Artis—uh, that's the town I came here from."

"Yeah, cold, dry air," Val said, nodding. "Well, anyway, I didn't want to keep you for too long. But thank you. Again."

"Yeah, you're welcome," I murmured, heading back into the hallway.

Finding out Keegan was fae pretty much discounted him from being my mystery heliotrope dropper, as it would have hurt him just as much as it would have hurt me. There really was no easy way for fae to transport heliotrope—even if he'd wrapped it up in something, it still would have made him nauseated and weak. He didn't seem like the sort to put himself at risk just to play a hunch, either. And if he was off the hook for the heliotrope, the pool was narrowing even further.

Based on what Val was telling me, it seemed like my next step was going to have to be tracking him down and seeing if maybe his tour offer still stood.

~

It only took a little bit of asking around before I was standing outside Keegan's door, poised to knock. He had a single room on the third floor, on the wing at the opposite end of the hall from Spooky Room.

He opened the door before I knocked, leaving me with my fist raised and blinking awkwardly. "Hey, Briar, what's up?"

I calmed myself and smiled. "I was coming to see if that tour offer was still good."

Like most of the students did after classes, he'd changed clothes, into jeans and a hooded sweatshirt; I was still in my school uniform, since I had a lack of anything other than my uniform and pajamas to wear. He leaned one arm against the doorframe, doing the exact pose I'd envisioned earlier, the one where he looms over me in a way that he thinks is cute and I find kind of menacing. I did my best to stand my ground, though, not wanting to shrink away from a dominating position just because it was dominating.

"I was just going down the hall to the bathroom." Keegan glanced back into his room. "Why don't you wait in here for a minute, then I'll come back and take you for a tour?"

"Oh, I can just wait in the hall, it's fine," I said, eyes growing wide. It wasn't against the rules for me to be in his room at this time in the evening, it just felt weird, like I'd be intruding on his space somehow, in a way I didn't feel entirely comfortable with.

"No, I insist." He stepped out of the doorway and held out his arm like he was presenting his room to me.

I took a tentative step forward and caught a faint scent of something familiar—a half-remembered aroma of Idyll. "Alright," I said, slightly breathless as I tried to identify the source of the smell, both in my memory and in Keegan's room.

It was a warm smell, a good one, and it took me back to my younger years, snuggled around the fire after a big meal, listening to stories from the other young fae. It gave me the faintest yearning for the Idyll of my early memories, but a stronger yearning to find the source of the smell and keep it as my own.

I took a moment to survey Keegan's room. It was about the same size as the one I shared with Lorelei, but had only a single bed, desk, and wardrobe, and the addition of a bookcase, which was nearly full. The bed and wardrobe occupied the entire left-hand wall, while the desk and bookcase were along the right-hand wall, the windows between them. The bed was unmade and the wardrobe open, and a quick step in that direction assured me that they just smelled like teenage boy, not the warm scent.

Stepping toward the bookcase, the aroma grew stronger, and I scanned the book titles, looking for something that I recognized. There was a middle shelf of school books and notebooks, a few shelves above and below of the sort of cheap paperbacks I used to occasionally find discarded in the park where I lived, and the lowest shelf packed tightly with old books, leather-bound and gilt edged.

I crouched to look at that shelf just as Keegan returned.

"Oh, you found my books!"

"Are these from—" I began, then cut myself off as I rose.

He closed the door behind him quietly. "Idyll? Yeah. I hope you don't mind me closing the door. I prefer to keep my past mostly to myself."

"Val mentioned you're ... fae, like me," I said, the last few words in a jumbled rush, as I was admitting my nature to him at the same time I was revealing that I knew his. "I didn't want to pry, but it came up when I was talking to her about Jaylin."

He nodded stiffly. "Ah. Yeah. That's a hard nut to crack."

"Jaylin?"

"Yeah. They suffered a lot in Idyll." He sighed. "They're not the only one who did, of course, but they take it a lot more personally."

"Val said you've got some sort of rapport with them. Meanwhile, they're just mad at me, and I don't even know why."

Keegan shrugged. "I've been out for a while, so I couldn't really tell you what you might have done to earn their ire."

"How long is a while?"

"A year or two?" He seemed a little unsure of his answer. "Give or take, I guess."

I hesitated for only a moment before blurting out, "Do you know about what I did?"

He arched an eyebrow. "Killed people, you told me."

"No, I mean, in Idyll."

He shook his head. "No."

I'd been ready to admit to what I'd done in Idyll, but Keegan's apparent ignorance of my past was almost refreshing. "I take it you're not a noble, then?"

"Hard to say," he said. "Let me explain something about Jaylin, that will bring us around to an answer to your question. They were treated abominably, by anyone's standards. They have memories of Idyll that they shouldn't be burdened with, and those memories involve things that we don't remember. There's something about leaving Idyll that normally takes away parts of us, fae and changelings alike, but something happened to Jaylin that made everything stick. They told me that I was kind to them once, so they trust me."

I listened with rapt attention to this new information. Did I remember everything I'd done in Idyll, or had I forgotten pieces as well? If I had, then there was every possibility I could have done worse things than what I recalled, and I could even have harmed Jaylin directly. "You don't remember what you did?"

He shook his head. "I wish I did."

"I feel like I remember most of what happened in Idyll too, though now I wonder if I've forgotten pieces as well. How do you find out?"

Keegan rubbed his chin as he spoke. "Sometimes for me, there's an obvious hole. Like I'm pretty sure I was a part of a family there, either by birth or by choice, but I don't remember anyone's names. But there are plenty of other things where I'm not sure if it's a real memory or something my brain has created to fill a hole. Like I remember the name Anya, and I've tried putting it together with the family members I remember, and sometimes it sticks to—" He trailed off, gaze searching the ceiling. "—a sister, maybe, or a cousin about my age? I just don't know. It's frustrating."

I nodded. "I wish I knew what I'd done to Jaylin that was so awful. If I could name the thing and apologize, maybe they'd accept it, and we could work on a little less hostility."

Keegan shook his head again. "I can't believe you'd have done anything awful, Briar. You ... I can tell that something happened to you in Idyll that didn't go well, but there's no way you could have hurt someone like Jaylin."

That statement didn't fit with the memories I did have, the memories of fighting with my teeth and claws, shredding fae and changeling flesh alike in my maw, in support of the nobility's aims, before my rebellion. I straightened my back, and my voice came out cold. "You don't know me."

"Right, you're right, I don't. But I just think—" He shrugged. "I get a sense of people sometimes, even here. And the sense I have of you is good and kind."

That pulled a sharp laugh out of my throat. "Your senses are way off then, Keegan. I'm not who you think I am. I'm a monster."

"No one is a monster."

"That can't be true. There are monsters in Idyll, and monsters on Earth. I've encountered them." I chuckled lightly. "One of my best friends from before I came here is a werewolf, and I can assure you, he and I could go toe to toe for viciousness and destruction. And he told me *twice* I was worse than him."

Keegan's brow furrowed. "I'm never wrong about my impressions of people."

"You are this time." I turned toward the door. "You know what, I should go and let you finish your homework. Maybe another time for this tour."

"If you'd rather, then okay," he said. His voice had taken on a somber note, but I didn't turn back around to see his expression. There was only so much sad puppy dog eyes I could take.

CHAPTER ELEVEN:
ROOMMATE TROUBLES

I was a nasty, snarly mess when I got back to my room, so it was probably good that Lorelei wasn't there, or I might have taken it out on her. She didn't deserve that, even if she had lied to me about what she was, and maybe more than that. If she'd been there, I might have called her out on it, and that could have ended badly, especially if we were stuck living together until I got off my one-month probation thing.

I tossed my books on my bed, and something crunched beneath the covers. The hairs on the back of my neck shot up as I tried to identify what might have made that sound. If the school didn't have ways of suppressing our powers, I knew my fangs and claws would have emerged.

I tiptoed back to the door and locked it, so I'd at least have some warning if Lorelei came back suddenly. Then I lifted each of my books off the comforter and stacked them on my desk, watching my bedding carefully for any unexpected movement. Once I'd moved my books, the comforter was rumpled enough that I couldn't tell if there was something hiding beneath it, or if I'd just made a mess of it by throwing my books down.

I debated for a moment if I wanted to grab the comforter from the foot of the bed or the head of the bed. Recalling the heliotrope placed neatly on my pillow, I opted for the foot. I gave it a solid tug, and it flew off my bed, scattering a bunch of dried leaves into the middle of the floor.

I blinked at the leaves. I recognized oak, maple, and aspen among them, plus a scattering of dried pine needles. All of those species were local—I'd spotted several of them in the woods, even though the branches had been bare. But what confused me was the why. Why would someone put a bunch of leaves in my bed? Heliotrope was one thing. Leaves? That was just weird.

A broom and dustpan stood in the narrow space between Lorelei's closet and the wall, and I retrieved it to sweep up the mess I'd made, giving all of the leaves a close second look. I didn't see anything poisonous in the mix, and I certainly didn't detect any iron somehow hidden by the debris. I unmade my bed, giving the sheet a thorough shaking before putting it back on, and then covered it up with my comforter.

When I turned back to the leaves I'd started to sweep up, they'd been scattered. I shook my head, reaching toward them with the broom, then paused. The leaves hadn't just scattered because of me shaking out my sheet and comforter. They'd somehow arranged themselves into the word "leave".

"Leave?" I asked aloud to the empty room. "And go where?"

Before my eyes, a gust scattered the leaves again, though they didn't re-form into any other words.

I checked the windows, both of which were locked tight against the chill outside. Then I felt the floor near our door, to see if a strong breeze came through there. Nothing.

Which meant there was something weird going on.

I edged over to my desk and flipped open one of my notebooks, laying a pen atop it. "Okay, I know there's someone here. I'm going to sweep up these leaves. Lorelei is not going to like it if she comes back to a mess all over the floor. If you've got something more to say to me, write it down."

The sound of my sweeping was loud enough that I wouldn't be able to hear if someone was writing in my notebook. But I couldn't keep my gaze on the blank page and do a good job of sweeping, so I focused on the latter. As I swept the last of the leaves into the dustpan, I glanced at the notebook. Nothing.

I checked to make sure my key was in my pocket, then headed toward the door. I didn't want to have to try to explain to Lorelei why our garbage can was full of leaves, so I figured I'd take it straight to the garbage chute. I pulled the door shut behind me and locked it, carefully holding the dustpan so it wouldn't dump leaves in the hallway, either.

Once I'd gotten the leaves all down the garbage chute, I headed back to my room. The door was still closed, and still locked, and I breathed a sigh of relief.

Nothing was written in my notebook.

"Fine, whatever," I muttered under my breath. I didn't know if there'd been someone invisible or a ghost in the room, or if my mind was just playing tricks on me. I'd seen patterns in nature before, and even though that was technically amongst my powers, and thus shouldn't work here, it could be that I'd trained my brain to see patterns outside of my powers. Maybe I'd just seen the word "leave" because a part of my brain wanted to do just that. It was impossible to know.

I sat down at my desk and started working on my homework.

~

Lorelei still hadn't returned after I'd poked at my homework for a few hours, and it was past the 10 p.m. cut-off for when she wasn't supposed to be in Jasper's room. But that was her problem, not mine. I had enough problems of my own.

I'd eliminated most of my suspects for the heliotrope, except for Lorelei and Jasper, and I wondered if that was why she was scarce tonight. I hadn't entirely ruled out Jaylin having something to do with it, either, but I had a harder time pinning it on them. They hadn't been in my room, as far I knew. And they hadn't known about heliotrope before I mentioned it to them.

But someone *had* been in our room to put the leaves in my bed. Even though that was a much more harmless prank, it was still disconcerting. I'd have to ask Lorelei about that when I saw her next. It could have been her, for all I knew, trying to freak me out by putting things in my bed and then claiming she didn't know how they wound up there.

I spun up all sorts of conspiracies about Jaylin working with Lorelei, and how that might have played out. Lorelei and Jaylin could be friends, a fact that neither of them had brought to my attention. I didn't know either of them well enough to guess on the plausibility of that. And if Jaylin had known I was fae from the moment I walked in the door, they could easily have gotten Lorelei on board with getting me out the door just as quickly. The leaves could also have been their idea.

Underlying all of my paranoid and convoluted thoughts, I kept returning to being mad at Keegan for thinking I was a good, kind person. He didn't know me. He couldn't know me, if he believed I wasn't a monster. He was just wrong. I doubted he'd believe me unless I proved it to him. And I was sure that, inevitably, I would.

I drifted off to sleep at some point, though when my alarm went off the next morning, it felt like I'd barely slept. Lorelei's bed was empty. Either she'd come in silently, slept, woken up, and made her bed all without me hearing her, or she'd never come in at all. I suspected that some of the students who had been here a while knew tricks and such to bend the rules, and since she said she'd stick to Jasper's room for naked time, I figured she'd just stayed with him overnight.

As I was leaving to go eat breakfast, though, I spotted Jasper wheeling toward our room.

"She awake?" He jerked his head toward our door, his bloodshot eyes revealing his exhaustion.

"Uh, she's not in there," I said. "I figured she was with you."

Jasper arched an eyebrow and rolled closer to me. "She didn't come in last night?"

I shook my head. "If she did, she's quieter than a mouse."

"Damn." He wouldn't meet my eyes, but he looked more worried than disappointed, his hands gripping the rims of his wheels tightly.

"Are you okay?"

"Yeah, fine."

"I mean you and her."

He still wouldn't make eye contact, but he nodded. "Just a difference of opinions. It happens. She probably just went to talk to one of her girlfriends and crashed in their room."

It sounded weird, especially since Jasper didn't name any of these alleged girlfriends. Jaylin wouldn't count as a girlfriend, either, though my brain did hook on Jasper using "their room," not "her room." Or was the grammar just weird because he didn't know which of her girlfriends Lorelei had crashed with? I shook my head to stop fixating on that detail.

I recalled what Jasper had said about what Lorelei did or didn't need when we talked after Group Therapy the previous day, and I wondered if maybe she'd gotten sick of him telling her what to do. If he'd been my boyfriend, I sure would have. But I didn't feel like he'd take it well if I pointed that out to him. Instead, I half-shrugged, and then nodded. "Well, I'll keep an eye out for her. We've got Psychology of Terror after lunch."

He had started rolling away before he responded. "Yeah, okay. See you in study hall."

~

Lorelei didn't show up to Psychology of Terror, and Jasper didn't show up to study hall, making me wonder what the rules on skipping classes were here. Finola hadn't said anything about Lorelei's absence, and Miss Whalen didn't really take attendance for study hall. As long as we stayed relatively quiet, she didn't seem to care what we did. With one group always out for Group Therapy, it was a rotating group of students, some of whom came and went seemingly as they pleased. Maybe it was optional. I'd have to look into that.

It wasn't until almost dinner time that I finally spotted Lorelei. But Jasper had already found her, since they were facing each other in the first-floor hallway, outside the cafeteria, with a huge crowd of students surrounding them.

Jasper's face was bright red, his breath coming out heavily. He glared in Lorelei's direction, seemingly unconcerned about the audience they'd attracted, and his expression suggested that I'd just missed a question from him to her.

Lorelei stood opposite him, arms crossed over her chest, hip cocked out to one side, attitude oozing from her pose. "What does it matter to you where I was?"

"I'm your boyfriend. I care about what happens to you, and I worry about your safety."

Lorelei gave him a tight smile. "I'm a big girl. I can take care of myself."

"I know you can," Jasper shouted back. "That's not the point!"

"No? Then what is your point?"

Jasper glanced away from Lorelei, his jaw twitching. His gaze narrowed when it reached me. "Briar said you didn't sleep in your bed last night."

Murmurs erupted throughout the gathered students, some scandalized, others seemingly unsurprised. Suddenly, I felt more than ever like I was back in Artis. At school, I'd always been on the outside of the big conflicts like this, but I'd generally stayed out of them by choice. This time, I felt like I was getting dragged into this, whether I wanted to or not.

In Artis, fights like this one usually broke apart when a teacher caught wind of the elevated tension. I scanned the crowd, but no teachers were present. We were right by their offices, though, so I figured it was just a matter of time. Maybe this would diffuse before teacher intervention was necessary.

I also spotted a handful of people peeling off the edges of the crowd after Jasper's revelation. The Spooky Girls were slipping away, and so was Gerard. The only other face I picked out of the crowd was Mason, from my Psychology of Terror class, the one who Lorelei had been watching so intently the first day I was there.

Mason was watching the argument with an oddly calm demeanor, unlike the students surrounding him. He was focused solely on Lorelei, much like the way she'd been watching him in class.

When I turned to look at her, she was glaring at me, but when she realized I'd seen her glare, she looked back at Jasper. "So what? I have to be in my own bed at curfew? Or what?"

"Where'd you stay?" Jasper asked, holding Lorelei's gaze.

Lorelei scoffed. "That's none of your business."

"It's a simple question," Jasper said.

"A simple question that I don't have to answer," Lorelei said, shaking her head. "You know what? I don't think I want to have this conversation with you right now."

Jasper's hand bolted out from his lap and grabbed Lorelei's wrist as she turned to leave. "Tell me," he growled, his voice suddenly lower and more gravelly.

Another wave of students suddenly found better places to be, a number of them passing by me on the staircase. In fact, it was starting to look like the only people still interested in this conversation were me and Mason, though he was still staring straight at Lorelei and likely hadn't noticed me watching.

I started to slink back up the stairs, taking my gaze off Lorelei and Jasper.

A clatter of metal followed, and when I spun back around, Jasper was on the ground, his wheelchair toppled. Lorelei was storming toward me, Mason had vanished, and Dr. Pudi had emerged from the office wing, hurrying to Jasper's side.

I froze like a deer in the headlights, so when Lorelei reached where I'd been watching from the stairs, I was still there. She cocked her head to the side. "You wanna judge me for not sleeping in my own bed?"

My words came out in a rush. "No. Not even a little. Jasper was just worried about you this morning, so I told him I hadn't seen you since Psychology of Terror yesterday."

Something in Lorelei's expression softened, and she shot one backward glance at Jasper and Dr. Pudi.

I followed her gaze. Jasper was back in his wheelchair, and Dr. Pudi had crouched in front of him, talking quietly, but Jasper was staring off to the side, his gaze away from Dr. Pudi and Lorelei.

"I do care about him," she murmured, "but he's a little stifling sometimes." She glanced at me. "You're probably better off not dating any of those guys who came by our room the other night. It's messy when you're dating them, and messier when you break up."

"Are you guys ... are you going to break up with Jasper?" I asked.

Lorelei shrugged. "I haven't decided. Maybe we just need a short break."

I wasn't sure if I was meant to dig further or if I should just leave this be. I tried to remember what I'd seen girls in Artis do when they were having hushed discussions in the restroom about breaking up with their boyfriends or being broken up with. I'd seen more of the latter, and that usually involved a lot of tears and hugging. Lorelei wasn't crying, but I figured the template was still useful. "Do you want a hug?"

Lorelei chuckled at that. "Thanks, but I'm not much of a hugger."

I nodded. "I'm not either, but it seemed like the right thing to offer."

"Sure. Let's just ground rule no hugs, though." She sighed. "I guess I better find out what I missed in classes today."

"We just watched video clips of jump scares in Psychology of Terror, and discussed how jump scares are horror, not terror."

"Awesome, caught up on one!" She smiled. "Thanks, Briar. I get that you were trying to help. But maybe just, I dunno, don't talk to Jasper about me until he and I are back on speaking terms?"

I bit at the inside of my lip. Now that Lorelei and I had talked, my instincts were to go straight to Jasper. But I realized she was right. Running back and forth between the two of them to pass messages back and forth wasn't likely to solve any problems. I wasn't a messenger, and I wasn't really involved. Unless ... "Can I ask you one more thing?"

"I guess?"

"Do you think Jasper could have put that heliotrope on my pillow?"

Lorelei started to shake her head but stopped abruptly and gave me a stiff smile. "You know, I'd say no, but I don't even know what's going on with him right now. Anything's possible."

I wanted to ask her about the leaves, too, but she let out a deep sigh and continued up the stairs, leaving me standing alone, awkwardly.

~

I met up with the Spooky Girls at dinner and filled them in on my conversation with Lorelei quietly, emphasizing the possibility of Jasper potentially being responsible for the heliotrope.

Echo shook her head, however. "I mean, he's still a decent suspect, but I think that sounds more like Lorelei trying to get you to go after Jasper, or at least to not trust him."

"Well, someone is getting into my room and putting stuff in my bed," I said with a sigh. "Last night, it was a bunch of leaves."

"Leaves?" Maddie asked. "What kind of leaves?"

"Random ones. No poison ivy or oak or anything." I hesitated. "What do you guys know about ghosts?"

Before any of the Spooky Girls could answer, loud laughter behind me drew all our attention.

Lorelei was sitting at a table with a stunning looking, androgynous, Japanese person. Lorelei's body language was open and casual, almost flirtatious, as was that of the person across from her.

"Who's that?" I asked.

"Kyo Uchida," Aimee said. "They're a shifter."

I turned back around to face her. "Shifter?"

"Shapeshifter. Kyo allegedly has access to infinite forms, and I've heard they know how to use whatever form they've taken really well, if you catch my drift."

"Rebound," Maddie said, shrugging slightly when I shifted my gaze to her. "Also, they were a drug dealer at one point, and I've heard they've still got a pipeline to the outside."

Echo shook her head. "You are the worst with believing everything you hear, both of you."

"Only when it's scandalous," Aimee said, grinning broadly.

"Kyo is in my therapy group," Maddie said. "They're quiet, but they've said at least half of what we just told Briar." Then she clapped her hand over her mouth. "Pretend I didn't say that. We're not supposed to talk about Group Therapy to other people."

I shrugged. "I won't tell a soul. I'm just curious why Lorelei would go to them, out of anyone else in the school."

"Probably to piss off Jasper," Aimee said. "Lorelei is making it look like she's going to hook up with Kyo, either for drugs or sex. Or both. Either way, Jasper will hate it. It's all about Kyo's reputation, even if she's literally just laughing at some dumb joke they made, or maybe even a dumb joke she made." Aimee shook her head. "Briar, your roommate is a social manipulator. Everything she's doing right now is calculated."

"To what end, though?" I asked.

"I don't know," Aimee replied. "Furthermore, I don't care, and I'm bored with gossiping about Lorelei and Kyo. What was that about ghosts?"

"First off, are they real?"

"Theoretically, yes," Echo said. "Have I ever seen one? No."

"I believe in ghosts," Maddie said.

"And I don't," Aimee said. "Do you?"

"I'm not sure," I admitted. "I'm just wondering about all the weird stuff in my bed. Ghosts could be an explanation."

"Or your roommate could be messing with you," Aimee said. "Show me proof of ghosts, and I'll believe. Until then, did you start the history homework yet?"

"The essay or the reading?" I asked.

Aimee pouted. "Ugh, which one is due first?"

Tires squealed on the linoleum of the cafeteria floor, followed a moment later by the thump of those wheels crossing the slight bump at the threshold of the cafeteria. I turned to catch a glimpse of Jasper's red hair and him and his wheelchair retreating rapidly from the cafeteria.

Lorelei had asked me to not talk to Jasper about her, but I felt like maybe Jasper needed someone to talk to him about himself, and how he was doing. That wouldn't be violating what Lorelei had asked of me.

"The reading," I told Aimee. "I'll catch up with you all later." I bussed my dinner tray and headed out of the cafeteria.

Jasper was waiting at the elevator when I reached the main hall.

"Are you okay?" I asked.

He glared up at me, then looked away. "Not really."

"I meant from falling out of your wheelchair earlier."

"Oh, that? I didn't exactly fall," he said quietly.

"What happened, then?"

His expression turned sheepish. "I lunged at Lorelei. I tried to hurt her. I'm not proud of it, but I have some temper issues."

I was beginning to think that most of the students here might have some sort of temper or anger issues, not all of which were entirely apparent. "So you're in Anger Management too?"

"Yeah." He arched his eyebrow at me. "Didn't realize you were." Then his eyes widened. "Oh, wait, you're why Jaylin switched into my section, huh?"

I looked away, suddenly intent on scratching between my shoulder blades, always a tricky prospect with my human body. "Uh, yeah."

"Huh. Okay. Hadn't pegged you as fae."

"No?" If he hadn't thought I was fae, would he have put the heliotrope in my bed? That didn't make a lot of sense. There might be items that could be used to test for other supernatural identities too (and I'd have to ask the Spooky Girls about that), but why would someone have started with heliotrope if they didn't have a guess that someone was fae? "What did you think I was?"

He shrugged. "Witch, shapeshifter, maybe? I don't know. I don't usually worry about it too much. I guess with you being Lorelei's roommate, I had a little more interest in who she'd be rooming with, but I hadn't figured out anything definitive."

I nodded, but then remembered that I wasn't going to talk about Lorelei with Jasper. Before I had to say something else, though, the elevator dinged, the doors opening to reveal Mason.

Jasper tensed beside me, growing paler beneath his freckles. He wheeled the equivalent of a pace backward.

Mason looked at Jasper, then at me. His gaze was intensely locked with mine as he stepped out of the elevator, even as he said, "All yours, man," which was clearly directed to Jasper regarding the elevator.

"Catch you later, Briar," Jasper said as he rolled past Mason and into the elevator.

"Briar," Mason said. Something about his voice made my name sound exactly like what it was—prickly and sharp.

My neck and back broke out in goosebumps, quickly racing down my arms, and I shivered despite myself. "Hey, Mason. How's it going?"

"Fine, thank you for asking." His gaze narrowed. "Did you have a question for me?"

I didn't, not really, but I somehow felt like I owed him a question, with the way he asked about it. It was unsettling, just like his gaze and his voice. It made the back of my head buzz, like a hornet's nest was trapped in my skull. I scrambled for something to talk about. "Uh. Terror ... horror ... what was the word you used with them?"

"Dichotomy." His voice was quiet, making me strain to hear his words, but it held an enormous gravity. "It has to do with the differences between two things. Some would say that it is more commonly used to draw a contrast between two things that are drastically different from one another, but I believe that what we often perceive as differences are not always as extreme as we see them."

I nodded, far more enthusiastically than I needed to. "That's it, thanks."

He continued, droning on as though he was giving a lecture. "One might also talk of the dichotomy between people. People like Jasper and Lorelei. Only there, I find more dichotomy than most outside observers might."

"Well, I see plenty of differences between them," I said, shrugging, "but I suppose that might come from living with Lorelei."

"And yet, one of them lives in horror, and the other in terror. Which do you suppose is which?"

I considered his question, recalling what we'd said about the difference between horror and terror in class. Horror was the revulsion after the fact, and terror was the anticipation of the horrifying thing. Jasper seemed to be experiencing remorse, so maybe he felt horror. But I wasn't sure that Lorelei felt either. She seemed to be pretty content with her lot in life, especially now that she seemed to be moving on from Jasper.

Mason watched me intently as I considered. He raised his eyebrows once, quickly, allowing a flash of a smile when he did. And then his face was deadpan and emotionless again. "Perhaps a different question is more applicable here. Briar Williams, listen closely, and choose carefully. Would you rather live in horror over what you have done or in terror of what you might do?"

I stared at him for a long time. His question had come out of nowhere. Aside from Psychology of Terror, we'd never interacted, and even there, he was clinical and detached, never making eye contact with anyone other than Lorelei and Finola. "I don't understand."

"It is a simple decision," he said, lifting a single slim finger toward my cheek. "Which haunts you more? Your past, or your future?"

His finger made contact with my skin, a shock travelling down my spine, and a rush of emotions flooded through me. On the one hand, there was the anger mingled with frustration, disgust, and shame related to my time in Idyll. And then there was more anger, burning red hot, untempered and fierce. For the first time since I'd arrived at Dedwydd, my fingertips and gums ached as though my claws and maw were about to erupt. My vision became hazy, and my nostrils flared.

I caught a whiff of Mason at a deeper level than just what he smelled like on the surface. And beneath that façade, Mason didn't smell human. He smelled like darkness, decay, rot, and searing flames.

I stumbled backward, breaking the contact between us, gasping for air. My vision cleared, and I held up my hands to make sure my claws had stayed where they were meant to be.

When I looked back at Mason, he had his head cocked to the side, watching me. "Interesting. Be cautious, Briar Williams. You have problems whether you embrace your horror or your terror. But I do look forward to seeing which one you will choose."

CHAPTER TWELVE:
THIS CHARMING KEEGAN

———

I ran.

I wasn't entirely sure where I was going, but I wanted to get as far from Mason as I could. Everywhere I looked, I saw shadows, and my subconscious filled them with his lurking form, his shining eyes, and his quiet voice. I knew he wasn't there, not really. He'd stayed at the elevator, and I'd run from him. But some part of my brain was sure that I'd only imagined that, and he was still here, menacing me.

Every time I got near a door, something made me turn away, unwilling to knock or try the doorknob. The hallway felt like it was pitching as I walked. When I reached the stairs, I clutched at the bannister, certain that if I didn't hold on, I'd somehow plummet up the steps.

It was like the visions I'd had about dying from the heliotrope, only these felt more imminent, more ominous.

I couldn't see after a while, my eyes grown blurry from the tears that were filling them. I just kept stumbling forward, somehow avoiding running into anything or anyone. It didn't make sense— people had still been in the cafeteria when I left, but no one else was in the halls, as though they were still all eating, lingering in the cafeteria for longer than normal. Or maybe I'd wandered far from the dorm wings.

A voice called out my name, and I spun in that direction. There was someone in the hallway behind me, but I couldn't identify who it was. I threw my arms up to block my face, hoping this was just another one of my visions of Mason, and that if I blocked it from my sight, it would go away.

"Briar, are you okay?"

I recognized his faint drawl this time. "Gerard?" My voice was a barely recognizable croak, thick with fear. Was it horror or terror? I couldn't tell the difference right now. I thought maybe horror, since something had happened (even if I couldn't identify what it was), but there was also the terror of what would happen next.

Warm arms embraced me, stripping away a layer of my fear. It was Gerard. It was *really* Gerard. I leaned heavily into him and gasped, "I need to get out of here."

"Okay, alright. Where?"

I needed air. "Outside."

"Okay. Just hold on to me, I'll steer you."

I let Gerard lead me, remaining pressed as close to him as I could. He was, literally and figuratively, keeping me upright and moving. Had he not been there, I'd likely have stumbled around or given up and curled up in that hallway until someone else, possibly not someone who cared, found me.

My tears transitioned into full-blown sobbing as I clung to Gerard. Only his sturdy frame kept me from shaking to pieces before we made it outside.

The blast of icy air that hit us took my breath away, but that fresh gust also calmed me even better than Gerard's presence had. It gave me the strength I needed to extricate myself from Gerard's grip.

"Are you okay, Briar?" he asked, concern etched across his features.

"I'm getting there," I murmured.

"What happened?"

I took a deep breath. What had happened? I'd hallucinated? It wasn't my ability to find omens in things. Never mind the fact that powers weren't supposed to work here. But Mason had touched my face ... I shuddered again at the memory of his finger gliding down my cheek. "I think I got whammied. But I don't know how."

"Whammied? Like magic?"

I shook my head. "Something nastier, I think. Because magic doesn't work here, right?"

"Spells don't," Gerard confirmed, but his gaze slid away from me, to the frozen ground. Then he glanced back toward the doors we had just exited. "You wanna take a walk around? Do you need your coat?"

I shivered a little bit. Strangely enough, our uniforms weren't really designed for outdoor wear. The shirt had long sleeves, and the sweater was decently thick, but the slacks I'd opted for felt like they were paper thin under these conditions. "How far are we going?"

"Just to the tree line. Wait here a minute, okay?"

I nodded and tucked myself into a corner near the entrance where the wind didn't reach as much. The stones were cold and damp every time my shivering knocked me into one of them.

Gerard jogged back inside, leaving me alone with my thoughts. Maddie had shown me a magical item that worked here. Did Mason have something similar? Was that what Gerard was preparing to tell me about? Or did he have different information?

Mason had asked me if I would rather live in horror of what I'd done or terror about what was to come. In this moment, I could identify what I'd been feeling as terror of the unknown. It still lingered, too. But that wasn't my own personal terror, about what I might do in the future. It was the terror of confusion in the midst of the unwanted visions.

I tried to push the terror from my mind. Outside, I was safe, even without my powers. The ground was solid beneath my feet, not just because it was frozen. The earth had a steadying effect. I crouched and placed my hand on it. If my powers had worked, I could have made the grass green and vibrant, rather than the yellowish withered form it currently had. I could have warmed up the dirt and let other seeds within it sprout. Even though I couldn't do any of that at the moment, thinking about it helped me calm myself.

About the same time I was getting really cold, Gerard came back outside in his coat and carrying a similar wool peacoat, which he handed to me. "It's my roommate's, but he said he didn't mind me borrowing it for a friend."

I shrugged into the offered coat, turning up the collar and wedging my hands into the pockets. It smelled of mothballs and spices, a weird combination, but somehow homey feeling. I let it envelop me, warming my limbs and making me feel cozy. "Tell him thanks."

Gerard started walking toward the tree line, and I trailed behind him. Once we were reaching the edge of the light cast from the windows of the school, he paused, letting me catch up to him. He looked back at the school, then at me. "Apparently the prohibition against powers works differently for different types of supernaturals. Who was it that whammied you?"

"Mason," I said quietly, my gaze darting around. It was quiet out here, but saying his name made me feel like his gaze was still on me.

"Mason?"

"Tall, thin, dark hair, pale, thick-rimmed glasses? Kind of nerdy looking on first glance?"

Gerard shrugged. "That doesn't ring any bells. Do you know what kind of supernatural he is?"

I shook my head. "Something that apparently still has powers here. Uh, he's in my Psychology of Horror class, so he *should* be something not normal."

"That doesn't narrow it down much," Gerard murmured, "other than to say he's probably not fae or a witch."

I frowned. "Where'd you hear about the rules not applying to everyone the same, anyway? The Spooky Girls haven't told me anything about powers that work."

"Spooky Girls? Oh, right, that coven." He nodded. "It's technically theoretical. We know—I mean, this is a thing that I've come across in my studies before getting here—that there are ways to limit the powers of certain supernaturals. Fae, for instance. There's a wrought iron fence around the place that does the trick. And they've done something with the ley lines to keep witches inactive. That's why I can cross them off the list of possibilities for Mason—there's no getting around the prohibitions for either of us."

"There are magical items that work, though," I said. "So maybe that's it?"

"Like what?" Gerard asked.

I didn't want to give away Maddie's secret, even to a fellow witch. I shrugged. "Stuff I shouldn't talk about. But I've seen a functional magical item on school grounds." I reached into my shirt pocket and pulled out the ring from the compound. "And I think this ring might do something, but I haven't figured out what it does, exactly."

"That creepy ring from that creepy compound?" Gerard shook his head. "What is it you think it does?"

"I'm not sure. It seems to react to my proximity to certain people." I frowned. "Though if there's some sort of connection between the people, I don't know what it is."

Gerard held out his hand. "Wanna try me?"

I shrugged and grasped his hand with mine, so that I had physical contact with both him and the ring, like I'd done with Maddie earlier. But I felt nothing. It hadn't reacted any time I'd hugged him, either. "I don't think it reacts to witches. It didn't work with Maddie, either."

"Maddie is ... oh, okay, Maddie from Occult Studies."

"Yeah, apparently all of you witches get a cool class, and I just get Psychology of Terror and Anger Management."

"You trying to tell me you don't need Anger Management?"

I stuck out my tongue at him in response, regretting it as soon as a cold breeze whistled across my face.

"Who has your ring reacted to?" Gerard asked.

"Nic Flores, Keegan Morris, and a girl named Val, whose last name I don't know."

Based on the blank expression on Gerard's face, he was about as familiar with them as he was with Mason.

"As far as the Spooky Girls know, Nic is a demon. Keegan is ... fae, and so is Val." I paused, wondering if the shock that had run down my spine when Mason touched my face was from the ring or from whatever he'd done. "Let's just say I've got anomalous results so far that I can't make any sense of."

Gerard pursed his lips but nodded. "Okay, so maybe this Mason has some sort of item, or maybe somehow he's not affected by the prohibitions here."

"Great," I said, rolling my eyes. "He's got an item for terrifying people or a get-out-of-prohibitions free pass? That's a lot worse than a ring that gives me shivers and zaps or ... you know, the other thing I can't talk about. If Mason really does have something that creates fear, it's definitely bad."

"In the end, it doesn't matter whether it's an item or a weird oversight in the prohibitions against powers. I get the impression he messed you up pretty badly, based on how you were stumbling through the hallway inside."

I nodded. Gerard had a point. Theorizing over *how* Mason had affected me wasn't important. That he had was bad enough. "Yeah, he made me see things. Hallucinations, except some of them were based in reality. From Idyll. Things I did. Memories. But he was there, too, without actually being there. Like he was forcing my brain to play back memories so he could watch them."

"But they weren't really real, right?" Gerard frowned. "This isn't like your brambles, is it?"

The brambles were something I had called to me when we were raiding the compound in Artis, and they were possibly what had kept me alive when things went really bad. The others hadn't known what to make of my sudden ability to summon some really nasty foliage out of seemingly nowhere. The seeds had all been in place, I'd only encouraged them along dramatically. But I had gotten the impression, in the limited time we'd spent together before I was taken to the institution, that my friends were all weirded out by that.

"No, the brambles were real. And the memories are real too, for the most part. It was like seeing the worst things I did in Idyll, without the sense of hope I had then. And bleak pictures of reverting to that behavior in the real world."

"So he was preying on your fears, maybe?"

I half shrugged, but then nodded. "Yeah, my horror over what I've done. He was explaining the dichotomy of terror and horror in class today, and he brought that up again."

"Okay, that might be a clue to what he did or used. Horror-based magic is pretty common."

"If magic worked here. Horror-based items?"

Gerard shrugged. "Anything's possible. You could ask the Spooky Girls about it?"

"Yeah, eventually." I took a deep breath of the cold air. Between that and talking through this with Gerard, I felt a lot better. "I'm not ready to go back in yet. Do you think your roommate will mind if I keep his coat a little longer?"

"Probably not, so long as you eventually return it."

"Okay, thanks. You look like you could deal with going back in, though."

"Yeah, this Southern boy ain't too fond of the cold," Gerard said, shivering in spite of his coat. "You sure you want to stay out here alone?"

I nodded.

Gerard shrugged out of his much larger coat. "Give me Sean's back. You can use mine and bring it back later. Just be careful, okay?"

"I will. Thanks, Gerard." I shucked off Sean's coat and wrapped myself in Gerard's coat, then gave him a big hug. "You're the best."

He chuckled. "The best, huh?"

"You are. Not just because you're the only person here I really know well. I'm making friends. But you *are* my friend."

"You're my friend, too." He ruffled my hair gently. "Just don't freeze to death and make me have to peel my coat off your frozen corpse and declare a vendetta against winter. That won't end well for anyone."

I headed into the woods once Gerard was safely back in the building. Even with his bulky coat, I was a little chilly, but I figured some walking around would help with that. I was also curious about this wrought iron fence, and I knew I'd sense it long before I ran across it.

It was close to pitch black once I got deeper into the woods, the light from the school only a faint glimmer in the distance if I looked toward it. Instead, I looked away, waiting a moment for my eyes to adjust, while relying on my other senses. It smelled like pine needles and plant material decaying on the forest floor, a lot like the park I'd lived in when I was in Artis. It was mostly silent, too, with a few crackles nearby that were probably evening animals making their way through the underbrush. But I caught a low murmuring, and then a faint burning smell.

Staying frozen in place, I tried to listen to the murmurs and locate the burning with my eyes closed. It wasn't far, a little to my right. But I stopped trying when I recognized the burning scent for what it was. Cigarettes.

Looking to my right, I picked out the faint glow of lit cigarettes—three or four, maybe more obscured by people standing between me and their cigarettes. I'd stumbled across the smokers, out in the woods to avoid the teachers.

As one of the figures took a drag, I reevaluated my assessment. The profile looked like Miss Hale. Maybe this was the teachers sneaking out for a smoke away from the students. Either way, they were easy enough for me to avoid in my attempt for a little solitude and a chance to breathe after my surge of fear and adrenaline.

As I wandered farther into the woods, I caught other faint murmurs. I wondered how many of the students (or teachers) snuck out here at night, and if they were all just clusters of smokers or if there was something more going on. The cigarette embers were the only light—the stars didn't penetrate the coniferous canopy very well—and I doubted everyone here had good night vision. Or maybe that was something people who wanted privacy learned quickly here.

A voice pierced the darkness, louder than the others, and more fervent. "She's gotten in over her head."

I froze again, trying to identify the location of the speaker.

"That's not my problem," a second voice replied.

The first voice spoke again. "No, but it could cause problems for my plans."

"So what do you suggest?"

There were only two speakers, but I couldn't be certain if there were more people with them, just listening. Both voices were nearby, but if they were smokers, they were doing a good job of keeping their cigarettes hidden.

The first speaker sighed. "I don't know. That's why we're having this chat."

Both of the voices sounded vaguely male to me, but I didn't want to jump to that conclusion. I couldn't tell if they were students or teachers or one of each. I also had no idea who they were talking about. For all I knew, they could have been rehearsing lines from a play.

"Any guesses on who she'll turn to?" That was the second speaker again.

"Oh, she's got plenty of people she's gotten friendly with. But it's easy enough to poison the well."

"Will that work for all of them?"

"Yeah, I think so. And I can deal with whatever outliers there are." An edge of menace had crept into the first speaker's voice.

My breathing sped up. I had no idea what was going on, but that menace made me wonder if I was overhearing a conversation between Mason and someone else. And if I was, were they talking about me? I stumbled backward, tripping over something in the underbrush. There was no disguising the sound of my fall or the grunt that escaped my lungs when I hit the ground.

"What was that?" the second speaker asked.

"Freshman, probably," the first speaker sneered. "We'll finish this later."

As I tried to regain my footing, multiple sets of feet shuffled through the underbrush, seemingly all around me at once. I couldn't get a sense of where any of them were, whether they were coming directly toward me or making their way back to the school. Instead of trying to get up, I curled into a ball inside Gerard's coat, tucked my head down, and stayed as still as possible.

The footsteps receded for the most part, but then a lumbering set of footfalls caught my attention. Those sounded like they were coming in my direction.

The dampness in the ground had seeped into my thin slacks, and I started to shiver in spite of myself, strongly enough that my teeth chattered together. I started to stand, ready to run if I needed to.

A light flashed across the ground, then directly into my eyes. I threw an arm up to block the glare, all the while frantically trying to remember if the woods after dark were prohibited in the student handbook.

A voice came from behind the light. "Briar? What are you doing out here?"

I recognized the voice. "Keegan?"

He lowered the light, so it was out of my eyes. "Yeah. Are you okay?"

I nodded. "Yeah, I just came out here to clear my head."

"That sounds worrying, you sure you're okay?"

"I'm better now. It was—" I trailed off. I didn't know how much I wanted to explain to Keegan. He'd probably just tell me that he knew I'd be fine, like he was some sort of weird psychic.

My eyes had adjusted to the light better, so I could see the confused expression on Keegan's face as he asked, "Is that your coat?"

Holding up my arms, I showed off just how huge the coat was on me. "No, it's Gerard's. I borrowed it because I went outside without my own coat, and ... anyway, here I am."

"Oh." Keegan paused. "So were you going to tell me what made you need to clear your head?"

I shrugged. My mind was still whirling from what I'd just overheard, Had Keegan been one of the voices? I didn't think so— I was pretty sure I would have recognized his voice if he had been, just like I would have recognized a handful of other voices of people I'd talked to. The more I thought about it, the more I was able to convince myself that maybe it wasn't all about me.

"Briar?" Keegan asked, a note of concern in his voice.

I looked up at him. I could only guess what sort of interesting faces I'd been making while I'd been thinking. I didn't want to tell him about Mason, so I decided to skirt it slightly. "Sorry. Did you hear about Lorelei and Jasper fighting?"

"Oh, yeah, I did."

"Yeah, Lorelei's my roommate, so I guess it was a little tense for me. You know, on top of this being my third day here, and this place is still just a lot to take in."

"Yeah, that's definitely true. It's still a lot, even after you've been here longer. But you're doing better now?"

"Mostly yeah," I replied. "But I do kind of enjoy the cold. You know, at least when I have a good coat."

"Yeah." He nodded, burrowing his hands into his pockets. "So, awkward question time. Are you and Gerard like seeing each other?"

"Like—" I trailed off, remembering the meaning of the colloquialism. "Oh, no. No. We're just friends. We went to the same high school before."

"Oh, okay, that makes sense." His posture relaxed slightly, and he lowered his voice. "Did you ... were you both involved with the multiple murder thing?"

I nodded. "Gerard had a rough time in that school. He likes it better here."

"Oh? And what about you?"

With a shrug, I said, "It's growing on me. A little, at least."

"Is that because of the place or the people?" he asked, smiling slyly at me. There he went again, trying to flirt.

But I didn't feel the need to lie to him. "The building is pretty cool, and it's arguably better than my last school in terms of interesting classes, but I think the people are more interesting. Some of them are just bigger puzzles to sort out than others."

"Puzzles, huh? Never really thought of people as puzzles."

"Some are, others aren't." I hesitated a moment. I wasn't sure how he'd take being told he was an open book, so I thought I'd steer the topic away from him. "Like my roommate. She reminds me of the cheerleaders at my old school, but I get the impression there's more to her than you'd think."

"Yeah, okay, I can see that." Then he smiled at me, all sparkling blue eyes and shining white teeth. "And me?"

Of course he had to put me on the spot. Was he more clever than he was letting on? Maybe, or maybe he just wanted to seem like he was. "I'm not sure yet," I said, "which I think puts you into the puzzle category, but I don't think I've gotten very far with that puzzle."

His smile grew wider. "Well then you clearly just need to get to know me better. And while Dedwydd doesn't exactly boast the greatest opportunities for dating, there's a movie showing on Friday evening. What do you think? Shall we make it a date?"

And there it was, the culmination of his flirting, in pretty much exactly the cheesy movie way I'd expected. It took everything in my power to not roll my eyes or laugh at him. I was going to have to let him down easy.

I was really not good at this human thing.

CHAPTER THIRTEEN:
I DON'T LIKE YOU LIKE THAT

I must have stared at Keegan in silence for a long time, because I was able to watch his face sort of melt in slow motion. His eyebrows slid back down to a normal position first, then his eyes drooped, then his mouth—I swear even his hair slumped as the realization set in that I had not responded to his overtures immediately and in the most enthusiastic of ways.

I finally found the right words. "So, you know we established that whole 'I'm not gay' thing, um, like two days ago, and I'm still not. I'm just ... I'm not interested in people in that way."

Keegan's drooping face shifted into something slightly more quizzical, but he said nothing.

"I am, however, totally into being friends. I like friends. I just don't want friends who I smooch and stuff. Does that make sense?"

"So not a date?" Keegan asked, his voice tight but with a hopeful note at the end.

"Not unless you're okay with a Platonic date."

Keegan nodded vigorously. "Oh, no, yeah, a Platonic date is totally what I meant. You know, just two buds, hanging out, watching a movie." He leaned forward with his fingers curled into a fist, swinging it toward my shoulder.

It was just like I'd done to him the previous day, trying to emphasize that we were just buddies, and totally not romantic in any way. Like football players did with their friends in Artis, as if any more physical contact was too much. Like in the movies. He was following my lead, but I sidestepped it all the same, instinctively.

Keegan's momentum carried him past me and falling to the forest floor, in the same slow-motion way I'd seen his face fall. All I could do was watch, not intervene.

A pained "oof" escaped his lungs when he hit the ground, and then I finally regained the capacity to move, crouching beside him and trying to help him up with my feebly grasping hands.

"I'm good, I'm okay," he said, scooting away from my reach and picking himself up. He dusted off his jeans and then grinned at me, both thumbs up. "We're all good. Sorry. Probably shouldn't have tried to bro-punch a girl."

I shrugged. "Force of habit. And I totally punched you the other day, so yeah, I should have just taken it. I'm not a fan of getting punched, though, even if it is just a 'bro-punch.'"

We were both crouched on the forest floor now, a little closer than I think either of us was comfortable with. Wordlessly, I scooted away from him and rose, while he also got to his feet.

It wasn't until he had brushed the foliage and dirt from his clothes that he looked at me again. "Cool. Okay. So. Do you want to hang out on Friday? Watch a movie? No smooching or date-like thing?"

I nodded. "That sounds nice. Could we also do the campus tour thing that you talked about earlier?"

"Oh, yeah, absolutely. We can do that right now, if you want. Just a couple of pals, walking around and seeing the campus."

His friendliness felt a little forced, but I imagined it was his way of saving face. It was awkward, but I forced a smile and said, "Lead the way."

~

Stepping back into the school after my run-in with Mason was a little terrifying, but once Keegan had started his campus tour, I was able to push most of my fear out of my head, instead focusing on how ridiculous the tour was starting out.

"So over here, we've got all of the teachers' offices. They have a kinda sweet setup, because they all have little apartments back behind their offices. Like a little dorm room of their own, but they get their own bathrooms and kitchenettes."

I had already known where the teachers' offices were, but I didn't want to bring that up, since part of the reason I knew was because I'd been taken to the Headmistress's office, and that was Keegan's fault. "Kitchenettes, huh? That sounds kind of cool."

He nodded vigorously, having easily shifted back to his slightly goofy over-enthusiastic dog-like personality. It really made me wonder what sort of fae he was, but I didn't think I should ask that flat out, especially not after our previous conversation about Idyll. "Yeah, did you know that they leave some food out—like non-perishable stuff—in the cafeteria, in case you ever want a midnight snack?"

I glanced down the hallway to the cafeteria. "Like, if I wanted to, right now, I could go grab an apple or something."

Keegan nodded again. "I know, right?"

"No, I mean it," I said. "Can I go grab an apple?"

"Oh, yeah, sure," he said. "I mean, I guess you already know where the cafeteria is, so it seems weird to include it on the tour, but there's not really that much to this tour, if I'm gonna be honest."

We walked into the cafeteria. About half of the room was dark, but a handful of lights remained on near the cereal station, and there were baskets of fresh fruit set out, along with some packages of jerky and candy. "Whoa, nice," I said, grabbing a green apple and taking a bite. "Can we walk around with stuff from here?"

"Yep." Keegan selected a red apple for himself, and we proceeded back to the main hallway.

"So most of the rest of this floor is classrooms and stuff. You've seen all that. So upstairs?"

I nodded and followed him up the stairs, still working on my apple. I wasn't hungry in the way I'd often been before arriving at Dedwydd, but having the apple gave me something to do while I looked around on what seemed to be a completely unnecessary campus tour. I'd seen pretty much everything he'd shown me, even having only been here a few days.

"Question," I said, as we reached the second-floor landing. "Aside from the fourth floor, which is a no-go, is there anything more than just classrooms and dorm rooms and offices and stuff?"

Keegan nodded. "There's the gym, which also has the rec room—that's where they show the movies on Fridays."

I pursed my lips. "Eh, I'm not really that interested in the gym."

We stopped in the middle of the hallway, and he looked at me. "What do you want to see then?"

I shrugged. "I guess I thought there might be more to see than what I'd seen already." I took a deep breath. "And, to be honest with you, part of the reason I'd taken you up on your offer, and shown up at your room, was because I wanted to ask you about Jaylin. And I thought I might have more questions for you, but ... I don't really want to talk about Idyll right now."

Keegan nodded, stuffing his hand into his pockets and looking around. A few people had their doors open, with music faintly emanating out into the hallway. More doors were closed than open, though there was a low rumble of conversations coming even from behind the closed doors. "There's one thing I could show you. It's not technically off limits, because the teachers can't enforce it."

My eyebrows shot up. Whatever this was, it sounded fascinating. "Okay, yes, what is it? Where is it?"

He chuckled at my sudden enthusiasm. "I thought you might be interested." He glanced both directions down the hallway, then leaned close to me. "We call it the ghost wing."

"Ghost wing?" I repeated. "So there are ghosts here?"

"Yeah, I guess it's an old wing of the school that was demolished for safety and then closed off, but there's still a way to get in there, if you know about it."

"Weird question, but can the ghosts get out of there, too?"

"Yep." Keegan tilted his head to the side, his shaggy hair falling away from his face like a veil slipping away. "Have you seen them already?"

I shook my head. "Seen, no. Interacted with? Maybe?"

"Okay, stick close," he said, picking up his pace and heading toward a window at one end of the main hallway.

I glanced behind us to the other end of the hallway, and realized that another wing extended off the building in that direction, without a mirrored wing on this side of the building. But from the outside, the building looked symmetrical.

As we reached the window, the texture of the hallway carpet and the wallpaper changed, both becoming more transparent. The carpet, however, extended beyond the wall, and walls covered in a faded version of the main hallway's wallpaper continued above the carpet.

"How has no one noticed this?" I murmured.

"It's easy to overlook. Most people know it's here, but they also aren't all that interested in it." He paused, biting at his lip. "Okay, so stuff you should know. You know how we've got people here who are witnesses to supernatural things? The thing about most of the ghosts who are here is that they were victims of supernatural things—a little more like Jaylin than say, Jasper, right?"

I found it interesting that he'd used Jasper as an example of a witness, not my roommate, especially since I knew Jasper was in Occult Studies with Gerard and the Spooky Girls, but I nodded. "Okay, so—"

"So it means some of the ghosts are a little bit vengeful. If they're in a mood, or if you do something to trigger them, they may attack you."

I blinked at him several times. "That makes a lot more sense as to why people wouldn't go down this hallway, Keegan. Why hit a hornet's nest with a stick if you don't have to?"

He shrugged. "You said you wanted to see something you hadn't already seen."

"I think I'm good with calling this close enough," I said, backing away from the transparent wall. "Anyway, I think I may have inadvertently upset one of the ghosts. I don't think I should go in there."

He frowned. "Really? How do you figure?"

I took a deep breath. "The first night I was here, someone—or maybe a ghost—put a piece of heliotrope on my pillow."

Keegan took a step backward, his eyes widening. "What?"

"Yeah." I sighed. "I honestly couldn't figure it out at first. Lorelei had told me that you, Gerard, and Nic had all come by to leave me notes that night, and I just ... I couldn't figure out why any of you would have tried to poison me on my first night here. Now that I know that you're also fae, I'm sure it couldn't have been any of you. Knowing that there are ghosts?" I shrugged. "That makes it all make a lot more sense. It explains why Lorelei didn't know what was going on, and probably how someone could have snuck past her. I'm guessing these ghosts are pretty movie-standard? Can't be seen if they don't want to be?"

"Yeah, the movies basically have that right. Still, though, from what I understand, it takes a lot of effort for a ghost to interact with our side of this wall. Carrying heliotrope to your room wouldn't be easy. Which means if a ghost did that, then yeah, one of them's got it out for you."

I sighed again. "Any good tips on keeping them out of your room?"

He chuckled. "Nothing that works here." Then he paused and pursed his lips. "Well, you might be able to find a witch who can at least craft a semi-functional charm that will mostly do the trick. Your other option involves figuring out which ghost you've upset and how to appease them, but that doesn't often go well."

"Wait, so the ghosts then still basically have their powers, right?"

"Yeah, basically. They aren't supposed to come into this part of the school, but everyone knows they do."

"I don't suppose anyone has a list of the ghost students?"

"The ghost faculty, probably. But before you ask, I don't know where their offices are." He inclined his head toward the ghost wing. "Probably down there, somewhere."

"Hmmm," I said, peering down the hallway. "Well, I guess I can see if the Spooky Girls have any ideas on that."

Keegan rolled his eyes. "You know they're not really all that spooky, right?"

I nodded, smiling. "Sometimes, it's not about what someone actually is, but more about what other people think they are."

Keegan nodded back, a faint smile tugging up the corners of his mouth. "And maybe, sometimes, a person believes what other people believe about them, and lets it shape their worldview a little too much?"

I got the distinct impression the someone he was talking about was me, and that he was back on his belief that I couldn't be a bad person—that I'd convinced myself I was a monster because other people thought I was a monster. I didn't rise to the bait. "Yeah, maybe so. Or maybe not." I glanced back down the ghost wing. "Whatever ghost I've upset, though, they don't want me here. They also put leaves in my bed, and then while I was sweeping them up, made them look like the word 'leave.'"

He laughed aloud at that. "Oh, that's just bad." Looking down the hallway of the ghost wing, he shook his head. "Leaves that said 'leave.' Wow, that's so juvenile."

I chuckled. "Yeah, it kind of is." I glanced back toward the dorm rooms. More of the doors were closed now, and I could only imagine how late it had gotten. "Well, thanks for the tour and showing me the ghost wing. I guess I should probably do my homework, still. I don't think they excuse you from doing your homework because you wound up creeped out and in the woods."

Keegan frowned. "Creeped out? Because of me?"

I realized I still hadn't told him about how I'd really ended up in the woods. At this point, though, it all seemed sort of ridiculous. "No, not you. Maybe it was a ghost," I suggested. "I don't know. At any rate, movie, Friday?"

Keegan nodded enthusiastically. "I wouldn't miss it for the world!"

~

The next morning at breakfast, I realized just how forced Keegan's friendliness had been. I waved when I saw him, not quite realizing who was beside him—Jaylin.

Their gaze bored into mine, and they sneered, linking their arm through Keegan's.

Keegan looked down at Jaylin's arm, surprised, and then glanced up, spotting me finally, my arm still poised in mid wave. He gave me a quick nod but didn't smile, and he looked away quickly, returning his attention to Jaylin's arm.

Well, if he didn't actually want to be friends, that was no big loss to me. I was just trying to be friendly to another fae. We might not have seen entirely eye to eye on a number of things about Idyll, but having a friend who understood me when I talked about my past might have been nice. If Jaylin had him wrapped around their little finger like that, though, it wasn't worth it.

I sat down beside Maddie, who was busy stuffing half a cinnamon roll into her mouth.

"Oh, hey, Briar," she mumbled around her food.

"Aimee and Echo sleeping in?"

Maddie nodded, finished chewing, and took a drink of milk. "Yeah. They're both last minute breakfast eaters. Meanwhile, I don't care if I haven't showered before I eat—" She trailed off. "And that's probably more information than you wanted."

I shrugged. "Have I mentioned that I lived in the woods before I came here, and that I only got a chance to shower before school if I could sneak into the locker room while the girls' soccer team was practicing in the morning? You get used to it. Anyway, can I ask you a question?"

"Sure, what do you want to know?"

"Do a lot of people hang out in the woods in the evenings?"

"Some people do, sure. We've even been known to test the boundaries of the whole 'no magic' thing out there." She cocked her head to the side. "Why do you ask?"

I shook my head, realizing that I had loads of questions for the Spooky Girls. Aimee had said we weren't doing *quid pro quo* any more, but I felt weird asking a lot of questions when I wasn't necessarily willing to talk about my past. I felt a little bad grilling Maddie when Aimee and Echo weren't around. I could recognize someone starved for human interaction when I saw them. Aimee and Echo were a couple, and Maddie was the odd girl out. I knew this was why she had latched onto me so quickly, just to have a friend who wasn't constantly making out with her other friend.

But I couldn't resist getting some answers. I told myself that if she asked me anything in return, I could answer her, which assuaged my guilt a little. "Well, first question is: what kinds of supernaturals can maintain their powers even in spite of the restrictions?"

Maddie shook her head. "Nobody. It's items only. That's the only way around it, as far as we've been able to figure out."

"That's what I thought. But I was talking to Gerard last night, and he said maybe not all supernaturals are affected quite the same. He told me about the iron fence and the ley lines. But how does that affect, like, an angel or something?"

"Oh, that's easy. The school has some holy relics like built into the walls or something? They work on angels and demons."

I frowned. "Really, it's that easy?"

"So I've been told," Maddie said with a shrug. Then she shook her head. "Why are you asking me all of this?"

I leaned closer to her. "Can we keep this between us?"

She bit at her lip. "Unless Aimee or Echo asks me. I'm awful at lying to them."

"Can we at least *try* to keep it between us?"

"Try to keep what between you two losers?" Aimee asked, setting her tray across from us and sliding into a chair. "And you know I mean that with love. You're my favorite losers."

Echo set her tray down as well, rolling her eyes at her girlfriend. "Morning."

I sighed. "Never mind."

"Does this have to do with you and Keegan?" Aimee asked, waggling her eyebrows.

I almost choked on my cereal. "What?"

Echo leaned forward, her voice quiet. "According to the rumors we overheard in the bathroom, you lured him into the woods with promises of sex and then left him out there naked."

I wanted to punch something, or someone, but instead I laughed, far louder than I ought to have. "Really? That's not what happened."

"Then what did?" Aimee asked, before digging into her breakfast.

"I was outside, in the woods, yes. Keegan stumbled across me, almost literally, and asked me out. But I'm—" I took a deep breath. It shouldn't have been a big deal. But I didn't want my friends to think differently of me because I wasn't like them. "I'm asexual."

Aimee opened her mouth, but then nodded. "Okay, that's cool. So I take it you told him no?"

I nodded, relieved that Aimee, of all the Spooky Girls, had made this no big deal. "I told him I'd be happy to be friends with him, but I'm not interested in dating in the sense of the word that most of the people here are going to mean it. So we're going to watch the movie tomorrow night together, just as friends."

Echo groaned. "Oh my gods, no. The movies they show here are all crappy PG-13 nonsense. Or if we get a rare R-rated movie, it's the edited for television version. And we never, ever, get to watch anything with any sort of supernatural elements. Movie night is the worst."

I shrugged. "Would it change your mind if I told you I've mostly only seen movies through other peoples' windows or by sneaking into the theater in Artis? And sometimes I didn't get to see the whole movie?"

Shaking her head, Echo looked like she was near tears. "Oh, Briar, that just makes it even worse. You'd never know what you're missing by watching the crappy ones here!"

"If you say so," I said. "Oh, hey, do you guys know about the ghost wing?"

Aimee chuckled. "Yes, we've seen the weird optical illusion near the allegedly missing wing." She arched her eyebrow. "Keegan showed you that?"

"Weird optical illusion?" I repeated, shaking my head in disbelief. "But the walls and carpet are like partially transparent."

Echo shook her head. "The ghost wing is a Dedwydd legend. There's something weird about the wallpaper near the window, and if you stand in just the right place, it looks like there's a whole other hall extending beyond the wall."

"So if there's no ghost wing, does that mean what Keegan told me about the ghosts is a big joke on me?" I asked, stewing about Keegan playing on my naivete.

Maddie shrugged. "There could still be ghosts here, even without a ghost wing. If you think about it, there's no good reason for there to be a whole section of the school just for ghosts. They don't need dorm rooms or anything."

I slumped in my seat. "Ugh. Tell me I'm not stupid for believing it was real?"

"You're not stupid," Maddie said. "Keegan's just showing his true colors." She glanced over my shoulder, then returned her gaze to me. "I mean, it figures, if he's friends with Jaylin, that he might have done some of this because they asked him to."

I nodded. "Yeah, you're probably right. This is just probably more of him getting back at me for turning him down, too, right? If he can't make everyone think I'm a tease, he can at least make me look dumb." I shook my head. "Whatever. If I cared what other people thought of me, I'd have never survived Artis."

"The good news is that you don't have to go see a crappy movie with Keegan tomorrow," Maddie said. "Echo's got *loads* of good movies on an external hard drive. So we can watch them on one of our computers."

The offer sounded fantastic. Whether the ghost wing had been his idea of a joke or if the story that Aimee and Echo had overheard came from him in any way, at this point, I wanted nothing to do with him. "Sounds like a plan," I said.

~

All throughout the morning, whenever I turned a corner or walked into a classroom, I felt a dozen eyes on me and whispers at the edge of my hearing. The rumor mill was in full swing.

I'd avoided its attentions in Artis because I'd been able to fly under the radar in a school that was maybe twice the size of this one. People didn't really pay much attention to the weird girl wearing last season's fashions that always had a faint mustiness to them. There were some people who picked on me, but the moment my claws popped out, they knew they'd made a mistake.

Here, without access to my power, I had no way of stopping this ridiculous rumor unless I could track it back to its source. And while Keegan seemed like the likely source of the rumor, I hardly thought it was his idea. Jaylin might have taken the truth and twisted it into something like this, but I wasn't sure they were that petty, especially since they seemed to just want me out of their life. Unless they were secretly into Keegan and figured this was the best way to separate me from him.

Ugh, I didn't even care, really. So what if they all thought I was some horrible tease? I knew the truth. And it wasn't as though I was trying to date any of them.

Mostly, I just hated the attention, the scrutiny, that it pushed in my direction.

I sulked through my morning classes, even with Maddie in my English class and Aimee in my History class. I hadn't mentioned my run-in with Keegan in the woods when I took Gerard's coat back to him, but Keegan had been waiting for me in the hallway, and Gerard had probably seen him. I nudged Gerard with my knee as I walked past his desk on the way to mine in Algebra. "Hey, lunch?"

He looked up, sheepish. "Sorry, Briar. I've got my solo therapy during lunch today."

"Do you still get food?" I asked, outraged that anyone might have to give up a meal to see their therapist.

With a chuckle, he nodded. "Yeah, I get a to-go bag and get to eat it in my therapist's office. Swanky."

"Okay, then later, after classes?"

"Yeah, I'll meet you in the library after sixth period."

I bit at my lip, knowing I needed to get to my desk before Miss Hale started class, but I hadn't seen any sign of a library, even when Keegan gave me the tour. "Where's the library?"

Gerard rolled his eyes. "First floor, east wing. To the right of the front door if you've just walked in."

I nodded as I comprehended his directions and headed back to my seat.

After Algebra, Nic was waiting in the hallway. He smiled when he spotted me. "You got a minute?"

"If that minute can be walking to the cafeteria, then yes."

He nodded and fell into step beside me, sticking a little closer to my side than I liked. But then he whispered, "So I heard you fell afoul of the rumor mill."

I sighed. "Yeah. What of it?"

"It sucks. I've been there, and it sucks a lot. I just wanted to tell you, though, that most people don't believe what people are saying, and the rumor will disappear in a day or two. Whenever the next big thing hits. Definitely by Monday, because weekends always kick rumors into high gear."

"Thanks," I said. But my tone of voice was anything but thankful. I didn't even want a day or two of people focusing on me. "I don't suppose you want to start the next big thing to take the heat off me?"

Nic grinned but shook his head. "Hey, I like you, Briar. You seem cool. But there's nobody cool enough for me to take the heat for them."

"Just as long as you don't like me because I'm an evil tease," I muttered.

"Nah," Nic replied. "I like you because I know you're not." He held up his hands. "And strictly in a friendship way, nothing more. You just seem like you could use a kind word from a friend today."

I nodded. "Thanks, Nic. For real." I let out a long sigh. "How is it only Thursday?"

CHAPTER FOURTEEN:
THE LIBRARY

I made my way to the library after classes. I was pretty sure that in a school like this, the library had to be sort of old and creepy, and I was not even slightly disappointed. The light filtering in through the stained-glass windows had just the right amount of dust floating around in it, all the shelves were just the right color of dark wood, and it smelled like old books—not like Keegan's old books from Idyll, but that still magical old book smell. I wished I had found it sooner, but I'm not sure I would have left if I had.

Gerard came in as I was still standing in the entryway, transfixed by the utter perfection of this place. It was like the Platonic ideal of a library. And it seemed like the perfect place to hide away until people had forgotten about the fake rumors about me.

"You found it," he said, smirking.

"You gave me good directions. Where's good for hiding?"

Gerard shrugged. "You know, that's not really the selling point for me. But there are some study nooks."

He stepped past me, and I followed, trailing my hand across the real wood shelves and tables. Maybe fae weren't often the types to spend a lot of time with books and studying, but we appreciate natural wood, whatever form it takes. Libraries like this were full of nature repurposed, between the wooden shelves and the wood pulp for paper. If nature was made to be used, this was how it should be done.

The study nook was a pair of mismatched overstuffed chairs with a small table between them, and I gladly flopped into one of the chairs, letting myself sink into it. Though the nook didn't have a door, a floor lamp cast a dull glow over the space, making it feel self-contained, separate from the rest of the library.

"So?" Gerard asked.

"This library is awesome."

"I meant about ... what happened after I left you outside? I know you well enough to know the rumors aren't true, but what really happened?"

I caught Gerard up on the conversation I'd overheard, but before I continued with running into Keegan and touring the building with him, he held up a finger.

"So you don't know who was having the conversation, right?"

With a shrug, I said, "I'm pretty sure it was two guys, but I didn't see them."

"And they didn't say any names, just 'she'?"

I furrowed my brow and tried to recall the exchange. "No, if they'd said any names, I'd have remembered that."

"Okay, so bear with me. You know this school is about half girls, right?"

"Yeah, I know." I frowned.

"I'm just trying to suggest that maybe it isn't all about you, Briar." He chuckled. "And I mean that in the kindest way possible."

I stuck out my tongue at Gerard, but he was right. Maybe it wasn't all about me. "But it could have been about me. In which case, I may have more problems than just rumors."

"Sure, it could be about you. I've got a different theory, though. What're the odds that 'she' is your roommate?"

"Lorelei? I don't—" But I paused, considering. In over her head? Maybe. Poisoning the well with whatever friends she's made? Maybe. "Okay, if it is her, then who do you think it was talking about her like that?"

Gerard shrugged. "I don't know."

Maybe it wasn't all about Lorelei, either. There were plenty of girls here, and not all of them were even in the same grade as me. Whatever I overheard could be something that predated my arrival here. I could have just stumbled into an odd conversation. I still hadn't confirmed that it wasn't people practicing lines for a play, for that matter.

But I pushed it aside for the moment. "Anyway, after that, Keegan practically tripped over me, asked me out—"

"Keegan asked you out?" Gerard said, stifling a laugh. "Wow. I thought we were beyond that sort of petty nonsense."

I frowned, unsure what Gerard meant. "What sort of petty nonsense?"

"It was classic in Artis. If a popular guy asked a girl out and she turned him down, his buddies would start rumors about how much of a slut she was. Completely unfounded. And pretty much everyone knew it, too. Didn't keep it from ruining some peoples' lives, but eh, that's high school in Artis."

"So how do you defeat something like that?" I asked.

Gerard laughed aloud now. "It's not like a compound full of whatever it was we fought in Artis, Briar. You can't just punch it or call down brambles on it, or whatever. It's not a thing that can be defeated." He pursed his lips. "I have one idea about how to make it stop, though."

"What's that?"

"Keegan reminds me of a golden retriever—"

"You too? I thought he was like a dog shapeshifter!"

Gerard shushed me. "Hey, we are still in the library. But yeah. He seems like he's pretty but not too bright. So if you just play friendly with him, it'll prove the rumor isn't true. And he'll probably just be happy that you're his friend and not realize why you're doing it."

I shrugged. "Okay, that's a thought. But I didn't finish telling you about my evening. After Keegan asked me out, he tried to bro-punch me, and then gave me a tour of the building. He didn't show me the library, but he did try to convince me that there's a ghost wing where the ghost students live. But the Spooky Girls explained that there's not really a ghost wing."

Gerard looked away from me, his mouth a firm line. When he finally spoke, he still wouldn't make eye contact with me, and his voice was even quieter than before. "That doesn't mean there's not ghosts here."

"Wait, do you know something about the ghosts?" I asked, my eyes wide.

"Yeah," he said slowly. "Apparently, my ability to see ghosts and spirits may not be a 'power' as far as the restrictions here go." His shoulders slumped a little. "I don't usually tell people about this, because they generally peg me as crazy immediately after. I've been able to see ghosts since I was a kid. So can confirm, there are ghosts here."

"Has anyone told you about the ghost wing?"

Gerard shook his head. "Most people haven't told me much of anything, but I haven't exactly been going around making friends like you have, Briar. Where's the ghost wing supposed to be?"

"Second floor, you know where there's that window, instead of a paired wing? Keegan said that the wing that used to be there got destroyed, so now it's where the ghosts are. The Spooky Girls said it's an optical illusion."

"Yeah." He paused, considering. "That's above where the teachers' offices and apartments are. I bet their wing is the addition, not the remnants of a destroyed wing."

I shrugged. "But there are ghosts."

"Yeah."

"I think some of them have been messing with me," I said. "I think maybe that's where the heliotrope and the leaves came from."

"Leaves?" he asked, his brow furrowing. "Is that new?"

"It was the other night. Uh, Tuesday, I guess. Someone put a bunch of leaves in my bed, and when I was sweeping them up, they spelled out 'leave'."

Gerard inclined his head to the side. "What, like the signs and portents you see?"

"I don't think so. I think someone was actually moving things around in my room." I frowned. "I meant to ask the Spooky Girls, but they were so busy telling me the ghost wing didn't exist that I didn't ask them about warding stuff. Then again, it was Keegan who suggested warding anyway."

"I've got something I can give you, that might at least make you feel better. I don't know if it'll work here or not. All I know is that I've seen some ghosts, but they've been steering clear of me."

"*Some*? Like how many?"

"Three or four. Most of them look about our age, I guess, so they're probably attached to someone here."

A chill crept up my spine. "Jasper's sister, Jade—twin sister— was Lorelei's best friend, and I'm pretty sure she died. It had something to do with why Lorelei and Jasper are here. Do you think one of the ghosts could be Jade, haunting our room?"

Gerard shrugged. "It's possible, but I'll tell you right now. If the amulet I have doesn't help you, there's not much else I can do without the ability to cast spells."

"Will you at least check out my room?" I asked.

"If that'll make you happy, then yes."

~

I wasn't entirely sure what I expected Gerard to do when he came into my room, but I was glad that Lorelei wasn't there. Somehow, I didn't think she'd be too thrilled about "spooky" stuff happening in our room.

Gerard looked around, scanning both sides of the room. "Which one's your side?" he asked finally.

I gestured toward my bed. "The one that doesn't look as lived in."

He looked at Lorelei's side of the room, which was pristine, and then back to my side of the room. "Yeah, I don't see a difference, sorry." He paused to scan the ceiling, then shrugged. "If you've got a ghost, they aren't in your room right now."

"Okay, so does that mean your amulet is working?" I asked.

"I haven't made the amulet yet. It's a gris gris. You know what that is?"

I shrugged. "It's a voodoo thing?"

Gerard nodded, a smile playing across his lips. "Good enough." He set down the small leather satchel he'd brought from his room. I remembered the students in Artis calling it his "man purse," but it was where he kept the tools of his trade, and he was never without it. Well, I supposed he would have been without it while we were in the institution, and he didn't carry it around at Dedwydd like he had in Artis.

From within its depths, he produced a scrap of red fabric, a length of twine, and a small plastic vial filled with indistinct grays and whites. He laid them all out on my desk.

"Door locked?" he asked.

I double checked the lock and nodded.

"Okay, I need a strand of your hair or a fingernail clipping." He chuckled. "I'm not going to ask you for blood or spit, because I'm pretty sure you *would* give me either, and I really don't want that."

"You're probably right," I said, tugging a strand of my hair loose and handing it to him.

He laid it atop the fabric, then opened the vial and emptied its contents on the fabric as well. He muttered quietly under his breath, but I could barely hear his words, let alone recognize them.

The latch on the door clicked. I hadn't heard Lorelei's keys, but maybe she was just being quiet. When I spun to face the door, though, ready to run interference, the door was still closed, though the lock was clearly no longer engaged.

I stepped toward the door, ready to lock it again, when a cold chill ran through me. "Gerard, I think the ghost is here."

He started to respond, but it turned into a yelp instead.

I turned his direction in time to catch a face full of whatever it was he had poured out of the vial, gritty and dusty.

"Sorry, Briar!" His gaze darted around the room. "Okay, good news and bad news. She's not here any more. But that was my last vial of the components for making a gris gris."

"Did you see the ghost?" I asked.

"Yeah, but only for a second. Assuming Jasper's twin sister looked a lot like him, but a girl, I think it might have been her."

"Can't we just sweep up what's left of the gris gris stuff and use that?"

Gerard shook his head. "No, it won't be enough to keep her out. You might sweep it all to the base of your bed, and that might keep her from messing with you while you sleep, but it won't last for long." He sighed. "The only other one I've got is the one my grandmom made for me, and I can't give you that."

"It's okay, I get it," I said. I grabbed the broom and swept the floor, leaving the dusty debris against the edge of wooden frame of my bed. "Lorelei won't be happy if that stays for too long." I crouched to pick up a tiny bit of white that stood out, surprised that it wasn't just a scrap of paper. "Is this bone?"

"Rat tooth, probably," Gerard said, scratching at the back of his head, sheepishly.

"Cool," I said, tucking it into my pocket beside the ring.

"Okay, then. Sorry it didn't work out, but maybe I've chased her away for a little while?"

"That's better than not at all. Thanks, Gerard."

He folded up the red fabric, handing me back the strand of my hair. "You don't want that floating around in a witch's bag."

"It's safe with you," I said, but I took it anyway, laying it neatly at the base of my bed.

"If she comes back, let me know, and I'll see what I can figure out." He gave me a quick hug, whispering a couple of words into the top of my head, and then slung his satchel across his body.

As he reached the door, Gerard stopped to look back at me. "So what are you going to do about Keegan?"

"I could try to make friends with him, like you said," I said with a shrug. "Or I could just ignore him, because if I found out that rumor came from him—"

"I'm pretty sure it didn't," Gerard said, shaking his head. "I don't think he's smart enough to concoct something like that. But it's something his friends might have come up with to help him save face." His shoulders slumped. "Gods, I can't believe I'm stooping to this level. High school politics is the bane of my existence."

If Gerard was right, I had a pretty good idea about who might be behind this rumor. I cracked my knuckles. "Do you think Jaylin could have started the rumor?"

Gerard frowned. "Who's Jaylin?"

"They're non-binary, dark hair, kinda wavy, about to their shoulders, sort of pale with some freckles, slender build, and they wear a tie with their uniform. Really angry?"

"I don't think I've met them, but if they're a friend of Keegan's, then maybe? My working theory of high school politics is based on Artis, where you were the closest thing we had to a gender non-conforming student. So in my limited binary worldview, it's guys who start these rumors for their buddies. But I guess Jaylin could have done it, too."

"Well, that's my main suspect at the moment," I said. "Anyway, thanks for showing me the library. I'll probably see you there again."

"So you're finally getting used to things here?" Gerard asked.

I considered that. Despite the fact that we were four days in at a new school, and already I'd had a rumor started about me, I didn't hate everything about this place. I'd made friends with the Spooky Girls, and Gerard and I could still hang out sometimes. There was still the possibility that Mason had powers in spite of the school's prohibition against them, which was something I realized I should probably talk to a teacher about. Tomorrow, I would see Dr. Pudi for my individual counselling session. That seemed like a good opportunity to ask some questions and get some answers.

Speaking of answers, Gerard was still waiting for mine. "I'm not quite there yet, and I'm not too thrilled about stupid rumors, stupid high school politics, and stupid Mason. But the library's cool, and I've got some friends. Maybe the rest will grow on me."

~

I knocked on the door of Spooky Room, but pretty much shuffled in and collapsed face down onto Maddie's bed as soon as she let me in.

"Rough day?" she asked.

My voice was muffled in her comforter when I answered her. "Rough life."

"Samesies. Okay, may I present you with options? You could sit in silence while I pet your hair, or tell me about it while I pet your hair? Or either option without the hair petting?"

I rolled onto my side and stared at her. "Why would I want my hair petted?"

Maddie pursed her lips. "It's a human comfort thing? It's really soothing for most people. I think it's basically the best. Aimee won't do it, but sometimes Echo will, if I make a really sad face and sit near her feet."

I ran my hand through my hair tentatively, arching an eyebrow at Maddie.

"No, it doesn't work if you do it to yourself. It only works if someone else does it."

I sat up, making room for her on the bed. "Okay, you can try it. And I'll tell you if I want you to stop."

"Of course." She sat beside me on the bed and started stroking my hair gently.

It felt strange at first, but soon I was calmer than I'd been all day. "Is this magic?" I asked.

Maddie chuckled. "No, not really magic. It just feels like magic."

Aimee and Echo came into the room, and Aimee rolled her eyes at Maddie and me. "Great, she's converted you to her weird hair touching cult."

"It's nice," I said.

"Thanks, but no thanks," Aimee replied, gesturing at her fauxhawk. "It takes a lot of work to get my hair to look like this, and hands just mess it up."

"Which is only acceptable if I'm doing the messing it up," Echo said, winking at Aimee over her shoulder.

"You are not wrong," Aimee said. "So, is this because everybody's spreading ridiculous rumors about you being a tease?"

It took me a moment to form my thoughts into something more coherent than a nod. "No, it's a lot of things, all piled up on top of each other. Keegan's a jerk, but Jaylin might be more of a jerk, also Mason's a scary jerk, and I don't know what's going on with Lorelei and Jasper, but I think there's something wrong, including our room being haunted, and things were never this complicated in Artis, even when I was the new girl in our class there." I had to take a deep breath after all of that explanation, and then slumped against the wall. "Why does it have to be so weird here?"

"Because you go to school with a bunch of freaks," Aimee said, "present company included, but know that I mean freaks in the kindest way possible for me to mean it."

"Okay, let's break this all down," Echo suggested. "Keegan is a jerk because?"

I sighed. "Keegan's a jerk because either he started the rumor or Jaylin did, but either way, it's gotta be one of them. And even if Jaylin is entirely responsible, Keegan still had to tell them what actually happened before they could come up with a ridiculous rumor. Plus the stupid ghost wing nonsense."

"That seems fair," Echo said. "And Mason is a scary jerk?"

I took another deep breath. "Right. I didn't tell you guys about that yet. I was talking to Jasper after he and Lorelei had their fight, and Mason came out of the elevator while Jasper was waiting for it. And then I asked him about part of the discussion in Psychology of Terror, and then he touched my face and did *something* that made me remember a lot of stuff I've tried to forget, and maybe see stuff from a dark bleak future too? Which is how I wound up in the woods and ran into Keegan." I left out the bits about the conversation I'd overheard for now, since my talk with Gerard had convinced me it probably wasn't all about me.

"Weird question," Maddie piped up. "Did you smell anything before Mason touched you? Or when he touched you?"

"Uh, yeah, actually. Like death and decay and flames? He made me feel like my claws and teeth were growing out, too."

"Claws and teeth?" Maddie asked, scooting away from me, even as she tried to keep petting my hair. "What kind of fae are you?"

"The not very nice kind, when I have my powers. But they don't work here." I shook my head. "Except Mason's powers must work, somehow, right?"

"Or he's got an item," Echo suggested, frowning. "But the scope of that, it sounds like something that would have been reported if he'd used it before. Have you considered reporting that, by the way? That goes well beyond appropriate conduct."

"I ... yeah, I was going to talk to Dr. Pudi tomorrow. For most of it, I felt like I was hallucinating, so maybe it wasn't even real?"

"Even if you were hallucinating, you didn't do that on your own," Echo assured me. "I'd definitely let a staff member know what happened, make it an official report. If Dr. Pudi is your therapist, I'd go see him sooner."

"Tonight?" I asked. "Is that a thing we can do?"

"The teachers live in apartments attached to the back of their offices," Echo said. "I don't recommend going to all of the teachers after hours, but Dr. Pudi has a pretty open-door policy. Like literally, a lot of the time, unless someone needs to talk to him privately."

I felt a little uncomfortable with the idea, but I nodded all the same. "Yeah, okay, I can do that."

"One more thing you mentioned," Aimee said. "Jasper and Lorelei and your room is haunted?"

I nodded. "Yeah, Gerard was going to make a gris gris for me, and apparently that upset the ghost or spirit that has apparently been trying to get me out of my room. I've got a theory about whose ghost it is—" I trailed off. "Okay, this can't go beyond this room. Jasper's twin sister slash Lorelei's best friend, Jade. I think she's dead because of something that happened, that wound up with Lorelei and Jasper here at Dedwydd, and I think she's haunting Lorelei, and now me."

"Yikes," Echo said. "And the gris gris?"

"Didn't work. The ghost disrupted Gerard while he was trying to make it. Which makes me think it would have worked if he'd finished. Instead, I have a line of dust or something along the edge of my bed frame until the next time Lorelei or I sweep the room."

"It's not dust," Maddie murmured. "It's … never mind, I'll tell you later."

Aimee nodded, then glanced at Echo and Maddie, both of whom nodded in response. "Okay, so all of us are allowed to have solo rooms if we want them, but Mads and I opted to live together, and we'd all three live together if they had rooms for trios. But if you really need to get out of being Lorelei's roommate, Echo and I will request to share a room, and then you can put in a request to move in with Mads."

I glanced at Maddie, who was beaming at me. She did definitely seem like a better roommate than Lorelei, but I felt a little guilt at the thought of abandoning Lorelei without getting to know her better first. "I don't know—"

"I'm not saying you have to decide right now," Aimee said, her voice surprisingly gentle. "I just wanted to present the option to you, in case things get worse."

"Thanks," I replied. "I'm hoping maybe it'll all blow over, and I won't have to disrupt everything after I've been here four whole days."

"Go talk to Dr. Pudi," Maddie said, giving me one last pet at the base of my skull, ending with a gentle nudge between my shoulder blades for me to move. "Then come back up so you can help me with that essay on *Romeo and Juliet*."

~

The office wing was dimly lit, only a handful of the office lights still on at this time in the evening. The light in Dr. Pudi's office was off.

I wasn't sure how I was supposed to approach this, and I really wasn't sure that talking to a teacher was going to make the situation better. In Artis, bullies were bullies, and asking a teacher to intervene generally just got you more bullying. It hadn't happened to me, but I'd watched it happen to other people, while I was trying to learn how to interact with my fellow students.

Dedwydd was supposed to be different from that, but I couldn't shake the feeling that this was a bad idea. It also felt really weird to be essentially going to a teacher's house to talk to them. I wasn't born human, but I knew doing something like this wasn't what high school students did. At best, they vandalized their teachers' houses. More likely, they just avoided them.

But Echo had been insistent in her suggestion that I report this formally. The thought made me itch a little—I was asking someone to write things down, even if it was about Mason possibly using powers he shouldn't have had. Maybe this could be an anonymous report, so my name didn't have to be on the record. That might be better.

I tested the doorknob to Dr. Pudi's office, trying not to make too much noise. If it was unlocked, I could go in and knock on his other door. If it was locked, maybe that was a sign to just go up to my room and let this whole thing blow over.

It rattled more loudly than I would have liked, but didn't turn. It was locked.

But then I felt more awkward. What if he'd heard the rattling, and made his way out of his apartment to see why someone was rattling his doorknob? I held my breath, peering through the frosted glass of his office door for any sign of the other door opening.

After thirty seconds, I decided holding my breath was a bad idea. Maybe I should just knock and get it over with. I raised my fist, then hesitated.

"Briar Williams." The voice was barely louder than a whisper, not inquiring about my presence, but stating it rather definitively, from the main area of the first floor.

I turned to see who was talking to or about me, but there was no one there. Forgetting about my intention to talk to Dr. Pudi, I headed toward the main hallway, the nexus point for reaching most other parts of the building.

Still no one.

Had I just imagined hearing my name?

"Briar Williams."

There it was again, this time somewhere off to my right. I spun in that direction, again to face nothing more than a shadowy nook not large enough for anyone to be lurking in. Still, I stalked toward it, looking for any sign of the voice.

The door that led outside rattled slightly, and as I turned to look at it, it opened, just a crack. And a third time, I heard my adopted name. "Briar Williams."

I was curious enough to walk toward the exterior doors. They were similar to the doors we'd had in the school in Artis, mostly glass, with the sort of bar that you had to push in order to release the latch. In Artis, the latches were worn down, and the doors open and closed as they pleased, frequently just from gusts of wind.

Here, the latches looked shiny and new.

And the doors were locked. They shouldn't have blown open with a gust of wind.

The faint lights that illuminated the stairs leading onto the grounds barely reached beyond the lowest stair, shining faintly on frosted grass. It was probably well below freezing out there, and I didn't have my coat.

I pushed the door open anyway.

A strong gust of wind ripped it from my grip, slamming it against the doorstop, which then sent it hurtling back in my direction. I caught it before it impacted me and took a tentative step onto the porch. "Hello?"

The darkness surged forward, enveloping me, and I heard what was identifiably Mason's voice. "Briar, Briar, Briar. I called, and you came. Thank you for making this easier."

Something writhed within the darkness, grasping at my arms and legs, pulling me away from the safety of the school. I flailed backward for the door, but found nothing there, even though I couldn't have moved out of arms' reach of the door so quickly.

"Seems you're a hot commodity among certain organizations. The bounty will get me far from this place. Let's go."

An iron-like grip clenched around my wrist and tugged.

CHAPTER FIFTEEN:
DAMSEL, MAYBE. DISTRESS, LIKELY.

Mason's face loomed out of the darkness, grinning wickedly. I wasn't even sure he had a body attached to his face, or maybe his body was the darkness. Nothing made sense, which meant everything absurd was possible.

"Let me go!" I shrieked, trying to pull my arm away from his grasp. The darkness bit into my flesh, searing it like iron would, and I had to look down to confirm it was just tendrils of darkness, and not actual iron manacles.

"The only place you're going is home," Mason whispered.

My whole body went cold. "Home?"

"Idyll, as you fae like to call it."

I shivered uncontrollably, between the roiling cold of the darkness and my fear. "I've been banished from Idyll. You can't take me back there."

Mason cocked his head to the side. "Oh, I'm aware you were banished. But that doesn't mean there's not a bounty on your pretty little head." He leaned closer to me, his breath fetid with rot and heat. "And that bounty's going to make me rich."

I lashed out at his face with my left hand, since he had only restrained my right hand. I didn't have my claws, but I had fingernails enough to rake across his cheek.

At first, I didn't think I'd actually pierced his flesh, but he drew back suddenly, a flash of surprise in his eyes. A moment later, a tar-like substance emerged from beneath his skin, the pattern a replica of the furrows my nails had dug.

Whatever he was, it wasn't human.

As I struggled to get away, I considered the possibilities. He'd exhibited several different powers, so either he had one seriously powerful item or an entire arsenal of items. Or, the tiny voice in the back of my head wondered, does he have some way around the restrictions?

His grip remained vise-like, and he was pulling me farther from the school building. Or at least I was pretty sure we were moving away from it. It seemed unlikely that he had lured me out of the building only to take me back inside.

Though he'd been surprised by me slashing his cheek with my nails, he didn't seem otherwise fazed by the attack. Without my own powers, there was little I could do. I wasn't going to get away from him by fighting him, so I had to try something new.

"Help!" I had no idea if sound would escape from the darkness Mason had surrounded us with, but I had to try. "Somebody help me! I'm being kidnapped!"

Mason chuckled, making me certain that he was about to tell me that no one could hear me scream, just like a movie villain. In fact, that's what this whole thing felt like. A stupid damsel in distress, in search of someone to rescue her.

Then again, at that moment, I was looking for a rescuer.

Mason winced, his face suddenly bathed in a luminescent glow. "No," he snarled, tugging me more vigorously than he had been.

The glow, whatever it was, got brighter and warmer, washing out Mason's pale face, except for the weird tar blood on his cheek, and pushing the darkness and cold away from both of us.

I tried to turn back, to find the source of the light, but it was too bright for me. Shielding my eyes with my left arm, I shouted, "Whoever you are, I need your help!"

Mason's grip vanished from my wrist, and I stumbled toward the light. Underbrush crunched beneath my feet. I was right at the tree line, and the light was coming from somewhere near the stairs.

I ran toward the light, only shooting a quick glance into the woods to ensure Mason wasn't following me.

He wasn't there. He had vanished.

The light was moving toward me now, and it dimmed as I approached, fading back into a ring on Keegan's finger.

"Keegan?" I gasped, stumbling toward him. "What ... Mason ... light?"

"Are you okay?" he asked me.

I looked back toward the woods, then back to Keegan. "I don't know where Mason went."

"It's okay, he's gone," Keegan said, wrapping his arms around me in a huge hug. "Are you okay?"

Panting, I nodded, shook my head, and then nodded again. "I don't know. Where'd he go?"

"Away. I banished him."

"Banished?" I looked up at Keegan. "How?"

He tapped his thumb against his ring. "It's a little something from back home."

I bristled at his use of the word. "Idyll isn't my home. Not any more."

"I know. I'm sorry." He put his hands on my shoulders and moved me far enough away from him that he could look into my eyes without it feeling like he was looking down at me. "Seriously, Briar, are you okay?"

I was shaky, still. Interacting with Mason seemed to have that effect on me. But now, all I wanted was for Keegan to keep hugging me. I normally hated hugs, but right now, I needed some sort of human-like contact to keep me from falling apart. "I still don't know. I just want to know what happened. What was Mason doing? What is he?"

Keegan sighed, dropping his arms to his sides. "Well, I can answer that last one. He's a demon. And based on what I just saw, I'd say he's found a way around the power restrictions."

I nodded. "This isn't the first time he's used powers on me. He needs to be stopped."

"He's stopped for now, at least." Keegan peered past me toward the woods. "I don't think he'll be back any time soon."

I stepped closer to Keegan. "Thank you. For rescuing me."

"I'm just glad I showed up in time." He glanced back toward the building, then lowered his voice. "I've got something else I need to tell you about, but we should go into the woods. I don't want to be overheard."

"Are you sure? What if Mason's still out there?"

Keegan shook his head, holding up his hand bearing the ring and tapping his thumb against it. "I'm certain he's a long way from here right now. That's what this ring can do."

I nodded, eyes wide. "Yeah, okay. Lead the way."

Keegan headed for the woods, his long stride putting him ahead of me with just a few steps.

I hurried to catch up to him, clutching at his right hand to slow him down. "Hey, wait up."

He looked down at my hand in his, then back up at me. "Yeah, sorry. I walk fast when I'm angry." He slowed his pace, gently cupping his hand around mine. The warmth from his body seeped into mine, banishing the last of the darkness and cold from my hand. Even my fingertips, which had felt like ice after touching Mason's face, warmed up in Keegan's hand. I wanted him to somehow hold my right wrist, too, which was still chilled from Mason's grip, but I couldn't find a good way to do that without standing in front of him and preventing him from walking us toward the woods.

We walked hand in hand, far enough into the trees that we couldn't see the lights of the school at all. Keegan's ring still glowed, just brightly enough that I didn't feel like we were stumbling around in complete darkness.

He glanced around, then stopped. "So everyone's known for a while that we've got demons and angels on campus. And without access to their powers, they're not really a problem—they're just like the rest of us. Restricted from accessing what makes us who we are. Atoning for their slights against the humans, whatever those might have been."

"Or at least perceived slights, in some cases," I murmured.

He chuckled, then stage whispered, "Pretty sure murder's a real slight, Briar."

"I didn't mean me."

Keegan nodded. "Point taken. At any rate, it appears that if a demon, or an angel, in theory, manages to find people willing to—" He paused, sighing. "—worship them, for lack of a better term, they can circumvent the restrictions on their powers. Somehow overpower the warding."

"So Mason has worshippers?" As soon as the words were out of my mouth, I felt coldness creep up my spine. I knew what Keegan was about to tell me. "Lorelei?"

"Not just her," Keegan said, his voice soft. "Lorelei and Jasper. If I had to guess, I'd say their fight the other day had something to do with Lorelei going all in, and Jasper feeling some hesitation to do the same. Either way, though, the end result was the same. Mason's got at least one worshipper who is devoted enough to him to get him his powers back."

My shoulders slumped. "A loophole. Somehow, I'm not really surprised. I imagine Lorelei being saddled with the weird new roommate tipped her over the edge. And then—" As I thought about the possible ghost, possibly Jade, I remembered I was mad at Keegan about the ghost wing. I pulled away from him, crossing my arms over my chest and glaring at him straight on. "You lied to me."

"What?" He seemed genuinely confused.

"About the ghost wing. There's no such thing."

"Oh, yeah." With a sheepish smile, he said, "I'm sorry about that. That was actually a bet I made. With Nic. To see how gullible you were."

"Nic?" I growled. I'd thought he was my friend, and now he was making bets with Keegan behind my back. "Seriously?"

"Sorry, Briar. You were new, and it's just something we do here to mess with the new kids." He turned his shoulder toward me. "If it'll make you feel better, you can punch me as hard as you want."

I considered it, but ultimately shook my head. "I'm only accepting your apology because you saved me from Mason, so clearly you're not a complete jerk. Jury's still out on Nic. Mason, on the other hand, is a total jerk. He's got my roommate worshipping him so he can have his powers work here, so he can drag me back to Idyll."

Keegan frowned, then looked around warily. "Keep your voice down. I don't really want the whole school knowing what's going on. Let's keep walking."

I followed him for a minute or so before asking, "Oh, hey, do you know where the edge of the school is?" I figured Keegan had been here longer than me, and being fae, maybe he had identified where this alleged iron fence was.

He glanced down at me. "Do you want to get out of here? Like leave?"

I considered Keegan's question. I was just getting accustomed to being here, and I didn't really want to run away. There was a chance that Dedwydd could actually be a good place for me. But with Mason having powers and ill intent toward me, maybe away was the best place for me to be. "I don't know."

He nodded. "I get it. It's a difficult decision. Like I don't love the idea that I'm here as a punishment, but I've come to kind of like this place. It might not be home, but it's a pretty good substitute."

"When you say home—"

"I mean California." Keegan chuckled. "Idyll has its own problems."

I nodded and took Keegan's hand again. "I hate thinking of Idyll as home. I just haven't been anywhere else for long enough to have a different one. Maybe it's here. With you."

Keegan frowned. "Sorry, what? I thought ... the whole not interested thing?"

I didn't understand quite what I was feeling, but holding Keegan's hand seemed right. Somehow, between Maddie petting my hair and Keegan hugging me, I was less resistant to the idea of physical contact with other people. And I didn't think that extended to anything sexual or romantic, but my head was kind of a mess at the moment, and I didn't know what I wanted. I shrugged. "Can we just walk?"

Keegan nodded. "Yeah, sure." He looked about as confused as I felt. "If you really want to see the fence, it's this way."

We continued walking hand in hand, now in silence. At first, the walk seemed like being anywhere else at the school, but as we passed a particularly gnarled tree, bare of leaves and unlike the pine trees around it, I felt sick. Doubling over, I began gasping for air.

"Briar?" Keegan asked, crouching to maintain his grip on my hand.

"Iron?" I managed to choke out.

"Yeah, we're close. I don't understand why this is affecting you like this, though. C'mere." Pulling me back to standing, he wrapped my arms around his waist and his arms around my shoulders, so we were pressed up against each other. It calmed me, though I could still feel my stomach roiling.

"I don't know if this is a good idea."

"Did you feel sick when you first got to school?"

Shaking my head, I said, "I was out cold. It was a long day leading up to that. And I'd been drugged in juvie."

"Huh, okay. Well, we can go back if you want?"

I looked at the gnarled tree beside us, barely lit by Keegan's faintly glowing ring. "How much farther is it?"

"A few more minutes of walking. But I've got an idea. Do you trust me?"

I looked up into Keegan's eyes, which were shining with a fervor that I hadn't seen before. He didn't seem like the boy imitating the movies anymore. He seemed like he really cared about me. Still confused, I nodded. "Yeah, I trust you."

"There's another point where the fence is starting to weaken. You have to promise not to tell anyone about it, though."

My stomach clenched, tighter than it had been. Keegan was fae; he knew the power of a promise. Most fae only used that word when it was something serious, because a promise was the one thing we were obligated to honor. Deals and bargains didn't mean anything without that single word. "You want me to promise?" I asked, my voice barely audible.

He looked sheepish. "I need you to promise, for this. It's … it's important."

I nodded slowly and called upon one of the most traditional oaths of Idyll. "I promise on the moon and sun."

Keegan's gaze faltered, and when he returned to looking me in the eyes, his eyes glimmered with tears, and his voice was husky. "I haven't heard that in a long time."

I didn't understand it, but suddenly I wanted to hug him tighter, pet his hair, and tell him it would all be okay. But I shook my head and the feeling passed. "Sorry. Old habits," I murmured. "I promise I won't tell anyone where the gap in the fence is."

That seemed to help him regain his composure, and I felt a little more comfortable with it as well. "Yeah, okay. C'mon." Still holding me close to him, he set off perpendicular to the path we'd been travelling.

It was a little awkward to walk while we clung to each other, but the reassurance it was giving me was enough to get over the clumsiness of suddenly being a four-legged creature traversing rough terrain. I couldn't imagine trying to follow Keegan or walk side by side with him. I'd be completely lost.

Keegan seemed familiar enough with the woods that he didn't stumble at all, but I was tripping over everything. I noticed, for the first time, that Keegan smelled like those books on the lowest shelf in his room—like Idyll. It made it even more difficult to focus on where I was stepping.

My foot found a hole, deep enough to tip me off balance. And with how entangled Keegan and I already were, I pulled him down with me.

Keegan let out an "oof" as he fell half on top of me and half on the cold ground beside me. He caught himself with his arms, preventing his full weight from crashing down on my torso.

"Oh my gods, I'm sorry," I gasped.

"It's okay. I'm fine. Are you okay?" His gaze met mine, and then he bit at his lip, choking back a laugh. "Did you fall down on purpose, Briar?"

I shook my head, starting to giggle myself. "No, I mean, I'm just clumsy. Sorry."

"It's a little complicated walking like that, I guess," he said, now allowing himself to laugh.

Somehow, it felt like the most natural thing in the world, Keegan laying half atop me, in the middle of the woods, in the freezing cold, but laughing together. I felt less like fae and more like a teenaged girl.

He stopped abruptly and looked at me. "I know you don't really ... would you be upset if I kissed you, just once?"

I could feel my heart pounding, and Keegan's had the same rhythm, the beating synchronized. I didn't understand it at all, but I nodded, once. "Okay."

His lips were warm and squishy, just slightly parted when they met mine. I wasn't entirely sure how to kiss him back, but I tried to match what he was doing, darting my tongue out to moisten my cold-chapped lips.

Keegan took that as an invitation, and his tongue darted into my mouth, just for an instant.

And then, just like that, I suddenly felt weird and awkward. I pushed at Keegan's chest, and he took the hint, breaking off the kiss.

"Are you okay?" he asked.

"It just got weird."

His lips started to curve downward, but he nodded, climbed off me, and stood. "Sorry. I just wanted to see what it would be like."

"It was kind of nice, and kind of weird," I admitted. "I guess maybe that's what it's like normally?"

"Yeah, something like—" His eyes went wide. "Was that just the first time you've ever kissed someone?"

I nodded, not understanding why that was important. Since I didn't think about people that way, it only made sense that I'd never kissed anyone.

"I really should have thought that through better," he said. "Maybe we'll try a do-over sometime when we're not in the middle of the woods, huh?"

"Yeah, maybe," I said, but again, I had a pain in my stomach. "Are we really close to this gap?"

"Uh, we're getting there, yeah. Hey, how about I give you a piggy-back ride the rest of the way?"

I laughed but hopped onto his back and held on.

Keegan hooked his arms beneath my knees, helping me maintain my precarious position, and then began walking through the woods as though he knew them like the back of his hand. "Hey, keep your head down, just in case we run into any branches."

I buried my face on Keegan's shoulder, near his neck, still smelling that heady Idyll scent somewhere on his person. I refrained from sniffing at him, knowing that would be weird.

As we made our way through the woods, I thought more about kissing Keegan. Every time I recalled it, my stomach turned again. Something felt off.

I stayed where I was, but I started noticing more things that seemed odd. Keegan's scent was changing, no longer reminding me of Idyll, but fading to something more like the other boys at the school. And now that I wasn't looking into his eyes, I felt almost constantly nauseated.

Everything since he had rescued me from Mason took on a dreamlike quality, stretched out and warped. Now that I was on his back, I could look at it with the clarity of analysis that I could do when I'd woken from a vivid dream, picking out all of the inconsistent details. Why had I kissed him? What was wrong with the tree that had caused my stomach to cramp so badly? Why did Keegan's ring glow? How had he happened upon me and Mason at just the right moment to rescue me?

Was he doing something to draw me to him?

CHAPTER SIXTEEN:
THINGS GET WORSE

I must have shifted how I was holding on to Keegan, because he suddenly asked, "Are you okay?"

"Yeah, fine," I lied. I could play along with this for now. I'd learned a lot about being human from movies about teenagers. I could pretend to be lovesick, at least until I could figure out what I should really be doing.

And then I saw the fence.

It was least ten feet high, made of wrought iron that inexplicably gleamed in the faint available light. I quickly realized the fence was glowing from within, probably a result of the various enchantments they used on it to keep other supernatural creatures from using their powers here.

Vines and other plant life grew across portions, but as I looked closer, I could tell that none of them were natural plants. Razor sharp thorns with jagged hooks and withered, sickly looking berries abounded. I knew my way around dangerous plants, and these were none I'd ever seen before. If I'd had my powers, back in Idyll, they're the sort of thing I might have concocted and used. Here, they menaced me, threatening and unknowable.

"Oh my gods," I murmured. "That's—"

"Yeah, it's a sight, isn't it?" Keegan asked.

"There's a way through it?"

Keegan shrugged. "That's where this all kind of falls apart." Without warning, he released his support of my legs. I still had my arms wrapped around his neck, but as gravity took hold of me, he twisted out from under my grasp.

I hit the ground hard, some of the wind knocked out of me. But I knew something was going on, so I bounded up to my feet as quickly as I could.

Keegan's face was twisted into a nasty sneer, his ring glowing brighter than before, and taking on a reddish hue. "Technically, you can go through it, but you'll be in pieces."

I scrambled backward. "What the hell, Keegan? I thought—"

"I know." He smirked. "You thought I was hapless, you thought I actually liked you, you thought I was rescuing you from Mason. You were wrong."

Everything started clicking. Mason had lured me out of the building, and Keegan had been there to rescue me, seemingly just by coincidence. But now, it seemed it wasn't a coincidence at all. They'd planned this—Mason making me terrified and Keegan assuaging my feelings, making me want to be in contact with him, to kiss him. Disgusting. "You're working with him."

"Actually, he's working for me," Keegan said, grinning. "On this project, at least."

"Why are you doing this?"

"Artis. The compound." He held up his left hand, so the glowing ring was prominent. And there it was, around the band. *"pacem undique quaesivi sed nusquam repperi."* In all things I sought peace, and I have found it nowhere.

He had the same inscription on his ring as the one in my pocket. And he knew more about Artis and the compound than I'd told him—I hadn't mentioned where I'd been or where the murders took place. I don't know how he'd arranged it, but he'd been waiting for me to arrive at Dedwydd, waiting for his opportunity to grab me, working with Mason to drag me back to face punishment in Idyll.

I was done with talking. I wasn't going near that fence or Keegan. I stumbled another step backward, then turned to run.

Fog shrouded the landscape behind me, thick enough that I wasn't entirely sure there were trees. Were we even still at Dedwydd? For all I knew, Keegan could have opened some sort of portal to Idyll.

"You killed my cousins, Briar. One of my uncles, too. The rest of them survived, surprisingly."

"Cousins? Uncles?" I managed to sputter out. "They were just humans. Religious fanatics."

"They were angelspawn."

I frowned. Angelspawn suggested the offspring of an angel and something else. They weren't related to fae. "How on earth could you be related to angels?"

"Clearly, you don't know our history. The original fae was the offspring of an angel and a demon, who got together to see what would happen if they made a baby. After that worked out, more followed suit. So all of us now are angelspawn and demonspawn. Some of us are a little more of one than the other."

I didn't want to believe what he was telling me, but it made some sense. I'd heard fae in Idyll talk about others being "on the side of the angels" or "touched by the Devil himself," but I'd always interpreted them as figures of speech, influenced by the mortal world, and the various snippets of their culture that seemed to be drawn from Idyll.

If he was right, I had killed kin to the fae. And it explained why their ring had a Latin phrase that ... the pieces clicked together. Idyll was another word for utopia. Utopia, literally speaking, meant "no place." "In all things I sought peace, and I have found it nowhere." Or no place. Oh gods.

It also explained the ring I'd wound up with. It reacted to the presence of demons and fae for certain, and maybe angels too. The fae and all their relations, in theory. While this was useful information to have, it wasn't particularly helpful in the moment. It didn't even glow, let alone hold the potential for whatever Keegan intended to do with his ring.

"Gerard's next, by the way," Keegan said, drawing my attention back to my situation. "We figured we could get you out of the picture first. Then him. We already know where Chris is. And we'll find Zee. The nice thing about hunters like her is that they'll always come running when people are in danger."

I had to get back to the school, back to safety. I could sort out this new information later. My gaze whipped back and forth, studying the misty terrain. If I squinted just right, I could make out the darker spaces. Those had to be the trees. Holding both my arms out in front of me, I started moving.

"Oh, Briar, there's nowhere to run. But don't worry. I'm not taking you back to Idyll."

I kept moving, though I slowed my pace just a little bit to see what he'd say next.

"We wouldn't be welcome there either, you see. And you and your friends are the only ones who know why."

"Because you're making deals with demons?" I spat out, feeling the space in front of me as I continued. The slight hill that the school was on felt much steeper now that I couldn't really see it, and it seemed like every step I took was like climbing a stair that was two times as tall as it should have been.

"Angels, demons, they all came from the same place once, and so did we. You and I both understand that Idyll has become a place of darkness that needs to be cleansed. The difference is that my family has recruited the right allies. The very allies you and your brambles tried to stop."

I heard what he was telling me. But if it had been that simple, if we were arguably on the same side, then why were the people at the compound trying to stop me and my friends in Artis? That didn't make any sense.

At the same time, I wasn't sure I cared about hearing his explanation. If we'd started on the same side, we weren't there any more. I should have known he didn't actually want to be my friend. He just wanted to lure me out and make me pay for what my friends and I had done at the compound.

I wasn't going to let him. He wasn't going to get me, Gerard, Chris, or Zee.

I ran.

The fog messed with my head. I headed toward what I thought was the school but found myself on a downhill slope. Turning around, I tried again. It was all uphill to get back to safety, but even when I was sure I was headed up the incline, I stumbled. When I rose again, I couldn't gauge whether I was going uphill or down.

It had to be Keegan doing something to mess with my sense of direction. Or this fog, which couldn't be natural. Maybe this was more of Mason's demonic powers. I didn't really know, and it didn't really matter. What I needed was to get out of here.

From somewhere in the distance, I felt and heard a snap. My fingertips and gums ached, and a reddish haze crept into the corners of my vision. It was like my powers were coming back, like I was about to turn into the snarly, messy killing machine I was in Idyll.

Keegan had done something to the fence and the wards around the school. Oh gods, this was not what I needed right now.

I leaned against a broad tree trunk, hoping it was between me and Keegan. I caught my breath from all the running, and then tried to calm myself, willing my fangs and claws to stay hidden. If my only choice was to fight Keegan or die, I could summon them back up in a blink. But if I was trying to get back to the school, to tell a teacher what was going on, the last thing I needed was to look like a ravenous fae.

I also had no idea what kind of fae powers Keegan might have, so I wasn't even sure if fighting him would come out in favor of me or him. I was a fierce enforcer in Idyll. For all I knew, he could have been one as well.

I didn't hear Keegan anywhere, but I seriously doubted he had just given up. Stealth magic, perhaps? I knew a little bit of that myself. I willed myself to be unseen and unheard.

The first step I took away from the tree assured me that while some of my powers might be coming back, stealth wasn't one of them. My foot crashed through the dead leaves and underbrush.

A snarl sounded from somewhere nearby, and I looked to see Keegan's glowing ring, still a ways off, but growing larger as he headed in my direction.

I ran again.

I wasn't meant for cat and mouse games, at least not as the mouse. I was supposed to be the cat. But I knew that even if I did defeat Keegan to keep him from dragging me to whatever warped sense of justice he and his family thought I deserved, my problems wouldn't end there. I didn't think the school would look too kindly on me murdering someone here.

My mind was awhirl with options, and Keegan's footsteps now crashed through the underbrush as loudly as mine. He was bigger than me, and probably stronger. Stealth was going to be my best option, but I needed a chance to collect myself to make it work.

A new crackling sound behind me drew my attention, and I turned in time to see Keegan release a crackling ball of white lightning. I dropped to the ground, watching it sail over my head and into a tree. I shielded my face peremptorily, sure the tree would burst into flames from the impact, but instead, the lightning rimed the tree in dagger-like shards of ice.

Lighting and ice? Was this some kind of non-fae magic? Or ... oh gods.

Keegan was an elementalist, and a powerful one from the looks of that initial blast. One hit like that one, and he could easily incapacitate me. I needed to hide, or I needed a serious amount of armor, and the latter was not my strong point. And ice instead of fire, from a powerful elementalist who had to know that what little armor I could summon would be nature-based and susceptible to fire, meant he didn't want this whole thing to draw a lot of attention.

I caught a glimpse of a lighted window and veered toward it. If he didn't want attention, then I'd make as big of a ruckus as I could. As I drew nearer, I shouted, "Help! Somebody get a teacher! Help!"

Imagine my surprise when the light went out.

Keegan chuckled somewhere behind me. "It's no use, Briar. You're a long way from help."

I studied the outline of the now darkened window and the wall that framed it. If this was the school, it was a portion I didn't recognize. I had no idea where we actually were.

But this building had angles and corners shrouded in shadows, so I ducked into one of those pools of inky blackness, again concentrating on being unseen and unheard.

I felt tingles of magic across my body for the first time in a month, and I grasped at them, willing them to be stronger. But they faded away just as quickly as they'd started, my vision still tinged with the red haze of the bloodlust that gave me my claws and fangs.

I took a deep breath, closing my eyes so I couldn't see Keegan's glowing ring bobbing up and down in the woods, and thinking about disappearing. Gone. Hidden. Quiet. Unseen. Unheard.

The magic surged across my body again, and this time, it clung to me. I'd finally done it.

Too bad Keegan was close enough to watch me vanish.

In spite of the fact that he had been staring straight at me, Keegan looked around frantically. Had I somehow made him forget where I'd been, too?

I crouched low and shuffled a few steps to the side, and his gaze landed on the leaves I'd disturbed. If he could track me that way, I was in trouble. The whole area was blanketed with leaves.

My claws were itching to come out, but I kept holding them in. We weren't quite to fight or die, at least as long as my stealth kept me hidden from Keegan. Flight was still on the table, even if it wasn't in my former nature.

I scanned the area again, looking for a way past Keegan. There was a sidewalk just beyond the corner of the building. It would take a little bit of cautious movement to get to it, but once I was past the worst of the leaves, I'd be able to run.

I kept my feet still and rose from my crouch, looking for the best places to step to disturb the smallest number of leaves. Tiny shuffling steps would be a dead giveaway, as would overly long leaping strides.

So maybe the answer was just to walk casually.

Keeping my back against the building so I could watch Keegan, I took one side step. The leaves were sodden enough that they didn't crunch under my feet, and if my sneakers were leaving impressions of their treads, I couldn't tell.

Keegan didn't look my way, though, so I figured that step had been safe. Instead, his gaze darted across the ground, his nostrils flaring, expelling plumes of warm breath.

Slowly but surely, one sideways step at a time, I made my way to the edge of the building. I paused after every step, sure it would be the one that gave me away, but Keegan's gaze stayed away from me the entire time. When I felt the corner of the building, I almost let out a sigh of relief, but I held it in, just in case my exhalation sent up a cloud where my breath mixed with the cold air.

I still had about thirty feet to cross before I'd be on the sidewalk.

Thirty feet of streetlight-illuminated, leaf-strewn ground.

I wasn't entirely sure about the extent of my ability to hide. It had generally been sufficient in Idyll, but again, I was usually the cat, not the mouse. Apparently I still made noise, if you listened closely enough. Would I cast a shadow?

I held my position at the edge of the building, slowly extending my hand into the light. I didn't dare look to see my shadow. I was too worried about Keegan's gaze narrowing in on me, and I needed to know the exact moment he spotted me, because that was the point when I should stop attempting to hide and start running.

He didn't seem to notice my hand in the light, so maybe I didn't cast a shadow. To be sure, though, I wiggled my fingers, sure that if my shadow moved, it might catch his attention.

Still no reaction.

I looked down, then, finally, confirming that my hand wasn't creating a shadow on the ground. If I could keep moving quietly, I'd make it to the sidewalk before he had a clue.

Keegan grunted and then lunged toward the wall, missing me by mere inches. His arms swept through nothing, and he waved them around, walking in my direction. It wasn't elegant, but it would be effective. The minute one of his hands connected with me, I'd be caught.

I crouched slightly and ran for the sidewalk, no longer watching Keegan, but focused on moving as fast as I could. I didn't hear my footfalls, but it didn't take long before I heard Keegan's behind me.

"Nice try, Briar," he said, his voice nearer behind me than I liked.

Just beyond the sidewalk stood a hedgerow, easily ten feet tall. In the darkness, I couldn't tell what sort it was, but my skin prickled the closer I got to it. Like calls to like. It had to be full of thorns.

I pushed myself to run faster, still angled toward the sidewalk, but at the last possible moment, I dove past it and into the hedgerow.

The briars took me in, scratched me, and somehow understood that we were one and the same. The gap behind me filled with foliage that I had disrupted, and maybe a little extra for good measure. I was safely ensconced in the middle of a brambly plant.

Keegan strode up to the hedgerow. I couldn't see his face through the few gaps, but I was sure he was smirking. He extended one of his arms toward the hedgerow. Before it even breached the perimeter of the plant, he leapt backward, hot blood trailing in his wake.

He hissed in pain, then began pacing back and forth near the hedgerow. He couldn't get near enough to touch it without yelping. I could only assume the hedgerow, previously trimmed into a perfect box shape, had extended thorny tendrils out into the open. At least, that's what I would have done, were I currently a plant.

While he paced, I began inching my way backward, through the hedge. I had no idea what I might be backing into, but I assumed it couldn't be worse than Keegan.

At least that was my assumption until I stepped out of the hedgerow on the other side and realized I had a bigger problem.

I really had no idea where I was.

CHAPTER SEVENTEEN:
LEFT ALONE

———

The nearby buildings were a mix of small run-down shacks and larger ones that looked more like houses, on one side of a gravel path that ran parallel to the hedge. It took me a minute to realize I was on the backside of a row of houses, with sheds or garages that hadn't been maintained as well as the homes.

I had somehow found my way into the town that everyone had told me about.

There was a road I could see at one end of the alley, so I headed in that direction to get a look around. From this angle, the town looked pretty small, but I also figured I had to be on the edge of it. I didn't know how far away from the school I had run, but I would have seen more houses already if I'd made my way into the middle of town.

Before I got much farther, my phone vibrated in my pocket. I had my phone. I had a signal. I bit back the cheer that bubbled up in my chest as I pulled the phone out.

It was a text from Zee. *"Where are you?"*

The text said it had just come through. I punched the button to call her back. Zee's phone rang four or five times before it connected to her voicemail. "It's Zee. You know what to do."

Hearing her voice made me miss her even more, but it was just the voicemail recording. I'd have to leave her a message. "Zee, it's Briar. I'm ... I'm somewhere in Idaho. I need your help. Call me."

I thumbed through the other numbers on my phone. Mostly they were for people in Artis who I really didn't know well, and who probably couldn't help me. Chris, though, he was a possibility.

"Briar?" His voice was crackly and distant, like one or both of us had a poor signal.

"Yes, it's me." I half-sobbed in response. "Oh my gods, I haven't heard your voice in so long."

"Uh, yeah, I know." He sounded confused.

"Chris, I'm in Idaho—"

His laugh was sharp. "Idaho? Gods, Briar, really?"

"Yeah, why?"

"I'm in *Maine*."

My sense of geography was mediocre, but I recalled Maine being far from Washington and Idaho. "So I guess that means I can't get you to come pick me up?"

Chris laughed again, more gently this time, and I missed his goofy smile and sense of humor even more. "There is zero chance that I can get to Idaho in a timely fashion. Do they even have airports there?"

"Yes, that's how we got here. A really tiny airport."

"We? You and Gerard are still in the same place?"

"Yes, we're both at a school in Idaho."

"A school?"

The words burst from me like a torrent. "Yeah, it's some sort of reform school for supernatural teenagers who broke the law, and I'm being hunted by a demon and a fae with a vendetta for what happened at the compound in Artis."

Chris was quiet for a long while after I finished, and I worried the signal had dropped, and that he hadn't even heard what I said. But then he spoke again. "I'm sorry, Briar. I don't think I can help you much. My family's keeping me busy and out of trouble here. Like you only caught me because they've got me waking up at 4 a.m. to do chores."

"4 a.m.?" I echoed. I glanced at the display on my phone. He was right. Not only was I lost physically, I'd lost some time—it hadn't even been 6 p.m. when I'd followed the disembodied voice outside. It was 2 a.m. here, and 1 a.m. in Washington. "That explains why Zee didn't answer."

"Zee's okay?" he asked, his words tumbling out. "Thank the gods. Last I heard, she'd gotten hit by a van—"

"Wait, you heard from her after she got hit by the van?"

"You know about that?"

"Uh, I was in the van. Not driving."

"Yeah, she mentioned hearing from Gerard before that, who told her he was with you. She broke her arm, but she found an old

180

family friend who patched her up. She said she'd keep looking for you, but I haven't heard from her in a few days.

I shrugged. "I don't know when she texted me. The school's a dead zone for phones. But it's been ... well, sometime recently." I glanced around, hoping no one in this town would wake up to this conversation and call the cops on me. "I need to find somewhere safe to wait until a reasonable hour, I guess."

"You don't know where you are in Idaho?" Chris asked, concern tinging his words.

"It's cold and flat-ish? Small town near a school?"

"Not helpful. Are there any signs on nearby buildings, like a post office or town hall?"

I glanced around, but it was only houses here. "Maybe if I was closer to the main part of town—" I trailed off when I heard an angry voice on Chris's end of the call.

He sighed when the yelling stopped. "Look, if you can figure anything out, if you can get to Montana, I've got family in Three Forks. It's a small town, but if you get there, they'll keep you safe."

"How far is that?" I asked, suddenly feeling very lost.

"I don't know where you are. Three Forks is on I-90, between Butte and Bozeman. That's east of Idaho. If you can find a freeway, maybe you can find a nice trucker who can get you there? Ugh, that's an awful idea, though." He paused, and I heard more loud talking in the background. "I gotta go, Briar. When you figure out where you are, text me the location, and I'll see what I can do."

"Okay. Thanks, Chris."

"Take care of yourself. And Gerard."

"I'll try."

And then the line was dead.

My face was freezing, not helped by the tracks of tears that were cooling rapidly. I didn't know when I'd started crying, but I had. I needed to find out where I was, but I also needed shelter—a diner or a twenty-four-hour coffeeshop. I dug through my pockets. I hadn't needed to carry my wallet with whatever minimal money I might have while I'd been at school. I had my phone and that was all, which meant I wouldn't get much shelter in any sort of restaurant or coffeeshop, unless I got really lucky with finding a kindly waitress. If the folks in this town knew about the school, I somehow doubted they'd look too kindly on a student who had wandered into town in the dead of night.

The only other number in my phone that had a chance of providing me any help at all was Gerard's, at least until I could get ahold of Zee. And Gerard was, in theory, still in the cell-phone dead zone of the school. But maybe he'd realized I wasn't around, and he'd come looking for me. It was worth a shot.

It rang once before I got an automated message. "The number you have tried to reach is unavailable at this time. Please try again later."

I fired off a text to Zee. "Call me back no matter what time it is when you get this. I'll be awake."

Making my way back to the row of dilapidated sheds, I checked the doors to find one that was unlocked, dry, and had something I could sit on. It took me five tries before I found an unlocked garage with lawn chairs hanging on hooks on the wall. There wasn't a car parked in the garage, so I hoped the owners were away. I pulled one of the chairs down as quietly as I could and curled up in a ball, keeping myself as compact and warm as I could manage.

~

I woke up to my phone buzzing, unsure when I'd fallen asleep. I didn't recognize the number, but I answered it anyway, in case Zee or Chris was using a different phone.

No one responded to my initial "hello," so I repeated it several times until the line went dead. I checked the signal on my phone, but it was still good, so I had to assume the problem was on the other end. Maybe it was someone calling me from the school?

I tried calling it back, but I got the same message I'd gotten when I called Gerard. "The number you have tried to reach is unavailable at this time. Please try again later." It could have been someone at the school. I'd just have to wait and see if they called back.

Blinking at my phone, I realized I'd slept seven hours. It was 9 a.m.

I stumbled to my feet and peeked out the garage door. There was no one around, so I slipped out and closed the door behind me, making sure it was unlocked in case I had to retreat back here later.

I hadn't worn my coat, again, but at least it felt a little warmer outside the garage than it had last night at school. I wandered down the streets, looking for any place that might be willing to feed a random high school girl with no money.

It took about ten minutes until I was in an area of the town that wasn't all houses and had more businesses and people. I hadn't spotted either a post office or a town hall, so I still didn't know the name of the town, like Chris had suggested. Cars slowed as they drove past me, but they sped up as soon as I made eye contact or waved at the drivers.

A woman pushing a stroller turned onto the same block I was on, and I quickened my pace in the hopes of asking her for some help. Her eyes widened, and she steered the stroller off the curb and into the street, looking both ways rapidly before running across the road and continuing on the opposite sidewalk.

I paused in front of a large shop window, running my fingers through my hair to straighten some of the wild tufts, and checking that my eyes hadn't gone jet black or anything weird like that. But I looked like a normal, if slightly disheveled, high school student from Dedwydd Academy.

My shoulders slumped. That was the problem. The people here probably only knew the students from when they were allowed to come into town. And though I suspected there were rules about not using powers on the locals, any group of high school students was likely to be a nuisance, powers or not. Plus, I was here alone, and I would be shocked if the school trips into town didn't have teachers for chaperones. I couldn't even begin to guess how many rules I was probably breaking right now.

I wasn't going to find anyone here who would help me. And since I hadn't heard back from Zee, and Chris couldn't help me, I suspected my only chance of dealing with Mason or Keegan would be to get back to Dedwydd and go straight to a teacher, or the Headmistress if all of the teachers were occupied.

The only trouble was, I had no idea where I was. I'd gotten a good sense of the directions in Artis out of necessity, but that had taken me at least a week. This town was different, and the sky was milky white with a directionless illumination, so I couldn't rely on the sun's location to get my bearings. Even if I could, I didn't know which direction the town was in comparison to the school, and I'd been asleep on my way onto the school grounds, so I had no landmarks to go on, either.

I knew one quick way to get myself back to the school, even though I hated the idea of it. But the police station was sure to be in this downtown-like area, and since I was just lost, not on the run after committing a crime, they shouldn't have any reason to keep me here.

I didn't have to go far, as it turned out. Either the freaked-out mom had called the cops on me, or they had nothing better to do than cruise around town on a Friday morning. And at least when I made eye contact and waved at them, they slowed and rolled down the passenger side window, right above the painted-on "Sheriff" in all capital letters with no town name mentioned.

"Hi, I'm lost," I said, forcing a smile.

"From Dedwydd?" the cop—or maybe the sheriff—in the passenger seat asked, eyes narrowed in an overly pink round face framed by close-cropped sandy blond hair, beard, and mustache.

"Yep. Can you point me in the right direction?"

He looked at the driver, and they talked quietly enough that I couldn't hear them from the sidewalk. Then he turned back to me and jerked his head toward the backseat. "We can give you a ride back up there."

Sweat broke out across my body, in spite of the cold. While getting help from the cops seemed like a good idea, getting into the backseat of their car terrified me in a way I couldn't explain. I forced myself to smile and keep my voice even. "I appreciate the offer, but I don't want to take up any more of your time. If you just tell me which way to go, I'll be out of your hair in no time flat."

His eyes narrowed even further, to the point where I couldn't even be sure he had eyes anymore. "You new around here?"

"Yes, sir." My sudden deference was a little alarming, but I ran with it. "I haven't even been here a full week. I got turned around while I was in the woods on campus last night and somehow wound up here."

Again he turned back to his partner, and I wondered what I'd said wrong. If they wouldn't give me directions, if my only way back to the school was riding with them, I'd have to take it at this point. At least their car probably had heat. And if things went pear-shaped, I theoretically had my powers back. It would be messy, and probably cause more problems than it was worth, but I couldn't just stay here on the streets of whatever town this was forever.

Finally, he turned back to me and gestured out the window with his thumb, pointing the direction they'd come from. "Head on down to where this street hits the state route, then hang a left. School's the first driveway on your left. It's a few miles."

A few miles was a long way to walk in the cold, but it still seemed like a better plan than being in the back of a police car. I knew I'd warm up as I got moving. "Thank you, officer."

"Just make sure you get back up there straight away. No more loitering."

I nodded vigorously and turned to face the direction he had indicated. "I'll be out of here quick as a blink."

~

As I started my walk back to Dedwydd, the more I reconsidered my options. I didn't have to go back. I hadn't wanted to be here just a week ago, and if I was honest with myself, being chased by Mason and Keegan really didn't make me like the school anymore.

I could keep walking, find a freeway, like Chris had suggested, and get my bearings enough to find Three Forks, Montana. I could handle a little walking and scavenging. I'd been on my own in Artis for months. Sure, that had mostly been summer, when sleeping outdoors was comfortable. And even though Artis was small, being in a town was different from being on the road in Idaho, which, from all of my understanding of it, was uninhabited for vast stretches.

But Gerard was still at Dedwydd, and I couldn't abandon him. We'd bonded in Artis over our hatred of the seemingly normal kids in our school, especially the ones with ties to the compound, and we'd raided their compound to stop them. Me, Gerard, Zee, and Chris. We were in this together, even if Zee and Chris weren't here.

The Spooky Girls were there too, and even though I hadn't known them for very long, I would feel awful abandoning them. For all I knew, that phone call earlier had been one of the Spooky Girls—Maddie, if I had to guess. They were probably worried about me, or at the very least, she'd be worried about me.

I even felt a little bit of friendship with Nic, even if he was a demon. The more I considered it, the less I believed Keegan telling me that Nic had put him up to telling me about the fake "ghost wing." Nic was a decent person, even if he'd been born on the side of evil. And who knew? Maybe Maddie had just assumed he was a demon because of his bad boy attitude. Maybe he was an angel. Somehow, I felt like that fit him better, in spite of appearances.

I had no idea if Keegan and Mason would take out their frustration about me slipping through their grasp on my friends. I had an arrangement with Jaylin. I doubted that extended beyond them and their immediate circle of friends, even if Keegan claimed that he and Jaylin had an understanding. And I hadn't put Nic on my list, which was an oversight on my part.

While Mason might still have his powers at school, thanks to my roommate and her maybe boyfriend worshipping him, Keegan wouldn't have his powers within the school grounds. If I ran into him again, I wouldn't have to deal with him manipulating my emotions magically.

Maybe I could convince Lorelei and Jasper that their worship was misguided. Maybe I could convince the administration that the fact that angels and demons could get their powers back through worship meant they shouldn't even be at a school where we weren't supposed to have any powers.

I paused on the side of the road, having gotten myself worked up enough that my fingertips and gums were tingling. I was tempted to let my powers loose. They'd keep me warm, and I could get back to the school in no time. But I also knew that letting my powers loose was what had gotten me into this situation in the first place. And there was a good chance that if I did, I'd just keep running past the entrance to the school.

I glanced back. I'd only made it a couple dozen yards beyond the left turn the cop had directed me to. This was looking like it was going to be the longest few miles of my life.

I pulled out my phone and typed up a text to Zee and Chris. *"I'm going back to the school. It's called Dedwydd Academy, somewhere in Idaho. Gerard is there, and I have to keep him safe. Miss you guys."*

I wasn't sure how either of them would react to the information, but at least they had it. Zee was smart. She'd be able to track us down if it was important. And if Chris had family in the area, they might be able to find out if there was any reason Gerard and I shouldn't be at Dedwydd. And then Zee and Chris would rescue us.

Or we wouldn't need rescuing, beyond what I was going to do when I got back to Dedwydd.

CHAPTER EIGHTEEN:
FRIENDS IN ALL PLACES

As I continued up the hill, I worried I would miss the entrance to the school. I had no idea how to gauge a few miles of walking, especially not on this poorly maintained country road that led from the town to the school, the shoulders crumbling into ditches on either side of the road. I hoped the sparse trees on my left would remain thin enough that I could spot the school building when I got closer.

When I noticed the wrought iron fence surrounding the school, I realized I didn't need to have worried about how to find my way back. The other fences along the road were crossed timber or metal and wire. This one stood out.

The only problem now was that I really didn't want to walk beside the fence. That much iron gave me the same sort of prickly feeling as the heliotrope had.

I scanned the opposite side of the road to see if maybe I could walk on that side. But the shoulder was completely gone on that side, whereas this side had at least a foot or two of shoulder in most places before it crumbled away. And though I hadn't seen a car since I'd left the town proper, this seemed like the sort of road that semis would barrel down, not expecting to see teenage girls walking at the edge of the lane. Facing traffic seemed like a better bet.

I eyed the fence warily as I walked, as though the iron itself could spring free from the earth and attack me. For all I knew, it could. My plan about getting back to the school suddenly felt more difficult than I'd anticipated it being.

I hadn't felt the power from the fence when Keegan and I had been in the woods, but now I could feel and identify it. I wasn't magically sensitive, but there was no denying the magic inherent in the iron, even beyond the hold that iron had over fae. There were threads of what I guessed were wards against the various types of supernatural creatures housed at the school. There were other threads that felt more outward facing, like they were the way the school hid from the prying eyes of the outside world.

I tried to remember how far I might have walked in the woods with Keegan before we were outside of the fence, but everything was fuzzy, and I was certain I'd lost some time. He'd said there were parts of the fence that didn't work as well as they were meant to, also, so maybe he knew about places in the woods where the fence was less effective, and took me there to try to lure me out into the world.

This was the first time I'd seen the woods in daylight, and I was surprised by the number of rock outcroppings within the fence. I could only suspect that I'd never been in this section of the woods, because I couldn't imagine having navigated this terrain in the dark without falling down repeatedly.

A portion of the fence was bowed outward, weighed down with a large chunk of rock similar to the ones strewn throughout the woods. I slowed as I approached it. Was this the kind of fence gap that Keegan had told me about?

More importantly, could I use this gap to cross back onto the school grounds, so I could get away from the fence and the road?

I took a deep breath and walked closer. The fence was still intact, but about a three-foot section was bent to nearly parallel with the ground outside it. The rock that crossed it was huge, and now that I was closer, I could see where it had been pulled out of the earth. This was probably someone else's escape plan.

In spite of having lived in a park for a while, I couldn't quite tell if the rock removal was fresh or old. I figured the school administrators had to be pretty careful about checking the fence regularly, but I didn't know what constituted "regularly" in their minds. Maybe Keegan had moved this rock the day previous, to give him another place where he might lure me away from the school. Or maybe it had been here for longer than I'd been at Dedwydd. There was no way for me to tell.

Finally, my desire to not be standing on the edge of the road and near the fence at the same time won out. I leapt onto the rock and scurried down it to land on the school grounds.

I had started to turn back to look at the rock when one flash of motion, then a second, caught my gaze at the corner of my eye. I turned back, hoping for a friendly teacher's face, so I'd be able to plead my case for being absent.

Instead, I turned back to look at Keegan and Mason.

Both of them looked well-rested and well-fed, the opposite of how I felt right now. Mason's hands were in motion, spinning a cloud of darkness around them, like he was wrapping cotton candy around a paper wand. Snowflakes danced from the tips of Keegan's fingers, even though the air didn't feel cold enough for snow.

"Well, well, well," Keegan said. "Welcome back, Briar. Thanks for dropping by."

I stepped back toward the rock, but it wasn't there, the fence unburdened by its weight. It had felt solid beneath my feet, and I'd clearly bypassed the fence without suffering any ill effects of proximity to iron. "What—?"

"Surely a fae would recognize an illusion," Mason said.

"If she weren't desperately trying to run back to what she perceives as safety." Keegan shrugged. "Too easily lulled into a false sense of security, Briar. That's your downfall."

I sucked in a deep breath, trying to calm myself. He was right. I'd rushed in without thinking. I thought the school would be safe, and they'd used that against me. And in spite of everyone saying the school restricted our powers, they were living proof that it was something that could be circumvented.

But then I realized that even here, I was trying to keep my claws and maw in check. The school grounds wouldn't keep me from doing so. And Mason and Keegan weren't about to limit their powers. Why should I?

My talons ripped free of my fingers in a rush, stained red by my own blood, and the taste of copper filled my mouth as my fangs erupted. I didn't have to see myself to know that my eyes were jet black and flecks of dried blood decorated every inch of my exposed skin like freckles. I wasn't Briar Williams the high school student, I was Briar of the Brambles, fae enforcer. And I was made to be unstoppable.

Mason didn't react to the change in my appearance, but Keegan at least had the decency to arch an eyebrow and pale slightly. Or maybe he was just pulling a rime of frost across his skin to use as armor against me.

I smirked. Clearly, no one had told him everything he needed to know about me at the height of my powers. I knew I could deal with him, even if he tried to use his elemental powers against me.

Mason, on the other hand, was an unknown quantity. I turned my attention fully to him, cocking my head to one side. The darkness at his fingertips had expanded, shrouding his entire torso from view. His limbs and face were still exposed, so I lunged toward him.

Mason sidestepped, turning to put the cloud of darkness between Keegan and me. But he didn't move out of the range of my claws, and I raked them down his arm, tearing through his coat and skin beneath it.

To his credit, he didn't scream or even wince, though he gritted his teeth audibly.

Keegan then launched a frozen bolt through Mason's summoned darkness. It changed as it passed through the cloud, darkening and developing a wicked looking sheen right before it hit me in the stomach.

The ice didn't have much to punch through in terms of my clothing, and it penetrated my skin just as easily. The pain burned far worse than even the coldest ice should have. It felt more like ...

Iron.

Barely capable of rational thought, I grabbed the bolt and yanked it from my flesh. My hands sizzled, but it pulled free and I tossed it aside.

Had I been thinking better, I would have sent it back at Keegan.

"Pin her to a tree," Mason snarled.

Keegan shaped his hands to form another bolt, but I took the moment to duck behind the tree that Mason likely had in mind as a good place to pin me down.

At this point, I knew we weren't playing by any fair rules. I wasn't capable of ranged attacks, and they were combining their powers to hit me harder than either one could individually, somehow combining the darkness and ice to create something close enough to iron that it might as well be the real deal. They'd clearly planned this, and I hadn't.

I needed help.

I scanned the terrain and found the most heavily wooded portion nearby. If I ran that way, Keegan would have a hard time hitting me, especially if he needed to send his bolts through Mason's cloud first.

I ran, ignoring Mason and Keegan's surprised shouts and their attempts to redirect the bolts in my direction. As I ran, I thought a litany of names—*Gerard, Maddie, Echo, Aimee, Nic*—on repeat. I didn't have the ability to contact them with my mind, but I knew Gerard had some telepathic abilities. The Spooky Girls might have the same ability. Maybe focusing on their names would let them know I needed them. And who knew what Nic might be capable of doing. Hopefully fighting was on the list.

If nothing else, it reminded me why I was out here, my shins alternately being scraped by underbrush and bruised by sticks and rocks. I'd come back to be with my friends.

I could hear Mason and Keegan running too, now. They were both likely faster than me, even with adrenaline on my side. I also had exhaustion and hunger weighing heavily on me, and everything was sure to catch up to me soon.

I shifted my path to run toward the school. It might make it easier for Keegan and Mason to catch me, but the closer I could get to other people, the more likely it would be that someone would see me or sense me, and maybe help out.

The hole in my side from the iron bolt was starting to ache, ten times worse than a stitch in my side from running. I didn't dare look at it, to see how badly it had destroyed the tissue there. Even if I made it, that level of trauma probably would never heal quite right.

I hadn't heard any more crackling bolts coming from Keegan, so I hazarded a glance backward.

He wasn't there. Neither was Mason.

I'd watched enough horror movies through peoples' windows in Artis. I knew they'd be right in front of me when I turned back. But if I didn't turn back, I'd be likely to run into a tree and knock myself out.

I turned my gaze back toward the school, surprised that I didn't see Keegan or Mason.

The plants below my feet writhed, encircling my legs. The thorns didn't bother me, but the vines pulled taut and yanked me off the ground, halting my forward momentum as I flipped upside down and dangled from a high tree branch.

Then I saw Keegan and Mason again, arms crossed over their chests as they stepped out from behind the trees where they'd been hiding. The cloud of darkness and faint snowflakes were both gone, and Keegan looked a bit more green than pale at this point.

Keegan held up a hand for a high five from Mason, and Mason obliged him, though neither of them took their gazes from me as they stalked toward me.

I struggled against the vines, but they held me tight. This was almost worse than hitting me with iron—using the only element I had any affinity with to trap me. But any ability I had to command plants only let them grow larger, not wither away. And between the pain in my side, being upside down, and all of the other difficulties I was facing, I didn't even have it in myself to try to pull up a shield of plant detritus.

I was done.

My hands were still free, but I wasn't sure how to indicate my surrender while I was hanging upside down. I tried flailing my hands around, but all that did was make Mason and Keegan slow their approach, as though they expected I was still trying to fight them.

Before I could vocalize my willingness to surrender, though, I felt Gerard's presence surrounding me like a shield. "We got you," he whispered.

Neither Keegan nor Mason reacted, so I wondered if Gerard had gotten into my head.

I didn't have to wonder for long, though. A fireball erupted just in front of Keegan and Mason, driving both of them back. The leaves where it hit smoldered—it hadn't just been my wishful thinking, then.

"Confirmed, wards are down," Maddie shouted.

"Uh, yeah, we got that, Mads," Aimee replied.

I couldn't see my friends, but I knew at least three of them were there—Gerard, Maddie, and Aimee. I had to assume Echo was there too, though I hadn't heard her voice.

And Keegan and Mason looked terrified. They shared a quick glance, and then bolted in opposite directions.

"I got Mason," Gerard snarled.

"I'm with Gerard," Nic said, alerting me to his presence. In spite of my awkward position, I smiled, glad he had my back.

"We'll hold the hilltop in case they circle back," another voice said. It took me a moment to place it, but I was pretty sure it was Val. And since she'd said "we," I had to guess that at least Trinity might be here to help as well. Who knew how many others they'd recruited.

"Great, give us the fae to deal with," Aimee spat back.

"It's fine," Echo said, her voice eerily calm. "He's the easy target. Mads, get Briar down."

Maddie came into view, looking up at the vines holding me several feet above the ground. Then she made eye contact with me and, to her credit, she didn't flinch from my fae appearance. Instead, she smiled. "Hey, Briar. We missed you."

"Likewise," I said. "So, you going to magic me down?"

She grimaced and shook her head. "No, my plan was to cut the vine. I was just trying to figure out how to not drop you on your head."

I swung forward and grabbed Maddie around the waist, careful to keep my claws from piercing her coat. "Will this help?"

"Eh, maybe?" Maddie said, her voice muffled against my leg. She grabbed my ankles with one hand, followed by a sawing sound somewhere above my feet. The tension holding me aloft lessened and then vanished, and I flailed to keep from knocking Maddie down as gravity re-exerted its full hold on me. It didn't help, and Maddie and I wound up on a heap on the forest floor.

Disentangling ourselves, I set to work on getting the rest of the vines off me, slicing through them easily with my claws now that I could reach them without straining. "We have a plan?"

Maddie shrugged. "Aimee and Echo, and even Gerard, have fast magic. I'm a ritualist. Nic's got ... well, it turns out angel powers, because he's an angel, not a demon. And he's steaming mad at Mason."

I grinned, glad to learn that Nic was theoretically on the side of good. "Okay, then where do I go?"

"Nowhere," Maddie said. "I'm going to get you out of danger and let them deal with it."

My shoulders straightened, my jaw set. "No. I've got to see this through. You go back in if you want, but I'm not leaving Keegan and Mason on the loose and hoping they don't kill my friends. The wards are down, right?"

"Yeah. But the four of them can deal with this, and we've got fae and a couple of other people as backup."

"Sure, maybe that's enough. I'm not leaving that to chance." I jerked my head toward the school. "Keep the backup here, but go find anyone else you can. We've got to comb the woods until we find them."

Maddie's eyes went wide. "What are you going to do?"

"Make sure they can't leave and come back later. Maybe get them sent somewhere where they aren't a problem for us."

"So not kill them?"

I took a deep breath. Killing them was an option. But I wasn't sure it was the best option. I'd wound up on Earth because I'd killed in Idyll. I wound up at Dedwydd because I'd killed in Artis. If we killed Keegan and Mason, who knew where I'd end up next. Any way you looked at it, me killing people ended poorly. I nodded. "Yeah, not kill them."

"I'll tell Echo and Aimee," Maddie said, tapping the side of her head. "You probably ought to tell Gerard."

Right. Gerard was telepathically connected to me. *"Gerard, no murder."*

"What? Why not?" came the response.

"So we don't wind up in more trouble. Where are you?"

A glimpse of another part of the woods flashed across my vision. The point of view was hot on Mason's heels, Nic slightly ahead of Gerard, with the previously rock-flattened portion of the fence nearby.

I started running that direction. *"Don't let him reach the fence!"*

Seeing both Gerard's perspective and my own was dizzying, but I didn't dare close my eyes and rely on his perception when I was in a completely different part of the woods. So I ducked out of the way of trees here while I watched Mason bounce off an invisible force field of some sort, just feet from the fence. Nic continued in a wide arc around Mason, finally coming to a stop when he'd positioned himself between Mason and the fence.

"Now what?" Gerard asked.

"I'm on my way. Just keep him down." I could only hope that Maddie had gotten the message to Aimee and Echo, and that they were having similar luck catching Keegan.

Mason staggered to his feet and came up swinging at Gerard. His initial punch seemed to surprise Gerard completely, but through our psychic link, I could tell Gerard was already laughing off the blow. "Is that how you wanna play?" he asked, his voice sounding different when it was aloud and filtered through the connection.

By the time I reached them, Gerard had Mason in a sleeper hold, and Mason's struggles were feeble, at best. Nic waited, body still tensed and ready to fight, but it seemed like Gerard had the situation completely in hand.

I cocked my head to the side, surprised to see Gerard fighting physically.

He chuckled at my expression. "What, you thought I was just magic and brains? I wasn't gonna go out for wrestling in Artis, but that doesn't mean I don't know how. JV champ of my weight class as a freshman in Baton Rouge."

I laughed. "Remind me to never fight you. Let's take him inside."

"Did the Spooky Girls get Keegan?" Nic asked

I glanced over my shoulder, straining to hear anything else in the woods. "I don't know. I sure hope so."

CHAPTER NINETEEN:
WHO CAN YOU TRUST?

_____

With Mason slung over Gerard's shoulder like a sack of potatoes, Gerard, Nic, and I made quite an entrance. I hadn't looked at my phone lately, so I wasn't sure what time it was, but even if it was between classes, there were an awful lot of students loitering in the hallway.

I spotted both Lorelei and Jasper amongst the crowd. Lorelei gave me a tight-lipped smile and then turned away. I couldn't tell if she was grateful, disappointed, or both. I figured I'd find out later, and probably take the Spooky Girls up on their offer to move in with Maddie. Somehow, that seemed like the best option for everyone involved.

Jasper's smile was more enthusiastic, and he even gave me a thumbs up, though he kept it pretty well hidden from everyone around him. So I guessed I'd scored some points with him by taking Mason down.

Most everyone else looked a little bit stunned, whether that was because Mason was passed out, Gerard was carrying Mason, Nic was following along but glowering at anyone who tried to get near us, or I was limping along with dirty and torn clothing wasn't clear. They started to disperse quickly, though, which revealed the likely reason for their departure—the Headmistress.

"I trust you have a good explanation for this?" she asked, one eyebrow arched high.

I nodded. "I've been—"

She held up a hand to silence me. "Mr. LeCroix, Mr. Flores, please take Mr. Sanders to the infirmary. Miss Williams, with me."

"Keegan is—"

"With. Me." Her tone discouraged any further argument from me.

Gerard and I shared a look. I glanced at Nic too, and he just nodded. On the one hand, I was glad the Headmistress hadn't said she wanted to see either of them too. On the other hand, I had no idea how much trouble I was going to be in.

Gerard squeezed my shoulder. "You'll be okay," he whispered.

"I hope so."

"Just don't make eye contact," Nic murmured.

That at least got a faint chuckle out of me. "Yeah, already learned my lesson on that."

I followed the Headmistress back to her office. She never turned to make sure I was following her, just assumed that I would. I could have run. But I didn't know where Keegan was, since the Spooky Girls and Val and the group she'd pulled together hadn't followed us in yet, so I had to assume they were still chasing him around in the woods, or that he'd lost them and was hiding somewhere, lying in wait for me to come back out.

I also knew that even if I had left the school grounds and gotten into a couple of fights, I was legitimately only defending myself and trying to get back as quickly as I could. I was in the right.

The look on the Headmistress's face when she sat to face me suggested anything but. "What do you have to say for yourself?" she asked, her voice taut and quiet.

I shrugged. "Where do you want me to start?"

"Miss Williams, this is not a game. I suggest that you begin wherever you feel is most pertinent."

"Idyll, then." I sat across from the Headmistress, since this could be a long explanation.

The Headmistress frowned. "I don't think—"

I cut her off. "I know it seems like I'm going back too far. But before I was kicked out of Idyll, I made enemies. Things got worse when I was in Artis, because those enemies had agents there. Things got worse again when I got here and one of the agents of those enemies was already a student. So. I was a rebel against the nobility in Idyll. Keegan Morris is, as best as I can tell, a member of the fae nobility or one of their agents, who probably arranged some trumped-up charges to get himself sent here with the expectation that I would eventually follow. That would explain how he could handle the heliotrope."

"Heliotrope?" the Headmistress asked.

"Yeah, I assume you know what that is and what it does to fae?"

"I am aware." Her tone was icy. "There's a reason it's on the list of banned substances at Dedwydd Academy. And you would know that, if you had bothered to read the student handbook."

I sighed. This wasn't going well. "I'd only just gotten the student handbook when I found it. I hadn't exactly had time to read the handbook. Lorelei took care of getting rid of it for me."

The Headmistress arched an eyebrow. "Miss Quinn?"

"Yeah, my roommate. Any rate, if it's banned, then whoever put it in my bed should be in trouble, right?"

"Your failure to report it previously will be noted."

I threw my hands up, exasperated. I was done trying to explain this nicely. "Fine, whatever. Mason Sanders and Keegan Morris managed to chase me off school grounds, through some gap in the fence. Also, did you know that demons can get their powers back if people worship them? And also, apparently the wards are down right now, which is why we just had a running battle across the forest, which may still be going on."

The Headmistress rose from her desk. "You will remain here, in that seat, until my return." She stomped out of the office, slamming the door behind her.

The force of her words was heavier than just a Headmistress instructing a student. It felt like a weight was pressing me into the seat any time I tried to move. I could look from side to side, but beyond that was too far.

So the Headmistress could use magic too, and didn't bat an eye at doing so? Great. I was beginning to feel like the deck was stacked completely against me.

Or that the school had been lying to us when they told us we couldn't use our powers here. What if there wasn't any power dampening, and everyone just believed there was, and that made it work? It seemed a little far-fetched, because if you've got a school full of supernatural teenagers, it seems like someone would have tested their powers at some point. And while maybe they'd keep it a secret for a little while, someone would be sure to let their powers loose at an inopportune moment, and then the secret would be out.

Before I could continue further on that line of thought, the door behind me creaked open. At first, I didn't hear anything else, but I couldn't turn to see if the latch had just come unlatched or if there was someone there. Then someone entered. From the soft and timid tread, I could tell it wasn't the Headmistress. But they didn't announce themselves or move into my line of sight. "Hello? Who's there?"

I didn't recognize the voice that responded. "I have questions. Is what you just told the Headmistress about your role in Idyll true?"

I struggled to turn my head, but to no avail. "Yes, one-hundred percent."

"Why did you do it?"

"Because the nobles are oppressive jerks who wave their power around willy-nilly and expect the rest of the fae to just fall in line. Like they deserve our deference. Like things in Idyll should mirror the way things once were on Earth."

My mystery visitor remained silent, then asked, "And the changeling children?"

My shoulders slumped. "The changeling children are one of their worst abuses. They treat them worse than they treat other fae. All their nonsense about the changelings bolstering fae numbers is lies. They use them as brood mares to create new fae and cannon fodder to save precious fae lives, and it's not right."

"Thank you. You're much more forthcoming with information than I anticipated. I'll be in touch."

The faint presence I'd felt behind me when the door opened faded away. "Wait, come back!" I had no idea who I'd given that information, nor what they were likely to do with it. But every word of it was true. I could only hope that their "thank you" was sincere, and that they'd use the information to further my cause, the one that had got me sent here, ultimately. Maybe some good could come of this after all.

A different presence entered the room, but this one moved into my field of vision. The Headmistress had returned, and she waved her hand vaguely at me as she passed, releasing whatever hold she had placed on me. "Mr. Sanders is to be removed from the school premises when he regains consciousness." She paused. "I am assuming that magical intervention is not necessary for his recovery?"

"Yeah, Gerard just put him in a sleeper hold," I said, frowning. "Is that it? Somebody comes in and asks me a couple of questions, and all of the sudden everything is fine?"

"Someone asked you questions in my absence?" she asked, arching an eyebrow.

I bit at my lip but decided to keep up my current policy of honesty. So far, it seemed to be the best defense I had. "Yeah, about the political situation in Idyll. I don't know who it was, or why they asked what they did."

"Interesting," was the Headmistress's only response. She didn't seem concerned in the slightest.

I pressed on. "Okay, I have questions too. How can Mason and Keegan and you use powers here when no one else can?"

The Headmistress gave me a wry grin. "Do you really think that any magical prohibitions here would include the staff?"

I shook my head, chagrinned that I hadn't realized the truth earlier. Of course the teachers had their powers still.

"As for Mr. Sanders and Mr. Morris, they seem to have enacted some sort of counter-ritual that did, in fact, allow for the use of powers in certain parts of the school grounds. We will be examining the wards as soon as Mr. Morris is retrieved."

"Retrieved?" I felt the blood drain from my face. "The Spooky Girls ... Maddie, Echo, and Aimee were trying to contain him."

"And they may yet still be. But he has not been recovered yet."

I rose from my seat. "Um, can I be excused? I've got work to do."

The Headmistress studied my face for a long while, my gaze immediately finding more interesting things to look at rather than meet her eyes again. Finally, she said, "While I cannot condone the use of powers against another student, I think it is safe to say that Mr. Morris will not be a student at Dedwydd for much longer. I will have the transfer paperwork completed shortly."

That gave me pause. "Transferred? To where?"

"There are other schools better suited to students who are prone to causing problems. Dedwydd is meant to be a place of peace and refuge for students and staff who wish to coexist with the mortal world, not continue the actions that threaten to expose our presence to humans."

"So just like that, they get whisked off to somewhere else?"

"Do you feel they should be treated more leniently?" she asked, her eyebrow rising again.

She had a point. Whatever rules I might have broken, it didn't seem like I'd done enough to get sent to this other school. They'd tried to kill me. "No, I guess not."

"Very good. You are excused."

I didn't waste another minute. I ran to see what had happened to my friends, and where Keegan was now.

~

I sent out thoughts in Maddie, Echo, and Aimee's directions as soon as I stepped out the school doors. *I'm coming. Show me where you are.*

I listened, too, for any signs of a struggle, but it was eerily quiet outside, like the whole world was holding its breath.

Val and the crowd she'd assembled still stood watch on the hilltop.

"Anything?" I asked her.

"No, it's been completely quiet," she replied, smiling. "We've got folks stationed at every entrance to the school, though, so he won't get past us."

"Thank you."

An image flashed into my mind of Maddie prone on the ground, pale and covered in blood, with Echo kneeling beside her, tears running down the latter's face.

I gasped, before pushing out the thought, *"Aimee? Where are you?"*

The image shifted, and I saw Aimee then, charging toward my perspective. Then nothing.

I hadn't connected to the Spooky Girls, I'd connected to Keegan. And somehow, I was seeing what he was seeing.

No, that wasn't right. Aimee's mouth had been open, her face red like she was screaming. But I'd heard nothing. Was this real, or some sort of illusion Keegan was trying to trick me with? For now, I had to assume the latter, though the images still nagged at me as though they were real.

"What is it?" Val asked.

"I'm not sure. I'm going to find out."

The trees in the background of both images had been sparse, and neither the fence nor the school had been in view. That could mean that they were closer to the fence than the school, and Keegan had his back to the fence. The only question then was which part of the fence?

I calmed myself as best as I could and crouched low to the ground. I hadn't attuned myself to the land here, since I didn't think it was possible. But maybe I could do it now, even if it was only going to be the loosest of connections. Anything that might give me a direction to run in, rather than just flailing about in the woods, would be better than nothing.

The grass was thin here, but its root structure ran across the school grounds. It met up with other roots as it went, extending the reach of my senses through the plants. I couldn't see out of the trees, per se, but I could tell where something might be interfering with their natural states.

I found two things doing exactly that. One was a group of people, three or four. Either the Spooky Girls were still fighting Keegan, or they'd lost him. Regardless, that gave me a direction to search.

But the other thing was a weird, twisted blight in the heart of one of the trees. Try as I might to focus on where the Spooky Girls were, this rot drew my attention. I had to force it from my mind, with a whispered promise that I'd look into it next. The tree heard and accepted my pledge. Now I was bound to it.

The bargain sealed, my focus shifted, and I launched myself from my crouch, running in the direction where I'd felt the human disturbance.

It didn't take me long to find them. None of them were on the ground or bleeding, not the Spooky Girls or Keegan. He stood just outside of the fence, which was now coated in ice, and he paced, looking like a caged tiger. His expression changed as I came into view, and Maddie looked back toward me.

A trickle of dried blood marred her face, but she smiled as soon as she saw me. She mouthed something, but no sound escaped her lips at first. As I continued running toward them, though, her voice became clear. "Briar, wait!"

My limbs went rigid, like they'd been frozen solid. I'd somehow managed to plant both my feet, so I didn't immediately topple to the ground. But I couldn't move an inch.

Aimee turned now too, cocking her head to the side. "Aw, man, Echo, can you unfreeze Briar?"

"Not right now," Echo said, her voice strained.

"Can I throw her at Keegan, then?" Aimee suggested, winking at me.

Echo sighed, sounding like she was gritting her teeth. "I don't ... you know, maybe. Briar, if you hit a wall, I'm sorry."

If I'd been able to move, my eyes would have gone wide. I floated a few feet off the ground, then spun slightly. Keegan watched the process with a bemused smile, and what little I could see of Aimee's face looked strained. When I caught a glimpse of Maddie, she looked as worried as I felt.

"Briar, are there any tree branches you don't want to hit?" Maddie asked. "Grunt once for yes, twice for no."

I stared at the plethora of branches between me and Keegan, not really relishing the thought of going through any of them. But they were mostly thin and bare. I grunted twice.

"Sweet," Aimee replied.

And then I was flying.

CHAPTER TWENTY:
EXPELLED

Keegan's expression shifted to panic as he moved to get out of the way of where Aimee had telekinetically thrown me.

Seeing as my claws had ripped free of my skin while I flew, I didn't blame him.

I also wasn't entirely sure what Aimee's plan was, now that I was across the school property line. Was she going to land me or keep me in the air? Or was I going to crash to the ground at any moment?

Keegan started to run, and I flew after him, gaining rapidly. He glanced over his shoulder, and his eyes got wider, like he wasn't expecting a creepy looking fae to be hot on his heels. He stopped and turned quickly enough that I flew straight past him.

My speed slowed, and I got closer to the ground. I readied myself to land at a run, which I did with only a brief stumble. Then I turned back toward Keegan.

Something shimmered in the air beside him, vague enough that I couldn't identify it at first. As I squinted in that direction, trying to determine if this was the portal Keegan planned to use to take me somewhere else, I realized that it had a faintly human shape. It was all shades of whites and grays, much like the weird image of the non-existent ghost wing, but this looked more real.

A gust of wind whistled past me, though the nearby trees didn't stir. Carried on the wind, a soft voice said, "Get out of here."

I stared at the figure by Keegan's side, picking out more details. A curvy figure. Familiar eyes and jawline. Hair that probably would have been red in life. "Jade?" I asked.

"Get out of here, and leave Lorelei and Jasper alone," the ghost said.

That confirmed it for me. "Not gonna happen, Jade. You need to get out of here."

"She's with me," Keegan said. "With you out of the picture, things are going to be much better around here for everyone."

I shook my head. "I'm not the one who should be worrying about not being here anymore. Mason's in the infirmary, and the Headmistress is already preparing his transfer paperwork. And yours."

Jade's ghost surged forward, spindly fingers grasping toward my throat.

I ducked, letting Jade sail over my head, but still felt the chill of her passing wash over me. Shivering, I righted myself and shouted, "Anyone got any warding spells to stop ghosts?"

"It'll take me a few minutes," Maddie replied.

Footfalls crashed through the underbrush on the school property, and Nic emerged into view. "Where?" he asked, his voice a low snarl that didn't sound remotely angelic.

I gestured toward Jade, pulling up a swirl of leaves and other detritus to surround her.

"Get Keegan," Nic growled as he leapt into the air and flew toward Jade, translucent shimmering wings carrying him across the fence.

I turned my attention back to Keegan.

"Can't keep this up all day, Briar," he said, shrugging.

"Maybe you can't," I spat back. "This is what I was made for." I charged toward him, claws slashing and seeking purchase in his skin.

He sidestepped me at the last moment, but he didn't retaliate with fae powers or a physical attack. Maybe he really wasn't able to keep going. Maybe he'd used up every bit of his power attacking the Spooky Girls.

No, that didn't seem right. While fae eventually tired, I could fight for days without rest. And the nobles weren't weak. He was biding his time for something. Despite me telling him that Mason was out of the picture, he hadn't seemed concerned. Maybe he had other allies lurking in the wings, like his family.

Suddenly, I felt exposed. I was off school grounds, and there was every possibility Keegan was just waiting for someone to come along to collect me. He could have lured me out here for this very reason.

Even if that wasn't the case, I had another big problem. I had no idea how to bring him back to the school alive. And though bringing him back dead was an option, I didn't think it was the best one, given my already tenuous standing at the school. And I'd already made the decision that murder was only going to be an absolute last resort.

I lunged at Keegan again, aiming for his lower body. If I could get him onto the ground, I could magically manipulate the vegetation there to restrain him.

This time, he both sidestepped and drove his foot into my ribcage.

It knocked the wind out of me. My stomach was cold, like his foot had been coated in the elemental ice he'd used earlier. I rolled on the ground, trying to overcome the pain. Out of the corner of my eye, I spotted Nic and Jade circling one another. Nic had produced a gout of brilliant white flame from somewhere, and he wielded it like a sword. Jade held her arms up and crossed in front of her, like that would shield her from his attacks.

Keegan's steps toward me pulled me away from watching Nic and Jade's fight. He leaned forward as though he was going to try to pin me, but I rolled out of the way. I stopped when I lay on my back again, and I kipped up from the prone position, ready to drive Keegan away from the other fight and get him knocked down.

He kept his distance from me now, moving to put me between him and the fence. He sneered at me, but his gaze darted around, like he was looking for something.

I shifted to my right, so the gap in the fence would be at my back, not the fence itself. But I, too, was looking for something. I needed some way to turn this to my advantage, so I could put an end to this cat and mouse game.

Before I could come up with a plan, a tendril of some sort of plant matter danced across Keegan's sleeve, wispy enough that he didn't notice it. I focused on the plant, still green, but developing brambles, and growing from a small rip in the sleeve of his jacket.

I braced for the possibility that he was using plant-based powers again but watched as the tendril wrapped itself around his arm. He still hadn't noticed. It was snugly wrapped, but not tightly.

I frowned. Had I actually hit him when he sidestepped me? Maybe. But why was it causing a thin bramble vine to grow from his torn clothes?

I brushed my claws across the palms of my hands. And there it was. Just a touch of wetness on my right palm. I'd drawn blood. And from his blood, brambles bloomed.

Ignoring the possibility that this was all a trap, I rushed toward Keegan again, my claws flying wildly.

He tried to sidestep again, but I was ready for it this time, weaving from side to side as I drew nearer. He threw his arms up to block his face, and that was the only opening I needed.

I slashed at both his arms, raking my claws down them and continuing downward to strike his legs as I crumpled to the ground. I made myself as small a target as I could to avoid any retaliation on his part and rolled away from his feet.

No blow came in return, and as I righted myself, I saw that my plan was working. Brambles sprung from all of the places I'd cut his clothing and his skin, now wrapping him up like a spider wraps her prey for later.

Snowflakes danced out from Keegan's fingertips, nipping at the edges of the brambles. A faint rime of frost tipped the thorns, but it didn't last long. The warmth his blood had infused into the growing plants dissipated the snow and ice before they grew into anything more forceful.

"What are you doing?" Keegan wailed, eyes frantic as he pushed himself to increase the amount of ice he was emitting.

It was to no avail. I was Briar of the Brambles, and I was made to stop my foes.

But not necessarily murder them. I smiled at Keegan, though it didn't touch my eyes. "Taking you back to the Headmistress. I think you might be learning to adjust at a new school soon."

~

Aimee's telekinesis came in handy for the second time that day as we hauled Keegan back up the hill, since none of the Spooky Girls wanted to touch him physically, for fear that my brambles wouldn't distinguish them from Keegan. I suppose I didn't blame them, even though I knew I could keep the brambles in check.

I did just that as we headed back to the school, keeping the majority of my attention occupied with Keegan's bindings. In part, I wanted to make sure he wasn't doing anything sneaky to loosen them. But I also wanted to prove to myself that I could be effective without completely letting loose. It seemed that might be important if I was going to stick around in the mortal realm.

Nic followed a short distance behind us, saying nothing, his gaze downcast. Though he wouldn't tell us what happened, I had the distinct impression that he'd done something to stop Jade, something he now had regrets about. I could only imagine he'd somehow gotten rid of her, though the details of how an angel dispatched a ghost might be the reason for his sudden withdrawn nature. I hoped he'd be willing to talk about it later. I owed him for all the help he'd given me, and I'd gladly listen to his angst if it would help him move past any shame or discomfort he felt in that area.

The blighted tree I'd identified before fighting Keegan tickled the edge of my perception, and I paused. "Hang on a minute. There's something weird here I need to check out."

The Spooky Girls stopped, Maddie and Echo eyeing me quizzically, but Aimee maintaining her focus on Keegan. "Don't take too long," Aimee said. "I mean, I *can* do this all day, it's just not fun."

From the outside, the tree looked like any of the others nearby, but I could still sense the presence of something *wrong*. There was a small hole in the trunk, and I peered into the darkness in the hopes of seeing what I was about to stick my hand into. I wasn't looking forward to disturbing a hibernating squirrel family that might decide they needed to make a snack of my flesh.

"Anybody got a light?" I asked.

Aimee thrust one of her hips toward Echo, and Echo dug around in Aimee's pocket until she produced a pink lighter.

"You don't smoke," Echo said.

"Candles, incense, people who annoy me," Aimee replied. "All flammable, as it turns out."

Echo smirked and approached the hole in the tree with the lighter.

The flame danced across something shiny and dark, too large to be an angry rodent glaring out at me. I reached inside and felt the cold radiance of iron before my hand touched whatever object was hidden there. Jerking my hand back out, I looked at Maddie. "Mads, can you—"

Maddie hurried over and looked in the hole, then reached inside. The thing in her hand was bigger than I'd realized at first, an ornate iron setting with gold and silver strands woven into the ironwork, with a chunk of heliotrope the size of her palm in the center. It might have been a pendant, if you weren't opposed to having a softball-sized rock hanging from a chain. She flipped it over and sucked in a breath through her teeth.

"You okay?" I asked.

She nodded but pointed to where some symbols had been etched into the exposed back of the heliotrope. "It's ward-breaking stuff. Demonic, most likely. Just surprised me is all."

"So then we have the cause and the effect," Echo said, nodding at the stone and then at Keegan in turn. "Should be pretty simple to explain all this to the Headmistress."

"She already knows most of it," I said. Then I looked up at Keegan, bramble-wrapped and hovering, and back at the stone. "I think we might want to keep it here for right now. If it disrupted ley lines, moving it might make that stop working, right?"

"Yeah, and then poof, no more magic," Maddie said. She tucked the stone back inside the tree and pulled her scarf off. Tying it around the trunk in a surprisingly fancy bow, she smiled. "Now we can find it again, after he's been dealt with."

~

We drew an even bigger crowd parading a floating, bramble-packaged Keegan into the building. Somehow, when Gerard, Nic, and I had brought Mason in, and there was no display of powers involved, that was one thing. Now, me and the Spooky Girls were *flaunting* the fact that powers were not suppressed. I might have felt more guilty about showing that off if I weren't so proud of having taken down Keegan with the very powers that made me such a threat in Idyll.

Jaylin standing with arms crossed over their chest at the near end of the hallway leading to the Headmistress's office took the wind out of my sails. Their glare said everything I needed to know. They were not happy about me taking down Keegan. This was likely to get awkward before it got better.

They shifted their gaze away from me, looked up at Keegan, then quickly across the faces of the Spooky Girls, then turned their attention back to me. "Can we talk in private?"

Only then did I recognize the voice from earlier, in the Headmistress's office. It had been Jaylin. I nodded. "Echo, if he gets out of hand, yell, okay?"

Echo chuckled. "Yeah, I think we've got this."

Nic put a hand on my shoulder and finally made eye contact with me. "You sure you want to talk to them?" he asked softly.

I nodded. "I'm sure. Are you okay?"

Taking a deep breath, he shook his head. "I've got some things I'll need to deal with later."

"I'm more than happy to help, Nic. If you like."

He nodded now, squeezing his eyes tightly shut to hide the tears that glistened there. "Yeah, okay. Thanks."

Turning away from him, I followed Jaylin part of the way down the hallway, until they stopped and turned to face me, gaze averted from mine. "I'm really not good at apologies."

"You've got nothing to apologize for," I said.

"No, I really do," they insisted. "What you explained earlier cleared some things up for me. It seems that maybe I was lied to."

"I don't feel any shame to tell you that fae lie. It's what we're known for."

Jaylin took a deep breath. "Lied to by Keegan, specifically. I'm sorry I trusted him and didn't give you a chance." Looking beyond me, toward the end of the hall, where Keegan hung suspended, they continued, "I have a tendency to jump to conclusions about people, and clearly, my judgement in that area was tainted by some dim memory of Idyll."

I nodded. "Your memory isn't the only tainted one. I don't blame you for any of it. Were I a changeling rather than fae, I wouldn't trust someone like me either. I mean—" I gestured backward, generally toward Keegan. "I'm trouble."

Jaylin smiled faintly. "Yeah, but I think you're the right kind of trouble. Keegan spun up a story about how he'd been oppressed and hurt too, and I think he was telling your story, claiming it as his." They finally met my gaze and extended a hand toward me. "Truce still stands, but maybe we can try talking rather than just glaring at each other?"

I considered Jaylin's extended hand. It wasn't just us who needed to talk. It was a lot of people here at Dedwydd. Teenage humans and supernatural creatures alike were so good at thinking they knew everything and that they didn't need any help, but that clearly wasn't true. More talking and less glaring would help all around.

I took Jaylin's hand. "Yeah. Deal." I paused, considering. "No, not just a deal. I promise."

ACKNOWLEDGEMENTS

Like a number of the books I write, this book was inspired by a roleplaying game that went more than a little bit sideways. Without Jeremy, Ariel, Marc, and Nate, I would have never thought to write a book about a murderous fae and her similarly violent friends. I hope I've done those friends justice (even if I did change a few names).

As always, I owe immense thanks to my beta readers, Amanda Robinson and Cyrano Jones, who make grabby hands every time I tell them I've finished a new manuscript. Additional thanks to Torrey and Dietrich Podmajersky, who talked me into an additional plot element that turned out to be just what this story was missing.

Cara DiGirolamo helped me with the Latin. (If the translation is off, it is surely because I didn't explain what I wanted it to really mean correctly.) J. Kathleen Cheney knocked yet another cover out of the park. Kath Nyborg provided an excellent proofread and caught plot things I'd missed after all my revisions.

And even though Jeremy gets thanks for the game that spawned the characters that spawned the plot misunderstanding that spawned the book, he also gets my everlasting thanks for his love and support. I couldn't do it without him.

ABOUT THE AUTHOR

Dawn Vogel's academic background is in history, so it's not surprising that much of her fiction is set in earlier times. By day, she edits reports for historians and archaeologists. In her alleged spare time, she runs a craft business, co-runs a small press, and tries to find time for writing. Her steampunk adventure series, *Brass and Glass*, is available from DefCon One Publishing. She is a member of Broad Universe, SFWA, and Codex Writers. She lives in Seattle with her husband, author Jeremy Zimmerman, and their herd of cats.

Visit her at http://historythatneverwas.com.